THE LYCANTHROPIRE SAGA

HALF BLOOD

Kat Sloan

Kathel Coven
Press

KNIGHTSEN, CALIFORNIA

Kathel Coven Press

3019 Knightsen Ave. #204
Knightsen, California/USA 94548

Publisher's Note: This is a work of fiction. Names, characters, places, and incidents are a product of the author's imagination. Locales and public names are sometimes used for atmospheric purposes. Any resemblance to actual people, living or dead, is a coincidence and not intended by the author.

Book Layout ©2013 BookDesignTemplates.com

Summary: When she discovers that she is a Half Blood werewolf and in love with a vampire, young Kalapuya Native American Lakota Avital is forced to choose between her world and his in an attempt to thwart a war of catastrophic proportions between their two rivaling sides.

Sloan, Kat, 1985-
The Lycanthropire Saga: Half Blood / by Kat Sloan. — 1st ed.

{1. Werewolves — Fiction. 2. Vampires — Fiction. 3. Hybrids — Fiction. 4. Oakridge (Oregon) — Fiction. 5. Oregon (State) — Fiction.} I. Title.

ISBN 978-0-9914514-0-1 (Paperback)
ISBN 978-0-9914514-1-8 (Hardcover)

CONTENTS

We live off the blood that runs through these veins.

With an animal being that cannot be tamed.

–ASPEN TAKAHASHI–

PREFACE

My existence was a phenomenon. I could not have imagined how the ghosts of my past would shape my future. Or how *he* would so completely and entirely enrapture my heart and my soul.

My life was a spectacle, a freak show from which there was no escape. But, somehow, within my dysfunctional existence, I found love, I brought honor back to my people, and I embraced my destiny.

His world became mine.

And in death, my life was given purpose . . . .

1 AGONY

I TOSSED AND TURNED IN MY RESTLESS SLEEP, painfully aware of the stabbing agony that emanated from dozens of places in my body. My ribcage felt like shattered shards of bone and cartilage, my legs and arms ached as if someone had tried to rip them from my torso, and my head throbbed with a migraine so intense I dared not open my eyes.

Against my closed eyelids, there were two figures. One was male, tall and strong in build. There was something familiar about his presence, but his facial features were ever shifting and unclear in my delusional dream. The other figure was female with dark, bronze skin and long black hair. She was very beautiful, and her face reminded me of someone . . . .

Somewhere halfway between a waking and sleeping state, I was trapped in that grey area where consciousness acknowledges your physical being, but the mind is still confined in subconscious dreams or nightmares.

Suddenly, a dark, ominous figure jumped at me in the dream, which was quickly morphing into a nightmare. It resembled a human figure, but had no definitive structure, features, or form. Like a black cloud, or a curtain of darkness, its presence exuded an evil intent.

The thing grew in size and hovered over the male and female in my minds' eye. In slow motion, the creature descended over the couple like a vapor. It began to envelope them.

Red liquid flowed like a river.

Blood.

My heart felt suddenly heavy with a deep sorrow that I could barely comprehend. I realized that the two who had once been living, breathing beings . . . were gone. The lack of their energetic presences left a gaping hole in my heart and all that remained was a dreary pall that pressed on my soul with a deathly weight. Hopelessness overwhelmed me.

In my dream, I felt myself collapsing to my knees, defeated, as tears streamed down my face. My cries, like a wounded animal, filled the air in the midst of the void.

"They will come," came the whisper of a voice in my ear, an unearthly voice devoid of human tone, waking me from my grief. The words echoed again and again, becoming more and more distant, almost ghost-like.

Fear seeped through my body as the echo disappeared and I was left only with the bleak darkness.

I jolted up in bed, drenched in sweat. Consciously, I took several deep breaths as I tried to regain my bearings, to discern reality.

"They will come again," the voice repeated.

I gasped and my heart thudded wildly. The voice hadn't sounded so far or oneiric this time. I was sure I wasn't dreaming anymore. It sounded like someone had whispered the words directly into my ear. The tiny hairs on the back of my neck stood tall as terror gripped me.

"Who's there?" I demanded frantically looking around my room, lit only by the rim of silver moonlight.

There was no answer.

It was then that the waves of agony came. I collapsed back into my pillow and curled into a tight ball on my bed. I grabbed my knees, digging my fingernails into my legs, pulling them into my chest in an attempt to quell the pain.

There was the quiet sound of my moaning for what seemed like an eternity. The nightmare, the voices, and the fear I had experienced only moments before were suddenly very unimportant. Pain was all that existed.

Yet as quickly as it had come, the agony evaporated, and I lay there, deeply brooding.

My heart sank as I realized that the vicious cycle was complete. The same dream, the same agony, and the same voice. For almost four years, I'd spent each night without peace, without change, and without hope. It was an experience that I could only describe as alien and foreign.

As the sun streamed its first rays of light through my window, I realized my life had become a broken record player. It just kept skipping and repeating itself.

Again.

And again . . . .

And again . . . .

Over the years I had tried to rationalize the incessantly repeating cycle. Time and time again, I shrugged off the physical agony thinking it was related to growing pains, and that the intensity of the dream was simply because I hadn't had a real night's sleep in over three years. I told myself over and over that it couldn't possibly be real, that I must simply be going insane, or that these episodes were psychotic.

I even tried convincing myself that I was living in some self-created, false reality, one I had fabricated so intimately in my mind that I truly believed it to be real.

But in the end, no matter how badly I wanted to believe that the incidents could all be logically explained, I knew they could not.

In desperation, I spent almost every waking moment of my consciousness trying to make sense of it all.

I simply had to believe that one day, somehow, someway . . . it would make sense. Oh spirits of the earth and sky, my heart ached for that day. But as the days and months and years ticked by, my supply of hope depleted.

I felt as if I was growing into the skin of some foreign creature, some monster. I was growing so unfamiliar with myself, terrified that I was literally going to lose myself. Admittedly, I felt like a zombie, neither dead nor alive. I tried to think back to the last time I felt even remotely normal.

Three years ago, high school. I shuddered as the word brought back memories of what normalcy had once meant to me. There had been a time when I was simply the young native girl from the tiny Oregon Kalapuya Reservation. I never did fit in. But that was part of the normality of being a native in a small town high school. If you were from the reservation, pursuing an education was an occupational hazard.

I just existed.

But now, I felt trapped in an existence that was larger than my own, neither moving forward nor backward, just suspended in time, as if time itself had forgotten me.

It became difficult to focus on anything as the anxiety continued to eat away at me. An urge for change hovered over me constantly. I felt every muscle tense in my body, waiting for something to happen, for something to change.

By day I fought the anxiety, and by night I fought the pain. And through it all the echo of the voice blew back and forth in my head.

"They will come . . . ."

As I slowly accepted the reality of my predicament, I was able to recognize more details. The voice I heard was not devoid of any tone, as I had originally thought. It was the voice of a woman with an accent, a melodic voice. Her resonance was unearthly and bitter-sweet.

"They will come . . ." she whispered again inside my head.

I jumped as the door to my bedroom swung open, waking me from my contemplation.

"Did you sleep Kota?" came a smiling face through the door jam.

Although he was only nine months older than me, my brother, Notak, looked as if he was three years older. I didn't remember his transition to manhood. It seemed to happen overnight. One day he was a skinny little native boy and then, BAM, he had become this big mass of rippling muscle under bronze-gold weathered skin. He still had that infectious smile though, the kind that could light up the cloudiest day.

Despite my anxiety, irritability, and my increasing unhappiness, Notak kept a watchful, worried eye on my fragile condition.

"I wish I were so lucky," I smirked. "Why would last night be any different?"

"One day it will end," he tried to reassure me. "Hurry up and get dressed, I have something for you," and then he was gone down the hall as quickly as he had come.

Then it dawned on me. I took a quick glance at my calendar hanging on the wall next to my bed to confirm my wary thought. It was Tuesday, the second day of February. It was my twenty-first birthday.

A whiny groan escaped my vocal cords and I collapsed back into my pillows in defeat. I wasn't sure which I hated more . . . the horrible nights or the birthdays that only reminded me that looming ahead was yet another year of the same frozen existence I called my life.

Reluctantly, I dragged myself out of bed and pulled on my forest green khaki pants with more effort than seemed warranted.

"Lakota!" came Notak's impatient voice trying to hurry me along. He knew all too well how much I hated my birthday.

Slowly, I pulled my long-sleeve brown shirt over my head, then hopped into my boots and fastened my belt as I headed down the hall. I swiftly grabbed my wide brimmed hat from the table in the entryway before I rounded the corner to the kitchen.

Notak stood there, waiting, with a small box carved from wood in his hands.

"Happy Birthday, sister!" his voice rang like bells in the wind as he shoved the box towards me. "Open it!"

Reluctantly, I took the wood carved box and turned it in my hands inspecting how beautiful the little thing was. It was the kind of craftsmanship our ancestors would have been proud of. My thoughts wandered to the time and care he must have put into it.

"It's beautiful, Notak," I whispered. "I wish you wouldn't spend so much time on me," I pleaded with him.

"Well you can keep wishing, because last time I checked I get to decide what I do with my time," he said with a smart smirk.

I just nodded my head in disapproval.

"You are my sister and my best friend, you know that," he said more seriously. "You are not a burden to me or to father," he went on, reading my all too predictable, melodramatic thoughts.

"I think I'm cursed, Notak," I said with sadness in my voice. "I pray that my curse will not harm you or father in the least way. I cannot help but feel that I will be your undoing." I turned the little box over again, still hesitant to open it.

"You can't punish yourself for what has not come to pass. Let the future be what it will. Our fate will be what destiny intends it to be. You can't ask me to pretend that you do not matter," he said with definitive purpose. "Now, I'm begging you, stop wallowing in your misery and at least attempt to enjoy your birthday. Shut up and open it!" he demanded with both impatience and excitement.

I sighed as I lifted the lid to the box. It opened easily on its little brass hinges. Inside was the most exquisite beaded bracelet I had ever seen.

Notak held the little box as I lifted the bracelet from its resting place. There were three intricate layers of small white beads with little bronze pieces chiseled into the shape of tiny leaves that held the layers together. In the center of the ornate thing was a large, smooth stone bead that contained many shades of white. It reminded me of the milky-way.

"My god, Notak!" I exclaimed. "This must have taken months to make." I knew the work that went into carving, smoothing, and polishing single beads from stone. It required skill, patience, and time, and I did not doubt that Notak had spent an excessive effort on the bracelet.

"It is meant to protect you," he said as he helped me fasten the clasp on the back. "I made the beads from the sacred stones of the Willamette River and the elders have consecrated them to bring you peace and protection."

I inspected the bracelet, turning my wrist over to admire its perfection. The white glowed against my bronze toned skin, and the little metal pieces sparkled in the light.

"Thank you," I said as I embraced him in a bear hug. I hoped he could understand what it meant to me. "Sometimes I feel as if you are the only thing standing between myself and insanity. Blood may not bind us, but you are no less a brother to me." Even though we were only brother and sister by adoption, he was still my brother in every sense of the word, my best friend and constant companion.

"I will always be here for you, Kota. You know that," he said. "My only prayer to the spirits is that you will one day find peace."

A long silence filled the air as his words sank in.

"Thank you brother," I said as I started towards the front door. "I have get to work."

"Be careful out there," I heard him call after me.

I stopped just before I walked out the door and turned back to him.

"Thank you again, Notak, for everything," I said. He just nodded with a smile, as if his support were no big deal.

It was strange how things had worked out for Notak and myself. Never in a million years had I expected us to become such good friends, much less best friends.

When my parents were murdered seventeen years earlier, the tribal leader, Wakiza, had adopted me to appease my father's dying wish. Wakiza's wife had died giving birth to his son, Notak. So it was by default that Notak had become my brother.

It's strange how situations sometimes find a way of working out. Sometimes I felt as if our lives were always destined to be intertwined.

A few moments later I was out the door and jumping up into the white Ford Explorer. I pulled the heavy door shut and started the ignition. Although we had several vehicles on the reservation, there were only a few that actually ran. Mine was the most reliable, a benefit of working for the Willamette National Forest Service.

I pulled out onto the tiny dirt road that led to the main highway. The trees grew thick and tall here, so much so that the sun seldom reached the forest floor. Their ominous branches climbed into the sky forever, stretching as far up and in every direction that the eye could possibly see. As I turned out onto the main highway my thoughts continued to wander.

Since I had taken the job when I was eighteen, I couldn't remember missing a single day of work. The eight to ten hour shifts, five days a week did wonders for my sanity. It gave me something to focus on besides the constant gnawing ache in my gut. It watered down my self-loathing just a little bit.

I arrived at the Willamette District office just outside the tiny town of Oakridge.

I pushed through the heavy doors and quickly made my way through the main lobby, turning the first right corner to a private office.

"Morning, Mr. Benson."

"Good morning, Lakota," came a gruff, older voice from the corner of the room. He was tall and built very strong. I smiled inwardly with my thought that Kyle Benson looked like a bear. With his dark brown beard, mustache, and long hair, he embodied the classic idea of the age-old mountain man.

"So what do you have for me today?" I asked as I strode towards his him.

"Actually, I have an unusual assignment. It'll be you and me today," he said, his voice filled with the unmistakable tone of worry and doubt.

"Ok? So no pile of paperwork for you today?" I said with hesitation.

The only time we ever scouted together was when it was a potentially dangerous situation. And that worried me.

"Spit it out. What happened?" I demanded, as I lopped myself down in a chair and threw my feet up onto the oversized desk.

"I think there might be something going on in the northeast just outside Blair Lake," he began, an obvious hesitation in his voice.

"A hiker came in yesterday, reporting a dead mountain lion with strange wounds around its neck. He said that in his twenty years backpacking in the wilderness, it was unlike anything he had ever seen." Concern was clear on Kyle's face.

"Thing is . . ." he continued, hesitating again. "It's the third report in the last month." His eyes strayed to the window and beyond.

"I don't understand. We get dozens of these reports every year. I mean, everything from mutilated squirrels to Bigfoot." He wasn't making any sense. "Why are these reports any different?"

He sighed, plopping himself into his deep-cushioned chair, silent for several moments. "All three reports claim that the animals were drained of their blood. All three claim a broken neck and bite marks in the neck. No other wounds, and the carcasses were just simply left there, untouched."

I put my feet down and leaned forward in the chair, taken back for a moment. That was not only odd, but decidedly unnatural.

"So not hunters, not poachers, and not natives," I concluded. Kyle nodded his head in agreement.

"Did you see any of the remains?" I asked.

"I went as far as Blair Lake, but the woods beyond there are thick and strange to me," he said, as his eyes glazed over with a fear I had never seen from him. "I just don't know if I should be getting you involved in all this. God knows what the hell is walking around out there, and if what these people say is true . . . ." Fear crept back into his eyes.

"Kyle, come on, it's me," I said addressing him more as a friend than my senior. "That's my home out there, your wilderness is my backyard," I said with a smile.

"I know, I wouldn't be able to find anybody who knows these woods better than you do. It's just—" he hesitated. "I don't know, maybe I'm going insane," he sat back and paused for a minute, thoughtful.

"This reminds me of cultish behavior, maybe vampirism or some other weird underground cult that harvests blood," he trailed off thoughtfully.

"You have been watching too many daytime drama shows. I mean, seriously? Vampirism?" I was lighthearted with my banter, but I secretly hoped he wasn't being serious. "I'm sure there's a perfectly good explanation. It's no big deal. We'll poke our nose around, find out what's going on and make a call to the proper jurisdiction. I seriously doubt that some cult or vampire club is out here drinking animal blood," I joked lightheartedly.

"I hoped I'd never have to tell you this . . ." he said, not amused by my light conjectures.

"Tell me what?" I was suddenly hit with a very bad feeling in my stomach.

"When your people were attacked, when your parents were murdered—" he proceeded cautiously "—we believed that it was a pre-meditated, cooperative act of an underground cult."

The words stung and my heart sank like a capsized boat.

I swallowed hard.

"You're not joking, are you? Who is this 'we' you speak of?" Now, Kyle had my attention.

"The FBI agents that oversaw the case, the protection officers here, and myself. They never found a single member of the cult to validate their suspicions, but I haven't forgotten," he explained.

"And you think this is related?" I heard a fear in my voice now that was strangely unfamiliar, even to me.

"I don't know, but I don't have a good feeling about it. Maybe this is a start-up of a new generation of the cult. Maybe it's an initiation of some type. Or worse, maybe the original cult is back." Kyle sighed, obviously overwhelmed. "It seems very unnatural and maybe a little too coincidental," he raised his head slowly. "It has been a long time though, almost seventeen years now. Basically, I don't know what to think," he said as he stood and approached me. "I don't want to drag you into this without your knowing what might be involved."

He towered over me by at least a foot. But despite his awesome size, his demeanor was gentle and loving. I knew he wouldn't hurt a fly.

"Danger, adventure, uncertainty, and maybe even get a lead on my parents' murderers. It's better than this mundane excuse for an existence I'm currently living," I ranted. "Let's go," I added, feigning excitement as I tried to relieve the distressing tension in the air.

Kyle drove for an hour or so before we reached Blair Lake. Neither of us said a word, and the weight of the silence hung heavy in the air. We were both lost deep within our convoluted thoughts and memories.

Normally, uncomfortable silences wouldn't have bothered us. But this was different. This struck a sensitive nerve in both of us that we simply couldn't ignore.

I imagined how strange it must be for him to have worked along-side my father for so many years as a Ranger, and then to suffer his loss only to have his daughter walk in the same footsteps several years later. The idea sent a chill down my spine.

When we arrived, Kyle hiked me out about three miles before I had to take over in the dense forest. I utilized all my tracking and search skills, second nature to me since I was a young girl.

A little more than thirty minutes later, we found the defeated beast. It was a female mountain lion.

"Huh," I said upon a preliminary inspection.

"What is it?" Kyle asked with cautiousness in his tone.

"You notice anything odd about this picture?" I hinted as I gently ran my hands over the smooth, untouched fur of the beautiful creature.

Kyle walked around me in a large circle, trying to figure out what I was referring to.

"Anything a little bit off about a dead animal that has been lying here on the forest floor for more than a sunrise and moonrise?" I egged him on.

Kyle paused for a moment, looking down at the ground as if he was trying to recall something to his memory. Suddenly, he looked to me with an expression of realization.

"Why hasn't it been a meal yet? It should be a carcass by now," he said, suddenly understanding.

"*SHE* should be a carcass, yes," I corrected him.

"So, what's wrong with her then?" he asked.

I turned back to her, brooding over the same question. Then I had a realization of my own and I stood and scanned the forest floor in a three hundred and sixty degree circle.

"Do you hear that?" I asked as I strained my ears to hear.

"Hear what? I don't hear anything," Kyle said, once again not understanding what I was implying.

"Exactly! It is deathly quiet out here. The absence of the expected is just as important as the unexpected discovery." I turned back to the lion.

"Her neck was broken first, then she was drained of her blood," I mentioned as I inspected the creature closer.

"How can you tell?"

"Look at the ground, there are no signs of struggle. Look around her body. There are no broken branches, no disturbed moss, not even a crunched leaf," I explained to Kyle. "She probably didn't even see it coming."

Kyle looked down by his feet beside the lion, then a look of bewilderment came into his eyes.

"How do you do that?" he asked, stunned.

"My backyard, remember?" I said lightly.

"See these small protrusions at the back of the neck?" I pointed as Kyle leaned down to get a better look. "These are the dislocated vertebrae from where the neck was broken. And see how clean the puncture wounds are? No torn tissue, or bruising, and barely even a stray drop of blood. Since there is also no evidence of a struggle in the puncture wounds, it would suggest that she was killed first, and then drained of her blood with great precision and care." I slowly circled around the beast, brooding. Kyle was silent as he waited for me to mentally process everything I was looking at.

"This was done by a very skilled hunter. It's too precise of a kill to be an animal, too premeditated and practiced," I thought out loud. "But I can't imagine a human being able to take her on either. So if it wasn't human, and it wasn't an animal . . . ."

"I don't understand," Kyle said.

"Neither do I, at least not yet," I said as I put my backpack down and procured my small evidence kit from the front pouch.

"What are you doing?" Kyle inquired.

"I think the lacerations are filled with some kind of fluid," I explained as I put on a pair of gloves and grabbed a cotton swab and sterile sample container. Gently, I touched the swab to the laceration. It ruptured and a clear, viscous fluid oozed from the bite mark. Carefully I put the swab in the sterile container and back into my pouch.

"I'll have Marcus take a look at this sample, see if he can make any sense of it."

"Marcus? Marcus from the bookstore?" Kyle asked as if maybe he hadn't heard me correctly.

"Yeah, he has a gift with chemistry and science. He has been the modern day medicine man for the reservation for years," I said.

"Huh, well I'll be damned. Just when you think you know everything about this town . . ." he trailed off in amusement. "So what is all of this?" he inquired. "What do you make of it?"

I stood and cocked my head to one side, visually taking in the beast once again.

"I don't know really. I've never seen anything like it before. Either that sample from the laceration has something very unfriendly about it and our forest critters can smell it, or whatever killed this beast is out there right now. Probably not far off, judging by the silence in the air," I added. "Something, or someone, is a very good and a very dangerous hunter and it's out there somewhere."

"Someone?" Kyle asked stunned. "I thought you said that's impossible."

Suddenly I sensed something from behind me. I froze and inhaled deeply, the hairs on the back of my neck stood high. I looked up at Kyle to see if he had sensed the same thing.

He looked completely unaffected, still craning his neck and squinting his eyes desperately trying to understand the mountain lion's fate.

I turned on my heel slowly, cautiously. There was something, or someone there.

I didn't know how I knew. I just knew.

"Stay here," I whispered and in the same instant I was off into a full sprint in the direction of the stranger.

I ran faster than I remembered possible, barely able to see more than five feet ahead.

I ran and ran, surge after surge of adrenalin coursing fast and hard through my veins. Suddenly something from the west caught my eye. It was a glimmer, a reflection of some type. The kind that would come from a light bouncing off of a mirror or metal.

An eerie feeling wafted over me and a chill went down my spine.

Something wasn't right.

I turned so quickly it made me dizzy, attempting to identify the source of the glimmer. There, through the trees about fifty yards away, was a woman.

Her face was shrouded in the darkness of a hood, but the few strands of golden hair that escaped glistened where the sun's rays hit them. She wore a gorgeous pale-blue dress that reached the ground, and on top of it was a jet-black cape that enveloped the rest of her body.

There was something very regal about her presence. She reminded me of a queen or a princess from a bygone era.

"Willamette Forest Ranger," I identified myself in a firm tone. "What are you doing out here? Are you lost?" I demanded.

Silence. I started to walk slowly towards the figure, so as not to scare her off.

"Hello," her greeting was strangely ethereal, like a whisper of an angels' voice. "Lakota Avital of the

Kalapuya people," she said as if she was simply confirming my identity in her own mind.

I stopped dead in my tracks and inhaled deeply again, as if I was trying to smell something in the air. I smelled nothing unusual, just the normal damp foliage.

The figure cocked her head to one side as she watched me intently. It was a strangely primitive motion.

"How do you know who I am? Who are you?" I demanded. I strode purposely forward.

She did not answer my question.

"They will come . . ." she whispered, but the sound of her voice traveled impossibly farther through the woods than it should have.

I froze again as the words echoed in my ear, the same words from my dream. And it was the same voice.

It echoed again, even louder.

"They will come . . . ."

I found myself shaking my head hard against the voices that chorused in my head.

"No! No!" I screamed. "Get out of my head," I yelled as I squeezed my eyes shut against the voices.

And then they stopped and there was nothing but utter silence. I opened my eyes, frantically looking for the woman.

She was gone.

"They will come," I heard her voice from behind me once more but when I turned to see her, there was no one there. Desperately, I scanned the forest floor, looking for the strange woman.

The woods were empty and the eerie feeling abruptly left me. It was as if the woman simply vanished, or maybe she never existed in the first place. Maybe I imagined the whole thing.

Of neither was I sure.

I trekked back to where I left Kyle, realizing how much distance I had covered. It took an awfully long time to get back to him.

"Lakota!" came a familiar voice through the trees. Then big hands grabbed me firmly by the shoulders, and shook me. "Lakota! Don't you ever do that to me again. Are you alright? What the hell were you doing?" Kyle demanded.

"How long was I gone?" I asked.

"Uh, I guess about fifteen or twenty minutes," he stumbled to get his thoughts together. "Why?" he asked, in a calmer voice this time.

"None of this makes any sense," I mumbled. I tried to figure the numbers in my head, but they just would not work out right. I had run at least a mile or so out into the forest, and I had walked back. Fifteen to twenty minutes should have only accounted for a one-way trip in the thick foliage of the forest.

I was struggling to keep my composure. What the hell was happening to me?

Everything felt horribly out of place and foreign all of a sudden. Without a word I started back to the truck with Kyle right on my heels.

"You look like you've seen a ghost. What happened to you out there?" Kyle demanded.

"I'm fine," I mumbled between my clenched teeth.

My mind tried again and again to deny what I had heard, what I had seen. It tried to justify, quantify, or explain it in some logical way.

But it just didn't fit. I couldn't recalibrate the distance I'd gone and no matter how much I tried to deny it, I knew I hadn't seen things. I knew I had really seen her, heard her, felt her presence.

We began the drive back and Kyle tried again and again to figure me out. "Please tell me what happened back there, Lakota. I knew I never should have gotten you involved."

"I'm fine—it's nothing. I just thought I saw something," was as much as I could mumble.

Finally he left the matter alone.

"I think we need to do something about that mountain lion," I said.

"Yeah, maybe in this case it's not such a good idea to let nature do its thing. Too much attention. I'll call animal services and come back first thing tomorrow and take care of it," he said.

"Don't bother," I said as I pulled out my phone and started to write a text message. "I'm letting Kotan and Yuri know now. She'll be gone by sunrise," I stated as a command with no room for interjection.

"Ok, thanks. You trust them right? No disrespect to the warriors, but I don't know Kotan and Yuri very well.

And what about your newest addition to the vampire clan, Jesse, isn't it? They won't tell anyone, will they? We need to keep this whole thing quiet until we figure out what's going on out there."

"I trust the warriors with my life. It's the best way to avoid unnecessary attention. We don't want the town to be in a panic," I concurred.

The rest of the drive back was silent and the rest of the day was uneventful. It seemed to pass in one big blur. Kyle kept a worried, watchful eye on me, but he didn't say another word about the subject.

At about half past four, Kyle insisted that I head home and get some rest. He did, however, remind me that he would want to talk about what had happened.

I consented, my mind still dazed.

Before I realized it, I was driving past the sign that read "Kalapuya Reservation" and pulling into the dirt driveway to our little white house trimmed in dark red. I cut the engine and hopped out. Leaning against the truck for a minute, I collected myself and noted how the setting sun cast beautiful amber shadows across the sky.

As I stood there, something from just east of our house caught my eye. I squinted to try and make out what looked like a figure.

With caution, I walked closer. As I approached, a familiar eerie feeling washed over me in waves that made me nauseous. I could see the outline of the figure against the dark forest scenery. I could see the familiar black cape, and a womanly silhouette veiled in the shadows of the setting sun. I could feel her heavy and intimidating presence.

It was her. It was the strange woman.

An unfamiliar fear tore at my innards.

I swallowed hard.

My bones ached with that familiar agony.

2 CREATURE

"WHAT DO YOU WANT FROM ME?" I demanded angrily as I proceeded closer.

This time the feminine figure took a few small steps closer to me. Within moments, we were within arms' reach.

I still couldn't make out her face in the shadows of the hood she wore, but I could see that she was slim in build, and she wore black gloves over delicate, thin fingers.

"The ghosts of your past . . . they have returned for you," her angelic voice whispered.

There was a pause and in that moment she raised her head to meet mine. Several strands of golden hair escaped the black hood and fell forward across her chest.

Within the darkness of the shadows that seemed to consume her, there were two things that were vividly clear, her rose red lips and her strange eyes.

They were eerie eyes. The color in them was almost as bright as her hair, but there was a darker ring around the golden color. Maybe a dark red, or an earthly brown. I couldn't quite tell. I had never seen such beautiful eyes.

They reminded me of something unworldly, almost alien.

"I . . . I don't understand," I stuttered as I shook my head and my eyes shifted down to the ground, my mind desperately trying to piece together what she was insinuating. But as I finished the sentence and looked up, the leaves rustled as if a wind had swept by abruptly, and she was gone.

"The secrets lie in your past," her voice echoed through the trees as if from the atmosphere all around me.

Spinning on my heel, I turned around to see where she had gone, but she was nowhere to be seen. Combing the ground with my eyes, I searched for any trace of her having been there; a broken twig, crinkled leaves, a turned stone—anything. There wasn't a single trace. Absentmindedly, I wondered if I had actually seen her or if she were a figment of my imagination. It was as if she had simply vanished into the ethers.

Mesmerized, I stood there in awe. I couldn't comprehend what I had seen, or what she had meant. I sat down on a nearby tree trunk and lost myself in the abyss of my thoughts until well past sunset.

When I was finally able to collect myself, I stumbled into the house in a daze.

"Hello? Anybody home?" I yelled as I stashed my keys on the tiny table in the small foyer. Turning the corner to the living room, I scanned the space for my father. Most nights, he would be there in his big brown leather chair catching up on the local news with a beer on the side table. But no one was there, which was strange.

"Lakota?" Notak, my brother came around the corner from the hall that led to the three tiny bedrooms in the house. He went to the fridge and grabbed an apple, taking a big bite as he shut the door.

"Where's Wakiza?" I asked, slightly concerned.

"Training drill with Jesse and the warriors," Notak mumbled with a full mouth. "Taking care of some dead animal in the northeast Willamette," he commented.

"Yeah, Kyle and I checked out a mountain lion today, and I asked Kotan and Yuri to get rid of it for him. Why is father involved though?"

"I don't know, Kotan called him not too long ago. Said there was something really strange about the whole thing." Notak's demeanor suddenly changed to that of suspicion. "What's going on? I mean, I thought the Rangers just left things like that to nature. What aren't you telling me?"

I sighed. There wasn't any way to hide things from Notak. He knew me too well.

"I'm not sure, but it was weird. Just little things that were . . . off. Maybe Kotan and Yuri can figure it out. They have more experience than I do. But I was hoping they wouldn't take Jesse. He's not ready," I said, concerned.

"Jesse didn't go originally. But when Kotan called, he asked Wakiza to bring him. He said something about this being good practice. They haven't seen anything like this in a long time. Give Jesse some credit, he's got some mad skills and he catches on quick," he said with comical animation.

"I just don't get father's obsession with making Jesse a warrior. I mean, he's just a kid," I mused. In the back of my mind I was instantly concerned about this having been seen before. What did that mean?

"Jesse is 14, he isn't a little boy anymore. It's not like they're hunting a bear or something. They're just cleaning up a mess. Why are you getting so worked up, Kota?" Notak's demeanor suddenly turned suspicious. "What is it with all the vagueness? Something you want to tell me?"

I paused momentarily, thinking back to the mountain lion, the strange wounds, the weird puss, and the woman. Were they connected? It wasn't that I didn't trust Notak. I trusted him with my life. It was just that I wasn't sure I wanted to get him involved in something I might regret.

"You just don't know what you're going to run into out there, and something just doesn't sit right with me about the whole thing."

"Geez, Kota, did you see big-foot or something? They'll be alright. I mean, I don't exactly understand the whole 'warrior' business but you know better than I do that father knows what he's doing. And lay off Jesse, the kid has the nose of a wolf. He's a born hunter and tracker."

In my hazy memories I thought back to the day Jesse was born. He was the first baby born to the tribe after the massacre. His arrival marked a turning point with our people. He was the dawn of new hope.

"Yeah, he definitely has something going on. Remember how Jesse refused to walk, he just never wanted to stop crawling. And remember how he used to talk to the wolves? And what was he, two years old when he shot his first squirrel?" I recalled all of it.

"Hey, I remember 'somebody else' I know who slept in the wolves' den. Oh, did I mention, with the wolves?" Notak said smartly, referring to my childhood days. "Come on, Kota. He's good at what he does. Let him be who he is. Don't be a hypocrite. You two are more alike than you want to admit."

"Yeah, that's what scares me," I said. "He's like a little brother to me."

"Well now you know how I feel," he said, teasing me with a wink.

I didn't respond. I opened the fridge and grabbed an apple for myself. "It's been a long day, I'm going to go lay down," I said as I took a bite.

"Alright, well, as always, I hope something changes for you tonight."

As I began to make my way to my bedroom, I quickly looked over my shoulder in time to catch the sad look in Notak's eyes. He knew as well as I did what the night would hold for me.

"Me too," I muttered.

My restless sleep came quickly. The nightmare came next, then the agony. This night was no different than any of the previous nights in the past four years. Except that now I recognized that the voice in the dream was *hers*. It was no longer a foreign whisper. It was the voice of the woman from the forest. The woman with the rose red lips, the strange eyes, and the unearthly voice.

When I woke in a sweat, as I always did, I could swear that I saw those unearthly eyes piercing through my window. For a while, I lay there contemplating what I had seen, but eventually I was swept into a dreamless sleep and the next thing I knew, the rays of the sun warmed my bronze skin.

I was up and dressed in less than two minutes, but this time I put on my deerskin moccasins instead of my boots. As quietly as I could, I snuck out of the house, escaping an encounter with Wakiza or Notak. I threw my boots onto the passenger seat, jumped into the driver's seat, and turned the key in the ignition of the

Explorer, pulling out onto the road that lead out of the reservation. Once I was cruising down the main highway, I took out my cell phone.

"Kyle, it's me. Hey, I have something I need to take care of before I come in today, will that be alright?" I asked.

"Yeah, of course," he said with slight hesitation.

"Thanks, I'll see you in a couple hours." I quickly hung up the phone so as not to allow any room for questioning or added conversation. In about an hour's time I stopped on the northwest side of Blair Lake. I got out, took a deep breath and broke into a full sprint towards the site of the mountain lion.

Before long, I was where she should have been. I could see where the twigs and foliage lay flat where she had once lain. A short distance away, I saw the fire that had claimed her remains.

The site of the fire was very neat and tidy and all that remained now were the ashes and smoke. My fear had been realized. The only time we ever burned the remains of an animal was if it had been diseased. I knew this meant that there was something very wrong happening in the woods. Dread started to fill the pit of my stomach.

Wandering the forests aimlessly for an hour or so, my thoughts wandered curiously on all the strange things that had transpired in the last day. Could they all be coincidental and unrelated? Or was there some connection between all the seemingly bizarre encounters?

Meandering through the woods, I was searching for something, but I wasn't sure exactly what that something was. It felt as if I knew where I was supposed to go, as if I was being drawn by some magnetic field.

Suddenly, I was aware of a twinge in the back of my mind, a painful feeling with which I was unfamiliar. It jerked all of my senses awake in a single moment. Surreptitiously, I scanned the forest floor taking mental note of which direction the moss on the trees was growing so I could get some sense of my location. But the twinge I felt wasn't because I thought I might be lost.

A lump had formed in the back of my throat and my breathing became heavy and laborious. My legs felt as if they were filled with iron, my vision blurred, and my head throbbed. I felt an uncontrollable urge to run, yet my legs refused to move. I tried desperately to pull myself from my paralyzed state.

I tried to turn back in the direction from which I had come; that seemed like a good place to start, but a wave of excruciating pain crashed down on me like ocean waves on the cliff rocks. It radiated down my spine, through my ribcage, and into my arms and legs until my fingers and toes were numb with anguish. There was an isolated stabbing twinge in the back of my head, like a migraine headache, that roared intensely.

It was almost like the nightly agony, only I was fully conscious and it wasn't night.

Unmoving and unable to bear the pain, I fell to my knees clutching at my head and my body at the same time. A distressing moan filled my ears, but I didn't realize until a second later that it was mine.

Time seemed to pass slowly, even stop altogether.

Clawing at my chest, I found myself gasping for air. It felt like there just wasn't enough oxygen in the atmosphere to satiate me.

And then as suddenly as it had all begun, the strange attack faded like a wave receding back into the ocean. The excruciating pain subsided to a dull, bearable ache. Now my eyes felt like they were on fire. My vision became incredibly clear, although the color in my world faded to shades of blacks, and whites, and grays. I felt my legs come back, but they felt itchy and hot. Every nerve in my body screamed at me.

I didn't understand what was happening.

In those few seconds that felt like an eternity, I became instantly aware of one, very disturbing truth.

I was not alone.

This time it was not the strange woman. This presence did not feel like the hovering of her angelic presence. No, this was a darker presence.

I flew to my feet, ready for whoever was there.

It, whatever or whoever it was, was behind me, in the direction from which I had come, following me.

I could sense it. A menacing, dangerous sensation.

It wasn't an animal, but it also wasn't human.

Wait! How would I know that? I thought.

Stunned, I found myself sniffing the air like a rabid dog. I froze, still as the dead, appalled at myself when I realized that I suddenly knew the difference in scent between animal and human.

Impossible!

My mind rejected the notion the instant it entered my head. I turned on my heel with a speed I simply could not have been capable of. A speed not humanly possible.

As I came out of my blindingly fast turn, I saw the figure of a man.

And then he was gone so quickly that I knew for sure that there was something very unnatural about the being. It was the form of a man, but I hadn't caught his face, just the shadow of the lingering ghost that he had left behind.

The whisper of rustling leaves was the only proof that something had been there in the first place.

The leaves in the trees rustled again, this time in a more predictable pattern, as if a bird had flown through and left only the sounds of his fluttering wings and the whisper of the wind in its wake.

A strangely intoxicating scent wafted down through the trees. I couldn't tell what the scent was, but I found myself inadvertently inhaling it.

It smelled almost like the fresh hides I prepared back home, but there was also something sweet to it, like maple syrup or honey.

I wasn't alone. He was up there . . . in the trees.

"I know you're there. Show yourself!" I heard my voice demand with an authority that baffled me.

I was no courageous hero. I found myself appalled at my uncharacteristic show of courage and determination, yet fear or terror or panic did not come back to me. I felt, instead, very steady, very calm, and very certain of myself.

I felt powerful.

"Come on, you son of a bitch. You want me?" I taunted him, or it, mockingly. "You want me? Come on."

For the first time in many years, I didn't feel so out of place in my skin.

I waited there, my eyes burning with determination as they scanned the canopy above me. I could hear every leaf as it floated to the ground, every drop of dew, every whisper of the wind. But I heard no response to my demands. I became suddenly aware that I was angry. I was furious that my demands had not been met.

And then just as suddenly as everything had happened it was all swiftly snatched away. That feeling of power and control was gone as inexplicably as it had come. I waited inevitably for something to happen. Somehow, I knew it would.

Barely a second later, it came. The lump in my throat, my heavy legs, the headache. Panic, fear, even terror. For the first time since my dreamy little stupor had begun, there was a terror that gripped me like nothing I'd ever felt before.

My heart pounded so hard I could hear it echoing in my ears. Then the pain came back ten-fold, my whole body quivering uncontrollably. My eyes were burning and blurry again, and there was a resounding scream in my head that made my ears throb.

I tried to force myself to walk, to get away, but instead I fell to the ground overcome with pain. "What the hell is happening to me?" I whispered. I was not alone. Despite everything, I was still painfully aware of this fact. But the pain was so horribly unbearable that I wouldn't have cared less if someone, or something, was out there to do me in.

I only wanted desperately for the pain to stop. It was more intense than I'd experienced in any of my restless nights. Writhing on the forest floor for several minutes, I finally dragged myself to my feet and succeeded in taking a few steps forward, moaning all the while.

I could feel his eyes on me. I pressed forward for three more steps. I expected each one to be my last and hoped my misery would come to an end. But the end did not come, and the agony continued to torture me until I became convinced that my brain would melt at any moment.

"What the hell is wrong with me?" I mumbled as I turned in a full circle scanning the forest. I could feel his presence was still out there, somewhere in the near distance still keeping an eye on me.

I stumbled forward step by step until finally I was back at the Explorer. I climbed in and collapsed into the seat, locking the door behind me. Gripping the steering wheel as if my life depended on it, I tried to calm myself and regain my composure. Minutes went by as I sat there trying to catch my breath, waiting for the pain to subside. My legs were shaking uncontrollably, my chest heaving hard.

"Just breathe, Kota," I told myself. And slowly but surely my breath evened out and my nerves relaxed.

"Lakota!"

I nearly jumped out of my seat and had a heart attack. I turned to find Notak banging on the driver's side window and yelling my name.

"Kota! Are you all right? Open the door!" he screamed at me in desperation.

Stunned, I obeyed his command and unlocked the door. As he swung it open hard and fast I realized I had been leaning against it. Suddenly overcome by weakness, I fell from my seat into Notak's muscular arms. Gently, he lay me on the ground and took my left hand into his.

"Kota, what happened to you?" he demanded, his eyes analyzing my body in disbelief.

I looked down at myself and gasped in utter shock. My white shirt was drenched in a combination of sweat and blood, and my shirt was shredded in so many places I couldn't begin to count. There were wounds everywhere, bloody gashes and scratches that looked like I had been attacked by a wolf or dog. I turned my hands over so that they were palms up. They too were covered in my own blood, mostly around my fingertips.

"Kota!" Notak insisted.

"I . . . I don't know." I stammered. "There was something out there."

"Damn it, Kota!" Notak yelled angrily. "I know you've been going through some weird shit lately, but this is too much," he said. "You've got to stop trying to be so tough and tell me what the fuck you've gotten yourself into."

I could feel tears welling up in my eyes. If there was one thing that I hated more than anything in life, it was to see how much misery I put Notak through. Turning my eyes to the forest, I tried to fight the tears. It was then that I saw Kotan, standing at the edge of the forest. He was tall and handsome, and his strong muscles rippled under his dark bronze skin. His long, black hair framed his strong, chiseled jawline. The look of concern in his face was undeniable.

"I got this!" Notak yelled towards Kotan, but his eyes never left me. Kotan hesitated for a moment, and then turned and ran into the woods.

"Notak please, you must believe me," I pleaded as the tears threatened to flow over. "I . . . I really don't know," I said, bewildered.

He stared at me trying to evaluate my honesty. After several uncomfortable moments, he let out a heavy sigh and sat back, his eyes staring straight ahead as if he was contemplating what to do next.

"There is something out here. Kotan saw something last night. You shouldn't have been out here." He looked at me once more before he effortlessly scooped me up into his arms. I wrapped my hands around his neck, welcoming his embrace. He carried me to the passenger seat and carefully sat me down. Without another word he got into the driver's seat and started the ignition. I knew he believed me. I knew he felt helpless and frustrated. But I knew he believed me.

After a short drive, he stopped the car and turned off the ignition. He got out of the truck, still wordless, and came to the passenger side to open the door for me. He carried my feeble body a short ways before we came to a small creek.

He sat me down on a boulder, took off his shirt and wet it with water from the creek.

"Notak, it's so cold," I protested him using his shirt on my behalf.

"Don't worry about me, I'll be fine," he reassured me. Gingerly, he began to wipe my face of the blood and dirt that had caked there. And then he proceeded down my arms, my stomach, and my legs.

After a while, I took the shirt from Notak and began to clean my wounds myself as he watched with concern in his eyes.

I took a big mouthful of water from the creek and swallowed. The ice cold liquid felt good as it rushed down my parched throat. I waited a minute for it to hit my stomach, hoping that it would help appease the knots that had accumulated there.

Notak rummaged around through a small pack he had brought with him, pulling out a piece of dried meat.

"Here, eat this," he said as he handed me the jerky. The smell of the dried venison made me queasy.

"Come on, Kota. It'll help," he pleaded.

I reluctantly took it and bit off a small piece. He was right, once I started I couldn't stop and the aching in my stomach subsided a little more with each bite.

It never ceased to amaze me how Notak knew exactly what it was I needed at almost any given moment. He didn't say anything, but I could tell he was waiting for me to explain. He just sat there patiently watching me finish cleaning up, sensitive enough to my predicament not to push the conversation until I was ready.

I wanted to say something, anything. But I didn't know where to start, or how to begin.

"How did you know I would be out here?" I inquired.

"Kyle called. He said you were acting weird yesterday. I could tell he was really concerned about what you might be up to. And he was right," he said.

"And Kotan?"

"We were hunting when Kyle called. And I figured with all this weird stuff going on, maybe I shouldn't be out here alone. Something you obviously didn't think about."

I sighed as I rolled my eyes.

"I can take care of myself," I said, but the words didn't sound as convincing as I'd meant them to.

"Uh huh, I can see that," Notak said. "What did this to you?" he asked as he motioned to the cuts and claw marks covering my entire body.

"Something was out there, but it never touched me. I can't explain how or why, but this was self-inflicted," I said as I extended my fingers to show him where the skin and blood had accumulated under my fingernails from digging into my own flesh.

"What the hell is going on with you Kota?" He nodded his head in severe disapproval. "And this whole 'I don't know' charade isn't going to cut it anymore. So spit it out."

"It's getting worse," I mumbled as I looked down towards the ground in shame. "Something in me is changing, brother. I can't explain it," I hesitated. "I have been seeing things, hearing things, sensing things . . . things that shouldn't be humanly possible," I said, staring past Notak into the distance. "I think my nightmare has been a warning of something that's coming. I was serious when I told you that I think I'm cursed," I said. My thoughts wandered momentarily to the foreboding words of the strange woman.

"There is something or someone out there . . . and I have a bad feeling about it," I trailed off lost in thought once again. "I'm sorry. You probably think I'm crazy."

"Yeah. Completely insane," he agreed sarcastically. Then he edged closer to me and took one of my hands into his.

"Kota. I've known you my whole life. I know who you used to be and I know how you have changed. But all this time, past and present, I have never doubted that your legacy will be . . . epic," he said. "I can't explain it, it's just this feeling I have. I trust you, and I believe you," he said looking into my eyes. "We're going to figure this out. I promise."

Then he turned trying to hide a chuckle. "Besides it must have been pretty serious. I have never seen you so pale in my life. Now I know what you would look like if weren't a half blood," he teased.

"Ha-ha-ha," I mocked him.

His laughter helped pull me out of my episode. It was nice to know that he had my back despite all my idiosyncrasies.

"I guess that bracelet didn't do such a good job protecting you, huh?" He glanced at the gift he had given me the day before, disappointed.

"Not true. I don't think it's supposed to protect me from myself. And there is something going on out there, but I'm still here." I gently rubbed the beads running along my bloody wrist and wondered belatedly how much danger I had really been in.

"So what now?" I asked Notak.

"You have a change of clothes?" he asked.

"Yeah, in the back," I motioned towards the Explorer. You never knew where or for how long you might be stranded on a job, so a good ranger was always prepared; food, water, extra clothes, blankets, flares, matches, radio. It was all basic survival stuff, but sheer necessity in some parts of the woods.

"Take me to the main highway, I'll walk home from there," he said. "Go to work before Kyle gets too worried. Get yourself back together and I'll come up with something to tell father so he won't worry too much. I'll tell him . . ." he paused thoughtfully. "I'll tell him you fell down a hill or something."

"What about Kotan?"

"Something tells me he has no intention of telling Wakiza about any of this," Notak said.

I nodded my approval of the plan.

"But promise you'll tell me if anything new happens," he demanded.

I agreed.

I gave Kyle the same alibi Notak had come up with; I had tripped and fallen down a hill. Fortunately, the long sleeve shirt and long pants I changed into were a dark navy-blue and hid the majority of the bloody evidence.

When he asked about the events of the previous day, I politely told him that when I understood what the hell it was that I had seen, he would be the first to know. The sad thing was, that really was the truth.

That night when I arrived home, I could have sworn that I saw a figure in the trees watching me. There was the scent of something rough and sweet in the air like earlier that day in the presence of that creature. But when I tried to approach to get a better view . . . no one was there.

And the scent was gone.

As I made my way up to my room, Wakiza gave me a bad time about how clumsy I was to be rolling down hills. I grabbed him another beer from the fridge and retorted back that I had just been very tired and a little off as usual. Thankfully, he didn't press the issue any further. He took the beer, opened it, and went back to watching the news on the TV without even a glance over his shoulder at me.

Back in my room, I peeled my clothes off my bloodied body, trying to be careful with the areas where the blood had dried with the fabric and adhered to the wounds. I took a long bath and cleaned the slashes in my skin, then retired to bed in exhaustion. The agony that night was so intense that I literally passed out from the pain and fatigue. My nightmare was the same as always, except that maybe there was a little more clarity to the dark, ominous figure. It was shadowy, and enormous, and black. It had great leathery wings, but the body of a man.

And then deep dreamless sleep took me.

For the rest of the night, my body and mind somehow found relief and the resemblance of peace.

It was as if the haunting creature had brought some reconciliation.

3 HONEY AND LEATHER

THE REST OF THE WEEK PASSED WITHOUT INCIDENT. The monotony of my strange, frozen life resumed. The days were a blur of disorientation, and the nights were a whirlwind of agony. I found myself looking, searching vehemently, for both the woman in the cape and the faceless creature. My senses were painfully aware, always on edge and waiting for the possible return of whatever or whoever was out there.

But their existences appeared to simply evaporate. Another week came and went, and then another. By the time my self-inflicted wounds had healed, and they healed faster than I had anticipated, my mind had yet again resorted to denial and repression. My thoughts dwelt on finding some logical explanation for all the strange events that had transpired.

It was a Sunday morning at the end of February when I finally decided to drive into town and make a visit to the local bookstore. Oakridge was about a twenty-five mile drive out from the Kalapuya reservation, the majority of which wound through the forests on a bumpy, old dirt road. My thoughts meandered and rabbit trailed as I made the hour-long drive into town. Before I knew it I was passing the "Oakridge, Population 3,148" sign on the right, just outside of the Hills Creek Dam Road.

Oakridge was a very small town, the kind that was barely recognized on a map. If you blinked while driving through, you would miss it entirely.

I pulled onto First Street and into the parking lot of the bookstore. It was my favorite place in civilization within a hundred mile radius and it was the only bookstore in town. The books I brought back to the reservation were always put to good use in the communal library. The Kalapuya loved to read and to learn. History books were the most common and the favorite among the people, but over the years we had accumulated a collection covering a broad range of subjects; geography, biographies, children's books, how-to books, cook books, a little of everything really.

The bell on the bookstore door chimed happily when I opened it.

"Hey, Marcus," I said to the old man behind the counter. He smiled in instant recognition.

"Lakota, good to see you. Where have you been hiding? Haven't seen you in weeks."

"Guess I've been a little preoccupied lately. I've been meaning to come see you for a while but some less than ordinary things have been happening in the Willamette. Sorry old friend, I didn't mean to worry you."

He chuckled to himself quietly. "I know you can take care of yourself, just missed seeing you around."

Marcus was in his late sixties, but he still had the energy and vitality of a forty year old. He was thin and tall, with the most inviting face.

"I have a favor to ask of you. I mean, if you can find the time." I knew he would have the time. In a small town like this, there just wasn't a lot of things to do. And sure enough as soon as I'd finished the words, Marcus suddenly came to life with anticipation and eagerness.

"I have this sample of something I pulled from a mountain lion a couple weeks ago," I said as I pulled a vial from my pocket. "It came from a strange . . ." I struggled for the right words. "I'm not sure, but they looked like lacerations from bite marks. I was hoping you might be able to shed some light as to what this might be, or if there is anything strange about it," I explained as I placed it on the counter.

"Anything for you, Kota. You know it's always nice when you bring me little projects. Gives me something to do," he said with a certain excitement in his voice.

"Thanks Marcus, I really appreciate it," I said with sincerity.

"Oh, before I forget," Marcus said with a pause. "I got a new book in yesterday . . . a history book about the Renaissance period," he fumbled around behind the counter for a minute. "Here it is. It's got lots of good pictures. I figured the elders would like that," he smiled knowingly.

I smiled as I flipped through the book. "It's perfect, thank you Marcus. Could you hang on to this for me? I'm just going to look around for a bit."

"Of course, take your time. I haven't got anything else new since you were last here though," he informed me.

It hadn't been more than a month or so since my last visit, but in this small town, we were always a little behind the pace of things. Including the timely arrival of new shipments.

"That's alright, I'm not looking for anything in particular."

"Well, I'll be right here if you need anything," he said with a gracious smile.

"Thanks," I said as I started towards the fiction aisle close to the back of the store. The shelves were very tall, and there were many aisles. I grabbed a stool on the way to the back so that I could extend my five foot three frame a bit to reach the upper shelves. I browsed through the hundreds of titles, lingering on the ones I had bought and read, trying to remember what I liked about each one.

I heard the bells on the door ring the entrance of another customer, and the quiet back and forth chatter between Marcus and the stranger as greetings were exchanged. Absentmindedly, I thought of how nice Marcus was, like a father welcoming his child home. I pulled a few books here and there, but was unsatisfied with my selections.

Suddenly, I realized a presence to my right, and looked over my shoulder quickly. There was no one there. Dumbfounded, I gazed down the aisle, confused.

I had sensed it. I knew I had.

A half-second late, *he* rounded the corner. I took a brief look at him as he hung his hat on the top of the bookshelf corner, and then turned my eyes back towards the books I had been mulling over. I spaced off, staring at the binding of some books, but not staring at any one in particular.

"Weird," I whispered to myself. It was almost as if I had sensed that he was coming before it actually happened. Although there were dozens of other aisles in the store, I somehow knew he would come down my particular aisle even before he had come around the corner. It was almost like in the forest . . . with that creature. I just knew.

I tried to shrug off the eerie feeling that threatened to take hold of me and cautiously glanced over at the young man. He was tall, maybe about twenty-five or so. I'd never thought much about what my idea of "handsome" might be, but he was it. He was ridiculously handsome. Stunningly good looking.

He was browsing at the end of the aisle as I felt my eyes glued on him. I hoped that he wouldn't notice my staring.

At that moment, he raised his head slowly and his eyes meandered in my direction. I willed myself to jerk my head away, not to look. But my head felt heavy. It was as if I was in a dream, the kind where everything you want your body to do seems to happen in slow motion, always just a moment too late.

He smiled at me from where he stood. I fumbled around with some books on the shelf, but my eyes never left him.

He was absolutely divine, his jaw so square and perfect. His tousled brown hair was like a model from a magazine. His thin button down shirt lay like silk on his broad, muscular shoulders and strained across the chiseled muscles of his chest.

The color tone of his skin was incredibly pale, as if he'd been holed up in some cave for the last several years. It made him look like a god or an angel sent from the heavens.

Our eyes locked for a second . . . two . . . three . . . .

He had the strangest two-toned color eyes. They seemed to be blue with a trim of brown, and I could swear that they almost glowed.

Four seconds . . . .

His eyes vaguely reminded me of someone I had seen before, but I couldn't quite put my finger on whomever it was.

Five seconds . . . .

The sound of several books hitting the floor startled me. I looked down to find that in my awe-struck stupor, I had managed to clumsily drop several books from the shelf.

"Let me help you with those," came the most angelic voice and suddenly he was beside me.

"Oh, it's OK. How embarrassing. I'm such a klutz," I said, as I knelt down to pick up the books. He had already begun to help despite my refusal.

I caught a scent from his swift movement to my side. *His* scent. It was strangely sweet but rough at the same time.

"Honey and leather," I whispered under my breath, and then I realized that I had said it out loud.

"I'm sorry, what did you say?" he asked.

I tried to answer him but the scent was intoxicating, like a drug. My senses screamed at me with fear, excitement, adrenaline, and . . . anger? The last emotion seemed out of place. I didn't understand how such a feeling could be in any way attached to his scent, or to him in any other way, shape, or form. I wanted to turn and attack him, to tear into his flesh. They were strangely predatory feelings. I took the stack of books from him and placed them on the shelf without a word.

"Have you read this one?" he asked as he handed me a specific book he had hung onto. His voice was soft, but rough all at the same time, like his scent. And he had the most sensual accent, not like anything I had ever heard before. It lilted and tilted in the most melodic way, simply mesmerizing me. I froze, afraid to wake from the dream I was sure I was living in now.

I looked down at the book. The title read *Tristan and Isolde.* Spoken words wouldn't come out of my mouth so I just nodded my head in a negative kind of direction.

"It's the tragic love story of two people torn between their hearts desire and what is right and noble," his voice trailed off as if he was somehow lost in the memory of the story.

"Umm," I stammered, my voice cracking. I cleared my throat with great effort. I felt a flush in my cheeks as all my blood seemed to go to my head. I hoped my bronze skin covered my embarrassment. I stood there staring at him, dazed. His eyes stared off behind me, their vivid colors dramatically accentuated against his pale white skin. I glanced over my shoulder as if to try and see what he was looking at, but I knew there was nothing and no one there.

There was an uncomfortable silence for a minute. And then he seemed to shake off whatever it was he was thinking about. His eyes caught mine again.

"I'm so sorry, I haven't even properly introduced myself," he said with that melodic accent that I was finding more and more enticing.

"My name is Aiden Kathel." I took his hand as he offered it in a friendly handshake. It felt cold as ice.

"Lakota Avital, of the Kalapuya tribe. Nice to meet you," I said, pausing to make sure I remembered his name correctly. Aiden. Our hands were still locked in greeting.

"The pleasure is all mine, love," he brought my hand up to his lips and planted a kiss there. A strange feeling, that kiss. Both stunningly cold, but utterly warm all at once.

Odd.

We stood there a moment, his two-toned eyes gazing into my earthy brown eyes. He still held my hand, but now his gloved hand seemed somehow warmer. My heart thudded hard, as if I had just run several miles. My face felt flushed again, and I felt my lungs deeply expanding and contracting. I could feel every muscle in my body twitch to life, every cell tingle. I was uncomfortable with the intimacy I felt with this stranger, but I was unable to pull myself away from him.

And then, as if he had suddenly sensed my uneasiness, he released my hand from his heavenly hold. I took a step back, willing my wild heart beat to calm down, focusing my energy on slowing my heaving chest and steadying my raspy breathing.

He took a step forward, closer to me.

"I'm sorry if I startled you." His accent sent shivers through my spine. It was such a foreign accent, but so melodic in a singsong kind of way.

"No, no. It's all right. It's just . . ." I hesitated a minute wondering if it was rude to say anything. "It's a small town and we don't get many outsiders beyond the gas station. Your accent is unique. Unfamiliar . . ." I trailed off waiting for *him* to say something.

He just stood there, gazing at me, as if lost in some dream or memory.

"I'm sorry if my inquiries are rude," and I meant it. I was momentarily embarrassed. I felt like I might be sticking my nose where it didn't belong.

"No apology needed love. I'm from Ireland, but I haven't been home in . . ." he looked down and stifled what looked like an amused laugh at himself. "Shite, it's been a long time. But I never could completely get rid of this accent, you know what I mean now?" A wry smile spread across his handsome face.

I felt my cheeks flushing again.

"Well, you shouldn't get rid of it. It's a becoming trait." I caught his gaze again and I could swear he was reading my mind. I was thinking how very sexy and intoxicating his voice sounded in my ears. He just had a look in his eyes, as if he completely understood what I was feeling, thinking, experiencing.

"I've never met anyone like you," he said as he took a step closer to me. He took a deep breath in, as if preparing to hold his breath.

Inadvertently, I cocked my head to one side in a very primitive way, confused. I wasn't sure what he meant or what he was referring to. But I felt like I should have known, should have understood what he was talking about.

He leaned in closer to me. Uncomfortably close.

He inspected me from head to toe as if he were trying to figure out what he was looking at. I didn't understand how my blue jeans and white collared long sleeve shirt warranted such attention. I fidgeted with a few strands of my long hair, twirling them around my finger, uncertain how I was supposed to respond.

"Umm," I stuttered. "You mean a native? Well, you're a few miles out from one of the last active reservations in Oregon."

He didn't say anything to confirm or deny what he'd meant. He seemed lost in some type of trance, just standing there staring at me.

"I mean, I'm not entirely Native-American. My father was from England, but my mother was full-blood Kalapuya."

"Was?" he inquired.

"They were murdered when I was four," I said. My voice was void of emotion, almost robotic.

"My apologies, I shouldn't have pried."

"No, it's OK. That was a long time ago."

His scrutinizing eyes met mine and there was an uncomfortable silence as we both stood there. He leaned in until he was but inches from my face and inhaled deeply, as if smelling a rose. I thought he was still trying to figure me out, although he had a strange way of doing so.

"You're an orphan." He smiled slightly as if the idea made him happy.

"I have an adopted father and brother," I corrected him. I didn't think of myself as an orphan.

Suddenly, he jerked upright and stumbled a step backwards. "I should go," he said in such a faint whisper that I could barely make it out.

It was as if he'd just remembered something terribly important. I noticed immediately that the rim of brown in his eyes seemingly grew brighter, almost a crimson red. His eyes bore into mine and I felt as if the crimson stare might tear a hole through my skull. The veins in his face appeared to ripple under his pale skin.

I wanted to run.

He blinked hard and tried to turn away from me to hide the expression on his face. But I had already caught it. It was sinister, almost evil, and it struck that cord of fear and terror you get when you're afraid for your life. My heartbeat erupted with frantic vitality.

"I'm sorry to have intruded," he blurted out so quickly I barely caught what he had said. He licked his lips as if they were horribly dry and abruptly shoved *Tristan and Isolde* into my hands. He kept his head turned away from me.

And without another word he turned on his heel, grabbed his large brimmed hat hanging from the edge of the book shelf, swiftly put it on and strode away with an urgency that seemed unnecessary. Not once did he look back at me.

The terror I had felt a minute before was suddenly gone, replaced by a strange sense of guilt. I felt as if it was somehow my fault that he had to leave so quickly. I felt that I had somehow repulsed him.

But what had I said? Or what had I done to warrant such behavior? I stood there holding *Tristan and Isolde*, open mouthed and confused as to what to think.

Something took over me in that moment. I felt incredibly . . . angry. My blood boiled under my copper-toned skin, my jaw was clenched tight. A split second later, I was bolting for the door after him. The little bells sang loudly and I was out the door so fast that I neglected to say goodbye to Marcus.

There was the roar of a motorcycle engine as it pulled out of the parking lot. I could only see a man on a red bike before it peeled out of the parking lot.

I knew it was him. I jumped in the Explorer, started the engine and followed as fast as I could. He pulled out onto the main highway towards Klamath Falls, but he was out of my sight within seconds.

There was no explanation for what overtook me, why I was so hell bent on *him*. It was just an overwhelming feeling that he was somehow important. I felt obsessed.

I followed the main highway for miles. There weren't many turnoffs in those parts. I knew the Willamette like the back of my hand, so I felt confident that I would find him.

Every time I blinked, I saw that menacing glare in his two-toned eyes. It burned in my minds' eye like one of my nightmares. It brought on that fear and a certain terror that haunted me. Yet I continued to drive, to seek him out.

Finally, there was a glimmer of red on the side of the road. I parked the truck next to the vacant bike and jumped out as quickly as I could manage. I inhaled the air around me as if that would somehow tell me if *he* had been there. And there was something there, a familiar scent now, the honey and leather. The scent was almost stale, as if he had been here a while ago and only traces of it remained.

I pursued the stranger on foot for miles, but the scent eventually died and the sun began to set. Frustrated, I relented and made my way back to the reservation. I tried to ignore the fact that I had been able to identify him by his scent. The idea was simply impossible.

"Lakota," I heard a familiar voice call to me as I realized that I'd arrived back home and had already gone up the steps to the house. Wakiza was just unlocking the front door.

"Father," I exclaimed as I focused on pulling the pieces of my disoriented mind back together. "It seems like I haven't seen you in days."

"Sorry Kota, I've just been busy," he said casually.

"It's nice out. You want to go on a run with me?" I asked.

"It's been a long couple of days for me. I'm in desperate need of a shower and a pipe, but you go ahead. Be careful out there," and with that he was in the door and down the hall.

"Kota!" came Notak's happy voice from around the corner. "Did I hear right? You going for a run?"

I nodded to him.

"Mind if I join you? I need to get some fresh air," he said as he began hurriedly putting on his moccasins. Within minutes the earth was beneath our feet, the cold evening breeze filling my achy lungs. Notak sped past me, taunting me playfully to keep up with his fast pace. We pushed and shoved at each other, teasing every now and then, and I realized how much I had missed his companionship lately.

There was a time—it seemed like so long ago—when we used to spend almost every waking moment with each other. We were inseparable . . . until three years ago, when my world started to morph into my alien existence.

It wasn't long before we reached the Sanctuary. It was my favorite place in the whole world. A circular chamber of tall trees broken only by the punchbowl waterfall that fed a calm pool of water, sparkling in the moon's light in the most magnificent way. The reflection of stars danced in the water. A soft, velvety moss covered the ground bordering the water and it glistened in the dim light.

Notak and I sat down by the bank. We were silent as we both caught our breath from our run. I picked a lonely wildflower and set it to float in the gentle current of the lagoon, tracing my fingers in the water here and there. It was strange how the icy, cold liquid felt so refreshing on my hot skin.

"What's gotten into you today? I haven't seen you this energetic in . . ." Notak paused reflectively. "Well, you know."

"I met someone today," I said nonchalantly.

"And might this someone have a name?" Notak inquired with intrigue.

"Aiden," I said recalling his name.

"Aww . . . a boy," Notak teased.

"Stop it Notak, he isn't a boy. He's a man, and there was something very odd about him. And about me around him . . ." I trailed off trying to mentally grasp what had happened earlier today.

"Go on," Notak urged.

"It seems so surreal to me now, but . . ." I hesitated, not sure if I really wanted to divulge such intimate information. "I felt drawn to him and repulsed by him at the same time. It was the most primitive, inhuman feeling I've ever had," I confessed.

"You have a crush," my brother continued to taunt.

"It's not a crush, although I did feel a little like crushing him. I don't know, it was strange. And he was strange," I added with a sigh before turning my eyes to the moon in contemplative thought.

"For so long I've lost sight of hope and I've forgotten about destiny. But—" I closed my eyes, relishing the memory of his presence "—he made me feel like there is something more out there, some big picture I'm just not quite entirely seeing."

"It took a boy to get through to you," Notak said. "Well, it figures," he chuckled.

"You think it's so funny," I mocked. He laughed again.

"Sister, can I tell you something I've never told another soul?" he asked hesitantly, but more serious.

I nodded my affirmation.

"I have these dreams," he said trailing off in thought for a moment. "In them, you become something incredibly amazing and powerful. You are covered in a blanket of white and grey, and I can't quite see your face so I try to get nearer to you. You push me away. It's not because you want to, it's because you have to."

"I would never push you away brother," I tried to reassure him. Slowly, I rested my head against his shoulder. "You're all I have tethering me to my sanity. I need you."

"Well, it's just a dream, right?" he said lightheartedly.

"Uh huh, just a dream," I mocked. "It's a bit ironic that we are both haunted by dreams we don't understand."

"It must be the curse of the Kalapuya." He tried to sound spooky.

"Will you stop it? It's not funny."

"We will get through this, Kota," he said as he wrapped one arm around my back and shoulder.

"We have to," I added, inviting his embrace.

We sat there for a long while, our souls losing themselves in the serenity around us and in each other. There was so much uncertainty in both our lives, yet somehow I felt at peace. All my worries, my doubts, my fears, seemed to wash away in the water.

That night was restless as usual, but there was a marked difference in this particular moonrise. The nightmare was altered. For the first time, it actually changed.

The same creature as before was there, but this time there was no couple, no man and woman being consumed by the thing. Instead there were long, black, leathery wings that stretched out wide and bore towards me with ferocious intensity. It was as if they would swallow me whole.

There was no dark, ominous feeling at the end of the dream. And this time there was no fear left behind. It was as if the great wings of the demon from my nightmare consumed me.

As I came back to consciousness, the familiar pain permeated through my body in waves. A miserable hour passed before I ceased tossing and turning in agony and fell into a deep, dreamless sleep. It was the first time in over three years that I would sleep most of the night. For three despondent years, I had been waiting for something to give, anything to change.

Change was upon me now. I could feel it coming, erupting in a grand finale. And although I saw no end to my nights of agony, to the nightmares, or the voices—I didn't care.

I knew not the purpose of my future, but that night I relished the present. Try as I might, I couldn't stop thinking about the man in the bookstore. Aiden. And when I slept that night all that existed was *his* intoxicating scent. Honey and leather.

4 INFATUATION

THERE WERE FOUR OF US sitting at the round kitchen table when the knocking came thundering from the front door. Wakiza got up to answer it, while Notak, Jesse, and I continued playing cards, laughing and otherwise very much enjoying ourselves. A few moments later, father summoned me.

"You guys get on without me, I'll be right back," I said cheerfully as I got up and proceeded towards the front door.

"Hurry up Kota, I'm about to take you to the cleaners," Jesse taunted me with a giggle. Although he was the youngest of the bunch on our game nights, he lacked neither skill nor an excellent poker face. He was smart and especially good at reading the rest of us. It was almost as if he had a sixth sense.

"Yeah, yeah, don't worry Jesse. You can't stay on top forever. I'll be taking my money back shortly," I retorted trying to sound more confident than I felt. Just then, I rounded the corner and in the doorway was the most unlikely visitor.

It was Marcus.

"Kota, I am so sorry to have disrupted you so late this evening," said Marcus, truly apologetic.

"Do you have a minute?" he motioned to me as if he would prefer to talk outside. He had a certain impatience about him.

"Yeah, of course," I said, surprised at his presence. For the fifteen odd years that I remembered knowing Marcus, he had not once made the trip to the reservation since my parents had been murdered there. I gently closed the front door behind me and walked to the far edge of the porch with Marcus. "What's going on old friend?"

"The . . . specimen," he hesitated, and looked around in paranoia. "I experimented with every crazy idea I could concoct," he said with a whisper. He continued to look around suspiciously as if someone might be listening to something he shouldn't be saying.

"And?" I pressed for him to continue.

"There is something very wrong about that specimen. It seems to be organic of some nature, but the DNA isn't like anything I have ever seen. It is highly resilient and adapted to every environment I put it in. It moves and acts like a living organism, yet I could not find a way to kill it or otherwise destroy it," Marcus explained with a fear in his voice.

"What?" I said, bewildered. "That's impossible."

"Precisely, my first hypothesis," Marcus agreed.

"So what is it? Is it toxic or deadly? Some type of chemical warfare substance?" I asked trying to put the pieces of the puzzle together, pulling my knowledge from the mass of books I'd read in the past.

"I call it 'Substance X' and it's completely unknown as far as I can tell. It didn't destroy organic tissue, so it doesn't seem to be deadly. Possibly toxic, but that depends on your definition of 'toxic.' It paralyzed, almost inhibited all cell function in organic tissue. Although there seemed to be some evidence of regeneration to damaged cells." Marcus explained.

"But . . ." I paused, thinking hard. "That's scientifically an impossibility, isn't it?"

"There is more to this world than mankind can begin to comprehend. But yes, our current scientific exploration is limited by our mortality. We live based on the assumption that all things eventually deteriorate and die. This substance, however, may disprove that. It reverses damage then indefinitely suspends cell function. As in no cell division or movement of any kind. Just frozen in time as it exists . . ." he trailed off in bewildered thought.

"So that explains why the mountain lion was in such perfect condition, even a day after her death," I postulated.

"Lakota, listen to me," he said with solemn purpose. "I don't know what this specimen is, where it originated, or what it came from. But of one thing I am very certain—" he paused grabbing my shoulder— "whoever or whatever this specimen came from is something the likes of which mankind has likely never encountered before," he hesitated to find the right word. "Whatever IT is—I pray we never find it. This substance is equivalent to the fictitious fountain of youth. If this kind of knowledge were to fall into the wrong hands, the fallout would be unimaginable."

We were silent for a while as the words sank in and my mind meandered back to the memories of all the perplexing things that had happened in the last month or so. For the first time in what felt like an eternity, I didn't feel so crazy. A foreboding truth began to articulate in the back of my mind.

"It was all a set-up," I whispered as I began to understand. "A creature capable of such skills and hunting prowess wouldn't have been so careless as to leave traces of its existence, much less an entire dead animal. This was a risky move, calculated and purposeful," I said, more or less just talking to myself. "I was meant to find that mountain lion, and the woman was warning me about the creature who hunts me."

"Hunts you? Lakota, what are you talking about? What woman? What is this creature you speak of? Have you seen it?" All his questions came one after another with barely a moment to breath.

"Thank you so much Marcus, you have been a huge help," I said as I hurried back in the house to grab my keys.

"Sorry guys," I called out towards the kitchen. "Jesse, you win this time. I have to go. Duty calls," and with that I was hurriedly out the door and down the front porch steps.

"Don't you be a martyr and go looking for it, Lakota. You hear me?" Marcus commanded with the unmistakable sound of fear drenching his every word as he followed after me. "You stay clear away from that—thing."

"That's the problem, I can't," I said as I jumped into the front seat of the Explorer and my gaze became fixed on the forest beyond. A chill went down my spine and an inevitable fear seeped into my every cell. "It's hunting me."

"Lakota, please, I beg of you. Don't go and do anything stupid," Marcus pleaded with me standing inbetween the door of the truck and me.

"I won't," I futilely promised him. "I'm just going to be prepared for that thing when I see it." I grabbed the door, forcing Marcus out of the way as I shut it.

"Marcus, I'm sorry for my rudeness, but I have to be ready. Please don't tell father," I said, turning the key in the ignition. I was down the road moments later.

There was a gripping fear that threatened to take hold of my soul, but I refused to give in. I had so many questions swimming around in my mind. Why had the woman warned me? Who was she and how did she know me? How did she know of the creature? What was this unknown creature and why was it hunting me? Were there more than one of them? I was afraid for my own life, but there was a far worse looming fear. I was afraid for the lives of the Kalapuya people. I was afraid that I would bring bad fortune to my brothers and sisters, and that was simply something I could not live with. I had to do something.

"Come and get me, you son of a bitch," I whispered under my breath. "I'll be ready for you."

I pulled into a small parking lot off the main highway a while later. The big red sign in front of my truck read "Jason's Auto and Towing". I immediately noticed a motorcycle parked to the side of the garage under a tree. It was a red sport bike. It was solid red except for the word "Ducati" in white on the tank. My heart skipped a beat.

"Nah, it couldn't be him. What would he be doing here?" I whispered under my breath, dismissing the notion.

I approached the dark garage and as I got closer, I could make out the figure of a man organizing some tools on the wall. A sigh of relief escaped as I realized it was only Jason and he seemed to be the only one in the garage. He was fairly tall and well built, his bare forearms rippled as he lifted a heavy bucket onto a workbench. His hair was long and grey from age, pulled neatly back into a ponytail. He heard me coming and turned, giving me a huge smile in recognition.

"Morning Jason," I greeted him. He rushed up to me and gave me a big hug. I returned the favor. Jason was like a father to me, I had known him since before I could even talk.

"Lakota! What a nice surprise," he chimed happily. "Where have you been?"

"I guess I've lost track of time lately," I mentioned.

"She about ready for an oil change?" Jason asked.

"Um," I stuttered as I realized he was referring to my vehicle. "Yeah, I guess so. But I'm actually here on other business," I said handing him the keys anyway.

"What's going on?" he asked curiously.

I hesitated for several moments as I contemplated the severity of my request. Looking back over my shoulder to the expanse of the Willamette, I felt a spooky electricity in the air as I remembered the creature.

"I need some . . . hardware," I said in a hushed tone.

"Uh, alright, no need to get all dramatic," he said with a chuckle. "What do you need? Wrenches, screwdrivers? You know I have just about anything. Name it," he said lighthearted again.

"No, Jason," I said with a stern tone. I looked around making sure there was no one else within hearing range of our conversation. "I need some HARD-WARE, you get my meaning?"

Jason stared at me in shock. A minute later he beckoned me into the protection of his office adjoining the garage. He quietly shut the door so our conversation could be more private, although there seemed to be no-one else for miles.

"What in god's name do you need stuff like that for?" Jason demanded.

"The less you know, the better," I said, my confidence faltering.

"What did you do, tick Bigfoot off?" he questioned as he laughed, dismissing me.

My lack of response, and the sternness of my stature surprised Jason and hushed his humor. I crossed my arms and glared at him.

"That serious, huh?" he said, thoughtful. "Did you try the police?"

I laughed, thoroughly amused. "Trust me. They would think I've been hitting the pipe too much. And besides, this is a reservation issue. Please, trust me on this one, old friend. I'll owe you one, but I'm begging you," I pleaded. "I promise to let you know what is going on as soon as I know it's safe."

"So . . . need-to-know-basis, huh?" he said, thoughtful and unconvinced. "You sure about this?"

"As sure as the sky is blue."

Jason was silent for several minutes as he contemplated my request.

"I've seen the look in your eyes before," he sighed. "It's the look a soldier has before he knows he'll be going into a battle he may not come back from."

There was silence for a while longer as he thought.

"I'll make a deal with you," Jason said. "I'll give you whatever you want, but I'm going with you."

"No, out of the question," I responded without hesitation or delay.

"Take it or leave it," he said firmly. "Think about it. I'm a better shot than you, I know my weapons like the back of my hand, and I have experience in combat. I have no wife, no kids—no life outside this garage. Whatever this secret is you're so scared of . . . we can face it together and you'll have a much higher chance of success."

I contemplated his proposal in silence. I knew he was right. As an ex-Marine, he had experience, knowledge, and expertise that would simply augment my more naturalist talents. He would be a valuable asset and a formidable opponent.

I nodded my headed reluctantly without saying a word. Jason smiled in triumph, and came alive with excitement as if he was a young man again.

"Follow me," he said as he headed towards the back of the garage. He opened the door that led into a large yard behind the auto repair garage. It was filled with old, broken vehicles and parts galore.

"Hey, Aiden!" Marcus shouted across the yard. "Where you at, boy?"

My heart skipped a beat.

"I hired this kid about a month ago. He has a real gift with his hands. I can't find anything he can't do," Marcus explained to me.

My heart picked up speed without my willing it to. The name made me shudder, and I realized suddenly that the red bike in front was no coincidence.

There was that scent in the air . . . .

Honey and leather.

Intoxicating.

The hairs on my neck stood up and every cell in my body screamed at me.

Then he was in front of me.

"There you are," Marcus greeted him. "Aiden this is my good friend La—."

"Lakota," Aiden cut Marcus off and finished his introduction. He beckoned to me with an open-gloved hand.

In the corner of my eye, I saw Jason's surprised face. Hesitating, I stood there, frozen for a moment. A sense of fear seeped into my consciousness. An ominous presence hovered over me in my mind's eye.

"I won't bite," Aiden said with an evil grin. It was almost as if he was taunting me.

"I'm not sure what you're going to do next," I said as I reluctantly extended my hand to his. My voice dripped with irritation. Those eyes I had tried so hard to block out and forget were peering at me from a deathly pale and wondrously beautiful face. He took my hand into his as delicately as a rose, and kissed it gently with painfully cool lips.

I felt a chill go down my spine from both the thrill and fear of his presence again.

"I had the pleasure of Lakota's presence once before," Aiden's voice sang like a melody. His lip curled up in a cocky kind of smile, his eyes never leaving mine.

"Well, this is a small town. It won't be long before you know everyone," Jason said.

I realized that Aiden was still holding my hand, and I jerked it away from him quickly, embarrassed.

"Alright-y then," Jason broke the silence. "Uh . . . Kota needs an oil change on the Explorer. Would you mind, Aiden?"

"My pleasure." Aiden made a short bow and rushed past me towards the garage.

Even though he was out of my sight, my limbs still felt heavy as I followed Jason. The one hundred yard walk to the hidden, underground bunker behind the garage seemed to take every ounce of my energy as I was sucked into some day-dream that I couldn't wake up from. Everything moved in slow motion.

I ducked my head down and into the bunker, jumping to my senses as I caught a gun that Jason abruptly tossed at me.

"That's a desert eagle. A good shot will take down a bear at close range," he said.

I shifted it uneasily in my hands before placing the machinery on the table in the middle of the room.

"What else you got?" I said shortly.

"Automatic assault rifle and she's got a kick you'll remember," he warned as he put a larger gun on the table. I picked it up, the weight of it strange and foreign to me.

"Maybe you want to take down, say, Bigfoot and you don't know where he'll be coming from or at what range you'll need to take the shot . . . combat shotgun should do the trick. You should have no problem handling this one. It has almost no recoil and it's an automatic, so you're bound to hit him at some point. This is one of my favorites because you can drop this thing in water or dirt and it'll have next to no effect on performance." He pulled another gun from the wall neatly layered from floor to ceiling with weapons.

I carefully inspected the guns laid out in front of me. I momentarily wished I had his confidence in them, or his skill in using them for that matter.

"Grenades, claymores, rocket launchers . . ." he trailed off as he touched one after the other of his personal arsenal.

"Your pick, Jason. I wouldn't know where to start," I said with no emotion in my voice. "Do you have a good knife?"

"You're so much like your father," he laughed and then drew instantly silent. "When we hunted together, he always pulled his knife before the gun." He handed me a large knife with a 7-inch long blade.

"Well, it's about time I gave this to you anyway. It's a combat knife that I made with your father when I used to have a steel mill here. It was his favorite, although he hoped you would never have to use it for something like this," Jason said with solemn devotion.

I inspected the blade slowly. The initials *T.A.* were engraved into one side of the blade near the handle.

"Trevor Avital," I spoke my late father's name out loud. The words stung my heart like a wasp. "Thank you," I said. "This means a lot to me. Sometimes I wonder what father and mother would do, or what they would say, if they were still here."

"I wish they were here too, but I know they would've been very proud of you," Jason said, gently touching my shoulder.

In silence we both sank under the weight of their absence from our lives. I had gathered over the years that Jason was one of my fathers' few close friends. In fact,

Jason was the only other town-folk besides Kyle that I remembered form my childhood.

"Why don't you go up and see how Aiden is coming along so I can get some of these packed up nice and quiet like?" Jason suggested, suddenly changing the subject.

"Yeah, of course," I agreed. I knew that I was one of a select few that had any knowledge of Jason's extensive weapons collection. And I knew that most of them were illegal in most states.

I headed up the steps and across the back yard to the garage. Dread began to fill my chest cavity with every step that brought me closer to *him*.

As I rounded the corner of the backdoor into the garage, *he* was there tinkering with some tools on a workbench. There was a smudge of dirt on the back of his neck. But somehow, he still managed to look perfect, majestic—maybe even angelic. I stood in the doorway, soundless for a minute, so that he wouldn't know that I was there, and I could watch him for a few perfect moments.

"Hello, Lakota," he said, startling me. He never once looked up or turned from his tools and his sudden acknowledgement of my presence made me jump a bit. At that moment I recognized the feeling that had been welling up inside of me for so long.

Infatuation. I was simply infatuated with this man, his perfect physique, his suave ways, his melodic voice, his angelic accent, his captivating eyes, and his tantalizing scent. And yet a new and unwelcomed emotion surfaced without my willing it to.

Anger. I felt so angry and betrayed by him whom I adored.

"What have I done to revolt you?" I demanded angrily.

I was shocked at the words that spewed out of my mouth. The feeling he had left me with after the bookstore encounter had never really left, and now it surfaced with unwelcomed ferocity.

Slowly, he turned his head in my direction and his eerie two-toned eyes inspected me cautiously.

"You think you revolt me?" he asked, amused. "No, no, love, it is quite the contrary," he said simply and then went back to his fiddling.

I blinked a few times, trying to understand his word of endearment. It seemed out of place when coupled with his previous actions in the bookstore.

"And what the hell is that supposed to mean?" I was agitated.

"It's complicated," he said calmly as he looked up at me once more.

Our eyes met. His didn't have the crimson ring as they did when I had last seen him. They were a vivid glowing blue with the brown ring around the color again.

"Complicated?" I exclaimed. "You are unbelievable."

"Were you born and raised here?" he asked, breaking the silence and changing the subject.

"The Kalapuya Reservation about twenty miles southwest of here. I went to school here in Oakridge though," I said, reluctantly.

"You fit in well, do you?"

"Not particularly. I've been an outcast to most, well, since forever," I said with a coldness in my voice. "The town turned on the Kalapuya after the massacre, thought we brought bad omens, demons, and the like to the Willamette. I am one with my people though," I said with confidence. "That's all that has ever mattered to me."

"Massacre?" Aiden did not hide his surprise.

"Why are you so interested in me? In my people? In this town? You're not from these parts so what are you doing here?" I blurted every question that I had been thinking, unable to bridle my curiosity any longer.

"I live with my aunt and uncle. They are here on business," he answered shortly.

Aiden rose and stood to face me only a few inches away. He peered into my dark eyes.

"What happened here?" he prodded.

I sighed in defeat. It was obvious that he would not relent until he knew the horrible truths these forests held.

"My ancestors have been here for centuries, since before there were white men. They lived up and down almost every river, in the plains, and the valleys," I said with great pride and conviction.

Deathly silence filled the air as the horrible facts of my past rose to full light.

"In the 1800s the 'fever', brought by the white men, wiped out over half of our population. Then they over-hunted the land, leaving us with no way to continue our way of life. One by one, our brother tribes were forced to cede their territories to the government and join reservations with tribes up north and in Wyoming. By 1950, there were only about five hundred of us left. We refused to cede our land," I said with a deep sadness in my voice. It all happened before I was born, but it still horrified me that the once powerful and strong Kalapuya nation had nearly been decimated and reduced to hiding in the trees of what was left of our once bountiful land.

"Seventeen years ago, we were attacked by . . . something. A hundred of our people were murdered, including my parents. Woman, children, elderly—it didn't matter. My people were butchered. I was four, but I can't wipe the memory of that day out of my mind," I couldn't look at him as I told the nightmare.

"Some never recovered from that day and what was left of our tribe split into two. Half of them went up north and joined with other struggling tribes to form the Three Sisters Tribe. The others stayed here."

"Why did you stay? There's so much pain and suffering for you here," he tried to understand.

There was a long silence as I contemplated his question.

"My father badly wounded one of them and single-handedly drove them away. But their leader killed my father and mother in retaliation. If it were not for him, they would have slaughtered every one of us. My parents sacrificed their lives for our people, I feel responsible for seeing things out here."

"Who did this to your people?" he asked.

"To this day, we do not know. But we live in fear of their return. They looked human, but they were inhumanly strong, blindingly fast, and had an insatiable thirst to kill. Some believe that they were genetically altered soldiers sent by the government to decimate us, since we would not cede our lands. But the authorities were convinced that it was some type of underground cult."

What color there was in Aiden's face drained completely, and he stood deathly still for a moment as if he had just discovered some horrible truth.

"Or maybe vampires," Aiden said thoughtfully, with a serious tone.

"Please don't mock me," I pleaded, insulted and hurt. "I have a friend who seems to think that's a logical explanation too. What is it with people and their obsession with vampires?" I mused.

"Immortality, of course. And vampires are immortal. They seem to be romanticized in these modern times," he said with a suggestive annoyance. "Human beings have been consumed with finding immortality for thousands of years. Wouldn't you want to live forever?" he asked with a slightly taunting demeanor.

That shouldn't be the way of things. Everything, everyone . . . has it's time and place. And all things have an end. Death is the balance of life and the living that nature demands."

"Well I have seen the strangest things in my travels with my family. There is more truth to those fairytales and myths than anyone wants to admit," he said with a distant demeanor.

"I think vampires are a little far-fetched. You travel a lot?" I asked, attempting to change the subject.

"Every couple months. My aunt, Enya, is a writer and my uncle, Draigon, is her publisher. We settle in one place for a couple years and Enya writes the stories of that place. It's the Irish way to be travelers."

"Kind of like gypsies?"

"Yeah, we've been called that before," he said with a chuckle.

"Lakota," I heard Jason's voice from around the corner. "Help me with these, will you?"

I asked Aiden to excuse me and politely dismissed myself.

"Of course. Just about done here," he nodded.

I helped Jason load the guns hidden in wooden crates into the back of the Explorer.

"Where'd you pick him up?" I asked Jason, curious.

"By accident, really, he came in to borrow some tools to adjust his bike. We just got to talking and next thing you know I was offering him a job," Jason laughed. "Truth is, he's been a big help around here. Guess I forget sometimes that my body ain't what it used to be."

"Good for you, it's about time you got some help around here," I said as I gazed through the front windshield towards Aiden. I admired his perfectly shaped eyebrows as they furrowed together. My head tilted to the side as I tried to imagine what he might be thinking about.

"You like him." Jason stated, rather than questioned.

"What?" I said, as my eyes jumped back to Jason. I tried to hide my embarrassment.

"I just say it how it is." He gave me a wink.

"All right, all finished," Aiden said, as he came around to the front cab.

"Thank you Jason . . . Aiden," I said and handed Jason cash for the labor.

"You know your money is no good here," Jason said as he refused the money. "It's our pleasure, Kota," he said with genuine emotion.

"Well, it doesn't hurt to try," I said, knowing how Jason was. "I owe you one."

"Just be safe, Kota. Promise me that," Jason pleaded. "I'll come by tomorrow? We can go hunting?"

"A deal is a deal," I agreed.

"Good," he said with satisfaction. And then he gave me a hug and went back to the garage. I knew he was trying to give Aiden and myself some privacy.

Aiden politely opened the door to the driver's seat for me.

"Would I be too forward in asking to see you again?"

It took me a minute to understand what he had asked me. The manner in which he spoke was foreign to me.

"I would like that," I whispered while still trying to process his invitation. I realized with shock how desperately I wanted to see him again. I was unfamiliar with the emotion I was feeling.

"I'll meet you at the reservation tonight," he said quickly.

My heart thudded fast with an excitement I had never felt before. Never in my life had I ever wanted any other person's company more than I wanted his now. I nodded my consent.

"Just head back out on highway 58—" I motioned in the direction of the reservation but he stopped my hand in mid-air.

He cut me off before I could finish. "Don't worry, I'll find it."

I raised an eyebrow in disbelief.

"You sure you won't get lost?" I asked with suspicion.

"I don't get lost," he said with that cocky smile I was already growing fond of. "I'll be there by sundown." He held out his hand to me, helping me up into the truck.

I hesitated for a minute as I looked at his gloved hand. His gentleman-like manners made me feel like a princess. His mannerisms were outdated by contemporary standards. They struck me as odd, almost creepy.

"Until sunset then, love," his melodic voice chimed as he took a bow, only confirming the anachronistic etiquette that made me wary. He held fast to my hand and pulled it to his lips slowly, never letting his eyes stray from mine. Gently, he placed a kiss there. The kiss was cool against my burning skin.

Speechless and mystified by his peculiar behavior, I could only nod my agreement. He shut the door for me and I pulled out onto the highway.

As I headed out, I caught Jason playfully pushing Aiden around. I'm sure he was teasing Aiden about how silly we must have acted around each other.

I meandered through the rest of my day, preoccupied the whole time by the stranger who was fast becoming not so much of a stranger after all.

Aiden.

Time seemed to pass so very slowly, as if it was indefinitely suspended in time.

When the sun had begun to make its descent towards the horizon, I quickly changed into a black long-sleeve shirt and some plain blue jeans. Nervously, I primped myself and brushed my hair, making sure I looked a little more than presentable. I threw on my warm parka jacket for the cold winter weather outside and headed into a light snow that had begun to fall.

I was anxious. And I felt guilty for having such emotions.

He's just a guy. I kept telling myself. And yet, I couldn't help but sense that he was so much more than that.

I waited as the sun continued dipping down towards the trees. And I waited.

I paced around the reservation, staying just out of range of anyone who might want to strike up a conversation with me. I didn't feel like talking to anyone.

Anyone—that is—except *him*.

I waited and began wondering if he was going to stand me up.

"Lakota, there you are," came a familiar voice. But it wasn't the one I wanted to hear. "I've been looking all over for you. What are you doing?"

"Hey, Notak. I'm, uh, waiting for someone," I said. I didn't want to tell him, but I couldn't lie to him. He knew me too well.

"Oh really?" he teased. "And would this someone be of the male sex?"

"Knock it off, would you?" I didn't want to talk to him about my interest in this stranger. I felt myself blushing just thinking about it.

"Geez! Don't be so defensive. I mean, really, it's about time!" he gloated. He paused as if he was thinking about something very interesting.

"He's important isn't he? He must be because you never bring anyone to the Res," he inquired, playfully punching me in the shoulder.

I pushed him back, but I knew he was right. I never brought anyone even close to our lands. Never before had I been interested in spending anything but minimal time with anyone from the outside.

"I don't know, he's different. I mean, I just met him." I gave Notak a stern look, "but yeah, he's kind of important." My tone softened. "Don't screw with him!" I commanded him as I waved a warning finger in his face.

"Ok, ok." He was still gleaming with mischievousness.

"You have to promise, for me," I said as I grabbed his muscular arm.

I could tell Notak was surprised by my sudden desperation.

"I promise," he said reluctantly and looked me dead in the eye to confirm his sincerity.

We stood in awkward silence for a minute. I wasn't used to sharing anything about romance with him. Not that I really had much of a romantic life to begin with.

But I knew I could trust him. I knew I could trust him with my life.

"I'm on night watch tonight with the warriors anyway. I just wanted to make sure you were ok," he said. "Be careful out there tonight."

Ever since that fateful night seventeen years before, the men and the warriors took turns on night watch for the return of the human beasts. Nothing had been seen or heard since that night, but it was a precautionary ritual of ours.

"I will," I said and I meant it.

He turned and disappeared into the forest.

I was alone again.

Waiting.

I was a little disturbed about what I'd said to Notak about Aiden being "different." I thought about what I'd meant.

It was almost dark now, and I was beginning to seriously doubt if Aiden was going to show up. His assumption that he would find me was disconcerting. I was convinced that he'd probably gotten lost and given up.

Or maybe he hadn't ever intended on coming at all. I pushed that notion to the very back of my mind in denial.

I waited. My heart was beginning to sink with the sun, lower and lower. It wasn't normal, how I clung to the hope of his arrival as if it was my dying wish.

I waited and waited. My infatuation with Aided consumed me.

5 Trapped

"Hello, love," his voice sang like a wave on the coast of Ireland.

I jumped up from the stump I'd been sitting on, surprised that I hadn't heard him coming. I hadn't heard his motorcycle, or any other type of vehicle for that matter. Certainly he hadn't walked the several miles off the main highway to get here.

Had he?

"Aiden!" The shock in my voice was obvious. I turned to meet him. "I didn't hear you coming. How did you get here?"

"The road closer to the reservation isn't exactly motorcycle friendly. I parked my bike a couple miles out," he said as he laughed, amused. Even his laugh had a melody to it.

But I knew he was right. The road leading to the reservation wasn't even paved, it was pressed rocks in dirt and mud.

"You should have let me know. I would have given you a ride." It seemed like too much energy and effort to put out just to see a little native girl. Was I that important?

It's alright, I needed the exercise anyway," he said with that infectious laugh.

"If I'd known this was going to be such trouble—"

"It isn't any trouble, and I'm fast. Forget about it," he reassured my trailing thoughts. The look in his eyes was sincere.

I stood there, blushing as my heart went wild.

"So this is the reservation?" he asked, as he parted two bushes to get a better view of our large communal grounds.

"Yup, this is it. Well this and the miles of forest around," I said, joining him to watch Jesse and the other boys splitting and stacking wood. Jesse's mother and a few of the other girls and women sat on logs around the large fire, occupying themselves by roasting camas and weaving fiber baskets. We listened to their whimsical laughs and hushed chatter. I saw Notak on the far side glance our direction. He gave me a wink.

Embarrassed, I quickly moved out of Notak's view.

"Um, can we walk?" I asked uncomfortably.

"Of course," he said with a suspicious look. He offered me his arm as a gentleman would in some past Victorian era. I politely took it and we meandered in no particular direction.

"Are you in a hurry to escape someone?" he prodded. "That young fella that winked at you perhaps?"

"Oh, you caught that?" I asked, disappointed.

He nodded slightly in confirmation.

"It's my brother, well half-brother, or—whatever," I stuttered at what Notak really was to me. "He's kind of protective over me."

"Should I be worried?" he asked with a laugh.

"Nah, he's just being the big brother and making sure I'm safe. But I think he's relieved that I'm talking with someone outside the tribe, or with someone at all for that matter," I mocked myself. "But never mind him, it's my turn to ask the questions now."

There was a short silence as I thought about which of the dozens of questions I should ask first.

"Have you always been a . . . traveler?" I asked, struggling with the very concept itself. Being born and raised in one place made it hard to imagine any other way of living.

"It feels like an eternity. I was born and raised in Ireland. My mother died giving birth to me so I don't remember her. My father married Enya when I was three, and we lived on a small farm in the country for seventeen years. It was a good life." He stopped and seemed to hesitate as if uncertain as to if he should continue or not.

"When I was twenty my father took ill and died, and my step-mother and I have been on the road ever since. We both just needed to get away from all the loss and grief," he said, obviously disturbed.

"Do you have any siblings?"

"My step-mother has a son back in Ireland. But we're not close." His eyes grew dark, as if that was a story he'd rather not tell.

"Enya met and fell in love with Draigon Kathel when we were in Japan, and they have since married. So now it's us three and Draigon's adopted daughter, Yuki Rin. I'm not blood related to any of my family and as you can tell, it's all a long convoluted story. So it's just easier to tell people they are my aunt and uncle," he explained.

I thought absentmindedly—what strange names his family had—but I didn't say anything.

"I get that. They aren't any less of a family just because you aren't related by blood," I said. It wasn't so much unlike my own situation. "So why did your family choose Oakridge? Why here?" I prodded on.

"Enya always picks the place, and they are usually small remote towns. She likes to tell stories about the littlest places on the map, places with stories that haven't yet been told. We stay in one place for a few months to a year, and then we move on. Draigon is her editor and publisher and sells her work as we go," he explained.

"Do you live with your brother?" he asked me.

"Yes, and my father. Before my biological father died, he left me in the tribal leaders' care. His name is Wakiza. I've been raised by him ever since, and Notak is his son. It's complicated, but they are my father and brother no less."

"Ironic," Aiden said with a sadness in his voice. "We are both orphans taken in by new families under dire circumstances. And now, they are all that we hold dear."

Abruptly, he pulled away from me and went ahead a few yards. He turned his head one direction, then the other as if he were looking for someone or something.

"What is it?" I asked in slight alarm. I realized with discontent that his behavior had caused me suddenly to feel insecure and almost unsafe. And his distance from my proximity only confounded the problem.

"I don't know . . . I keep thinking that I see someone," he said cautiously. My mind jumped to the creature in the forest several weeks back. That certain fear and terror started to creep back into my soul.

"There is something that isn't quite right about these woods, but I can't put my finger on it," he commented.

"It's almost as if you're always being watched," I added, as he turned back to me. Our eyes met. I couldn't pry myself away from his strange two-toned glowing eyes. They were simply mesmerizing.

Everything about him was mesmerizing. Everything about him was divinely . . . intoxicating.

Besides his obvious attractiveness, charisma, and maturity, something else drew me to him. Something forbidden and mystifying about him that made my heart beat hard and fast. And in his presence, I didn't fear the creature.

"I want to show you something," I grabbed his hand and pulled him to the north, walking at a brisk pace. I noticed that he tightened his hand around mine, a seemingly welcoming gesture. I looked back at him, but his face was stone cold as if he was concentrating on something. I felt his displays of emotion were contradictory.

As I pressed on, wordless, I embraced the racing of my heart. All my senses were in tune with everything around me. I didn't feel lost anymore. It had been a long time since I'd felt this—well, this *alive*.

We stepped onto the grassy outskirts around the pooling water, just as the moon began to rise in great splendor. It looked almost full, but not quite.

The white and blue waters of the waterfall crashed down onto the boulder that sat in the middle of the water with a deafening roar. It swirled in circular patterns onto the shallows of the bank.

"We call this the Sanctuary. It is a sacred place to the Kalapuya people," I said.

"It's beautiful," he said, looking back at me.

I walked to one of the trees that created the circle around the body of water. It was a mature tree, but fairly young in comparison to the other trees in the forest. I pressed my hand to the bark, and closed my eyes.

"This is my father, he was Trevor Avital," I said as I opened my eyes and caught his gaze. I jumped effortlessly to its sister tree.

"And this is my mother, she was Hot'ne," I said as I looked up into her tree branches.

"All of these trees were planted atop one of the brothers or sisters who were taken from us in the massacre seventeen years ago."

"There are so many of them," Aiden said, saddened as he turned around and grasped the sheer weight of how many trees created the circle.

"I am the only one that survives my blood line," I said with a sadness in my voice. "And there are many like me."

"I am sorry for your loss," he said. His two-toned eyes bore into mine with a sincerity that I hadn't expected. "You hold a sanctity for life that most have forgotten." He turned back to the waterfall, deep in thought.

"Human life is such a fragile thing, and it is so short. It's tragic how so many people rush through life, never once really learning what it is to have lived." He seemed lost in a heavy sadness as he watched the waterfall in its never-ending flow.

His words seemed too insightful and wise for his young life, but true nonetheless.

"You are different, love. You understand what it means to live, to be alive, to honor those who have passed or been taken, and to remember them for their lives and sacrifice," he said as he looked at me again.

"That's an interesting perspective on life. It's not un-like our own," I reflected. "The Kalapuya believe that we all have a purpose, we all have a destiny, even if we don't understand it or see it come to pass in our lifetime. We are all connected, and even in death there is purpose and design," I paused for a moment, thoughtful. "I struggle with it. I feel like I've been wandering through my existence with no purpose. Lost . . ." My voice trailed off as I became lost in my own disillusioned thoughts. "Yet I have been raised to believe that I have a purpose, a destiny. Maybe I just don't understand it."

"You just haven't found your place in life yet, that doesn't make your existence meaningless," he said, as his gaze returned to mine.

A chill went down my spine as his words sank in. I didn't understand why they meant so much to me . . . but they were terrifyingly comforting. It was almost as if he was my kindred spirit.

A twig cracked nearby and my head spun so fast in the direction of the noise that I had to blink several times to clear my eyes. I froze, a certain sense of antici-pation at the edge of my every nerve.

I listened intently. Crickets chirped their serenade, the wind whispered through the trees like air through organ pipes, and the leaves rustled as the wind washed through them. There was a *pat-pat* of what sounded like tiny feet from a short distance away.

"You hear that?" I asked, my eyes still peeled in the direction of the noise.

"Hear what?" Aiden asked confused, but instantly concerned.

I inhaled the air and I could smell the wet earth beneath my feet, and then, there was something else. Something barely there. A scent that was new to me, yet strangely recognizable.

I couldn't see anyone on the forest edge, but I could sense that someone or something was out there. Maybe the creature, or the woman again . . . .

And then there it was, a split second later.

A wolf.

I saw him through the brush about a hundred feet away.

"What is it?" Aiden asked, suddenly aware of the creature as well.

"Uh, I think it's a wolf," I said as I squinted to try and get a better look. "He's watching us."

Aiden grabbed me and pushed me behind him in a protective gesture. I stood there captivated by a feeling I didn't understand.

I unconsciously took a step forward away from Aiden's protective stance.

"What are you doing?" he whispered in a very demanding voice.

"Wait!" I whispered and his gaze turned into a deathly glare. "There's something about him . . ." I trailed off.

"Don't make eye contact with him. You'll be challenging his dominance. He'll attack us," Aiden warned in a serious tone.

"Like I don't know that? This is my land," I spoke the words as if ownership made a difference with this wild creature.

I inhaled again, taking in the somehow familiar scent of this strange wolf. I had already inadvertently locked eyes with him.

The wolf stared back at me, and I could sense that he wasn't intimidated by me. He was still shrouded in the darkness of the brush, so I cautiously crept forward a few steps more.

"Lakota! Please stop!" Aiden begged in a hushed tone. I could hear the desperation in his voice.

Warily, I pressed forward, closer to the wolf that stood still as ice.

"Stay there, trust me. I know what I'm doing," I whispered, not entirely convinced myself.

The wolf took a step forward towards me, and then one more. We were mere inches from each other now. In the moon's light I could see that his shiny coat was a vivid black with accents of brown here and there. And there was something odd about his eyes, something kind and understanding.

Tentatively, I reached my hand out to touch the wolf. He did not make a move, nor a sound. As I stroked his long, soft fur he stepped into me and nuzzled his nose towards me as if he were a domestic dog. It was almost as if we had some unspoken bond between us.

Behind me, I heard a twig snap as Aiden approached us.

The wolf suddenly pulled away from me and towards Aiden's presence, obviously distraught. He growled viciously, the hairs on his back standing high and his stance was one of hostile dominance. Then he turned and bounded into the forest, and he was gone.

"Am I missing something here, or did you just have a moment with a wild wolf?" Aiden inquired, both amused and shocked.

"I used to sleep with a wolf pack when I was a child, but I honestly have no idea what that was about," I said as I pushed passed Aiden, back towards the water.

"Things just keep getting more and more bizarre around here," Aiden said distantly.

"What's that supposed to mean?" I asked as I lay down on the soft grass just a few feet away from the lagoon.

"Never mind my idle contemplations, forget about it," he dismissed my inquiry as he stooped down to lay on the grassy shoreline next to me. We stared into the heavens and listened to the sounds of the water, the wind, and the trees.

"You seem very confident in your own skin," I said, breaking the silence. "Do you believe that you have some pre-ordained purpose in life?"

"There was a time when I thought I knew where I belonged, and then my world fell apart when my father died," he said, with sadness in his voice.

There was a long silence as he recalled the sad memories of his past.

"Certain . . . phenomenon happened to me, to my life, that made me question any supposed divine purpose," he said, as he looked at me with eyes that suddenly looked very old and very tired. "As time has passed, I feel that I have become cold and heartless."

"I get that. Sometimes I feel like I'm not even living in my own skin, like somewhere along the way I lost myself," I contemplated.

"Whatever happens, don't lose hope. When you lose hope, you lose your humanity," he said almost in a whisper.

My eyes drifted back to the heavens as I reflected on the weight of his words. There were so many things in my life that I didn't understand, and I was finding it increasingly difficult to hold on to hope. It was both comforting and disturbing that he somehow understood my plight.

The moon was high in the sky and I shivered as the cold night air wafted around my body and nipped at my nose.

Aiden noticed, pulled his jacket off and put it over me. He wrapped his arms around my waist and drew me closer to him. I curled myself in his embrace trying to absorb what heat I could. He felt so cold though.

"Is that why you're so sad?" I asked as I looked up into his eyes. "Have you lost your hope, your humanity?"

"I don't even remember what it feels like to hope for something. Sometimes, I don't even know if I'm human anymore, or if I've become some monster that simply consumes," he said with a distant voice.

"Well, you're not a monster to me," I said as I shivered again and burrowed closer to his muscular chest. "If this is all we have, if this life is the only one we get, what legacy would we leave behind?"

Aiden sat silently, as did I, lost in our convoluted contemplations.

"That's a beautiful bracelet." Aiden gently caressed my wrist and the ornate beads that adorned it.

"It was a gift. My brother made it for me. It's supposed to protect me."

"I think it's working."

As I yawned, I tried to understand how he could possibly know that. But exhaustion had begun to consume me.

"Maybe we should get you back home," he commented, as he felt my body shudder.

"No," I whispered. "I like it here." I closed my eyes and inhaled his intoxicating scent. I could feel his body warming a little, but he still felt cold. I realized how curious it was that I felt so comfortable with him, how effortless things felt when I was with him, how just breathing and existing felt like enough in his presence.

We were both trapped. Trapped in existences we did not understand. Trapped inside our own thoughts. And trapped in the grief of days past.

I woke up suddenly, jolting into an upright position so fast it made me lightheaded. I looked around, expecting to still be on the bank by the water with him.

But to my utter disappointment, I was back. I was in my own room. It must have been a dream after all—I started to panic. It couldn't be. It had all seemed so real. I couldn't bear the idea of not seeing him again. Had he ever shown up? Had I imagined the whole experience?

I felt myself begin to hyperventilate as the anxiety came flooding back.

And then I saw it.

My heart skipped a beat, and I found myself holding my breath.

A note.

It was folded in half, and on the outside was my name written in the most beautiful handwriting I had ever seen. I grabbed it and slowly opened it with trembling hands. Penmanship that reflected a bygone era was neatly inscribed on the page.

Lakota,

Please grant me the pleasure of your company again.

There was no name signed at the bottom, but I knew it was him.

I must have fallen asleep by his side in the Sanctuary, and somehow he'd silently brought me back home. I realized something else about the night. Something profound and truly amazing. I hadn't woken up once, not for restlessness or agony. And for the first time in three years . . . there was no nightmare. I had slept the whole night! I couldn't remember the last time I had slept that many hours in a row.

I felt invigorated and enthusiastic, as if I were floating on clouds.

Abruptly, I realized I was late meeting up with Jason for the hunt. I hastily got dressed and snatched a roll to cram down my throat as I headed for the door. Notak was there, with a wry grin on his face.

"How was your date? I didn't hear you come in last night."

"Uh," I stuttered. "It was great, I have to go though. I'm so sorry brother, I was supposed to meet up with Jason a half hour ago." Without waiting for his response I was out the front door.

As I drove, I wondered absentmindedly how Aiden had gotten into the house, and laid me to rest so quietly that my ever watchful brother and the warriors hadn't noticed.

I met Jason on the outskirts of the reservation, and we hiked, loaded with an artillery of guns and other weapons that seemed like entirely too much, to the place where I had seen the creature several weeks before.

"So can you give me any idea what it is that we're hunting?" Jason asked.

"I have no idea. I didn't actually see it," I admitted. "But trust me, you'll know when it's here."

We walked slowly and quietly for several hours, with only the sounds of a quiet forest to serenade us.

Then, I heard something in the trees. It wasn't a bird, or a branch breaking. It was something else. I put a closed fist high in the air, signaling Jason to stop and be still. Cautiously, I looked up into the trees for the source of the foreign noise. A horrible sensation of darkness came over me; it was just like the sensation in my dream and it permeated every cell in my body.

"What was that?" Jason whispered.

"It's here, up there in the trees somewhere," I whispered back. My ears felt like they were on fire. My legs were beginning to burn. I slowly took the automatic off my shoulder and clipped a magazine onto it. I heard Jason as he followed suit. I took a few steps forward, and with each step came excruciating pain. Desperately, I tried to keep my wits about me and hide my grimaces of pain from Jason.

"Come on, you son of a bitch, show yourself," I whispered under my breath.

A loud shriek filled the air and a huge black . . . thing swooped down from the tall trees towards us. In a split second, as if déjà vu, I recognized the figure. It was identical to the beast in my dreams, the same thing that killed my parents and my people. Kyle had been right. The creatures were back. An indescribable rage filled my gut, threatening to implode inside me. I pulled the trigger towards the thing, spraying bullets everywhere. And then it was suddenly out of sight. It was blindingly fast, just as Wakiza had said. I heard another shriek, and then it seemed to disappear.

I turned to Jason. His face was pale white and he was frozen in shock.

"What the hell was that?" he stuttered.

"That, old friend, is what murdered my parents and our people," I turned to Kyle, anger seething from every word. And then I caught it. The trace of a familiar scent.

I screamed out in excruciating pain as my legs collapsed beneath me.

"Lakota, are you all right?" I heard Jason's desperate voice as an echo in my burning ears. "What the—" I heard him say in utter shock.

Before I realized it, I was on my feet again. I dropped the automatic and grabbed the desert eagle on my hip. Then I ripped the same gun from Jason's side, wielding the unfamiliar weapons, one in each hand.

"Lakota, you can't handle them like that," Jason screamed at me. "You're going to tear your arm off."

I was in a sprint towards the scent and I could feel the presence of the creature just ahead of me. I heard Jason's running steps behind me.

And then as quickly as it had disappeared, the creature reappeared in front of my eyes again. All I could see was its massive black wings against the grays and whites of the forest.

"I've got him," Jason yelled out behind me before letting off a volley of bullets. The creature dodged every single one.

My legs propelled me towards the creature without my willing them to. I took aim and fired, again and again and again until the clips were empty. It eluded every bullet as if it knew where they were going before I even pulled the trigger. Frustrated, my rage overtook me and I threw the useless guns to the ground and bounded by foot towards the beast. In some miraculous feat, I somehow scaled the side of the trees with a speed I did not own, I propelled myself off a large trunk with a confidence I hadn't earned, and I collided with the great black wings in mid-air.

We spun uncontrollably through the air until both our bodies hit the ground with a terrible thud.

"Lakota, are you all right?" Jason asked as he approached cautiously, firearm at the ready. "Move out of the way, give me a clear shot."

Dazed, I rolled away from the beast and as I did the great black wings expanded to their full width in one quick motion. It had at least a ten-foot wing span.

"My god." Jason was awestruck.

The creature was in the air and gone in less time than it took to take a single breath.

"Damn it!" I exclaimed as I turned back to Jason. "How the hell do I kill something I can't hit?"

I realized that Jason was standing there staring at my lower half with the most ghostly white face I had ever seen.

Expecting to see something horrible, I looked down, simultaneously realizing the pain in my legs had subsided. My feet were bare, which was odd since I'd been wearing boots when we'd started. The lower part of my pants were torn to shreds, but I had no apparent injuries to my legs.

"What are you staring at?" I demanded, irritated.

"You had . . . your legs . . . they were . . . not human . . . . Wolf or . . . ." He couldn't make a complete sentence.

"Come on," I said as I headed back. "You're not making any sense. I knew I shouldn't have let you come," I said.

"What if it comes back?" Jason asked, as he followed after me while obsessively glancing back now and then over his shoulder.

"Doesn't really matter," I said shortly.

"What do you mean? We have to kill it," he exclaimed.

"Oh?" I stopped walking and turned to him in annoyance. "And how do you propose we do that?" I inquired, "Because your arsenal didn't do shit."

We walked the rest of the way back to our vehicles in silence. The reality of what had just happened weighing heavily on both of us.

"What are you?" Jason asked as we reached the clearing where we had parked.

"What are you talking about?" I retorted angrily.

"You don't know, do you?" he said. "You're not human anymore."

"You've lost your damn mind, old friend," I snapped.

He grabbed the guns I carried in my hands and ripped them from my grip.

"You fired these at the same time as if they were a child's toys. You only see stuff like that in the movies. That doesn't strike you as maybe, oh, I don't know, just a little bit off?" he snapped back at me. "I watched you change right in front of my eyes. You are not human anymore and I suggest you figure out real quick what you really are, or that beast out there is going to get the better of you."

Any words I would have retorted were trapped in the back of my throat. Any thoughts I had were trapped deep within my mind. The denial was all that existed.

"I have to go, I'm sorry you had to be involved in all this," I told Jason abruptly.

I went home and holed myself up in my room for the rest of the day. Notak and Jesse knocked on my door at one point to see what I was up to. I told them that I didn't feel well. I didn't want to see anyone, I didn't want to talk or think—I didn't want to exist. My stomach was tied up in a knot and my palms were sweaty as I reflected on everything that had happened. I didn't feel right. I didn't feel like me, and Jason's words echoed again and again in my ears. *You're not human . . . .*

If he was right, if I had somehow changed, then what was I? Hours passed and the sun began to set, my head was spinning and my body began to ache. Curling up into one corner of the room, I sat there chagrined and anxious. I was trapped. Shackled by invisible chains to something inside of me that I didn't understand. I realized with a heavy sadness that I was desperately trying to hold on to hope. And just as Aiden had warned, my humanity seemed to be vanishing right before my eyes. I did not fear, hurt, loath. I just wanted it all to end. I felt as if my heart was icing over. Yet, sitting there trapped inside my own mind there was one strand of hope I frantically clung to.

Aiden. I wanted to be with *him* again. When I was with him, somehow it all made sense, it mattered, it fit. And I ceased to be trapped.

"Lakota, are you alright love?" His voice danced through the air.

I gasped. I couldn't recall him coming in through my window, but the curtains rustled as if someone had just been there. He looked as perfect as ever, but concern was written all over his faultless face.

6 Haunted

"How do you do that?" It donned on me that I could hear a single leaf as it touched the forest floor, but somehow I could never hear him coming.

"Do what?"

"Sneak up on me like that." I could not hide my irritation.

"You just don't know what to listen for." He knelt down beside me and leaned into me dreadfully close. I braced myself, anticipating his touch.

"Come with me," he said as his lips touched my left ear. I could feel his breath against my skin, and my heart pounded against my breastbone. His breath was ice cold, and it sent a chill down my spine.

I felt intoxicated, and a single, lonely breath escaped my lips.

He took my hand and pulled me up from my wallowing corner.

"I . . . I'm not in the mood," I complained, but my words did not sound convincing.

"You owe me this," he said with a smirk. "Jason left an hour ago for his cabin in Montana. He was very distraught after your adventure this afternoon. I'm without a boss now, and I think that has something to do with you, love. And besides, it'll be like a date."

"My god, what's happening to me? What have I done?" I whispered contritely under my breath. "This is all my fault." My heart sank a little with the weight of the burden.

"He'll be fine, don't you worry. Seems you dredged up some old memories of his he couldn't deal with. He just needs some time to mull it over." He turned to the window and the rising moon as he slid deep into thought. "If you keep pushing away your past, it'll kill you. It's you and yours you should be worried about."

"I don't understand what you're trying to say. Is my family in danger because of me?" Everything suddenly felt very complicated.

"Come on, let's get some fresh air and we can talk," he said as I conceded and quietly snuck out the window after him. He took my hand as we headed to the edge of the forest. He had gloves on, as he always did, but still

I embraced the closeness. He made me feel safe and secure, and all my troubles melted away. We hiked a mile until I saw his red motorcycle parked on the side of the road.

"I am not getting on that thing," I yanked my hand from his and took a step backwards. He mounted the massive machine, pulled the clutch and started the ignition. The engine fired up with a roar of thunder, scaring every creature for miles.

He didn't say a word, he just patted the tiny back seat signaling to me with a nod of his head.

I gritted my teeth. I didn't want to ride on that thing, but I didn't want our time together to end either. "Damn it, Aiden," I muttered. I reluctantly swung my leg over the tiny back seat. The machine vibrated and churned under me.

We were on the main highway within seconds, my stomach in my throat. I wasn't used to this kind of open speed. There was nothing between myself and the hard pavement going by at ninety miles an hour, or whatever god-awful speed he was going. I looked down at the ground and immediately regretted it. I felt like I was going to throw up.

My arms were clasped around Aiden's waist so tightly that I was sure I must be suffocating him. Neither did I want to release my hold around his body, for fear of not being able to touch him. I alternated between clenching my eyes tightly and staring straight ahead, trying to decide which one was less nauseating than the other.

Finally, after what felt like an eternity, we pulled into the parking lot to the right of a large building with old train cars flanking it. I recognized it immediately as the Oregon Electric Station, a popular restaurant in Eugene among locals and tourists alike.

Aiden dismounted first and then helped me off. He grabbed both my shoulders to steady my trembling body, as my feet touched the ground.

"Wasn't so bad now, was it?" A mischievous smile crept across his face.

"I've never been on one of these before," I quipped, looking at the bike.

I could smell the delicious scent of fire grilled steaks and seafood in the air as we approached the restaurant. I noticed that my stomach was slightly queasy.

"I don't know how you expect me to eat after that," I mused. I only heard him stifle a laugh.

The fire pit by the front door was blazing high and many of the outdoor tables surrounding it were occupied by customers entertained by their food, beer or wine.

I watched them as they laughed. My heart ached a little as I wished for that kind of happiness.

Aiden went ahead of me and opened the small front door, beckoning for me to enter. The foyer was adorned in old-fashioned style, including several antique newspaper clips artfully displayed in shadow boxes along with 1950s artifacts from the old railroad days.

In a few moments we were led to one of the old train cars that had been converted into mini dining rooms. The attractive hostess walked us to a small circular table in the very back of the car. It was a nice and quiet, semi-private little corner of the restaurant. No doubt, Aiden had requested it. He pulled the chair out for me and waited for me to make myself comfortable before he, in turn, took a seat two feet away.

It was dim in the quaint little train car, each table lit by a single candle resting in a glass. Sweet sounds of violins and classical music floated through the room. It set a decidedly romantic mood. Near the roof of the train car, antique suitcases that had once been used by travelers long ago stood against the wall. Other antique items were scattered here and there to add character and ambience to the old restaurant; old lanterns, vintage luggage carriers, and numerous trinkets to keep the eyes busy and the mind engaged.

I smiled at the strange churning in my stomach, the butterflies that flitted to and fro, although I knew the sensation was not from the motorcycle ride. I looked across the table at Aidan's unspoiled composure and I was suddenly embarrassed at the intimacy of the moment.

Just then, a waitress approached our table with an infectious smile on her face. Her frame was thin, but curvy, and she looked to be about twenty-one or so. She had dirty blond hair cut to just above her shoulders, and her complexion was very fair.

I realized that I was silently envying her, daydreaming for a moment about how I might look with her hair and her skin. I might be prettier that way. More like an angel.

"Hello, my name is Melissa and I'll be your server this evening." Her vibrant, happy personality seeped through every word. "May I get you started with a glass of wine or a cocktail?"

"Uh, yes," I heard his soft, sensual voice awaken me. "A bottle of your best Riesling, if you will."

I opened my mouth to protest, but he shushed me before I could utter a word.

"Of course, sir, two glasses?" she asked him without ever once looking my direction.

"Yes," he said, almost in a whisper as his eyes locked on mine. He ignored the girl as if she was some type of wall art.

The waitress hesitated a moment, and I knew she was inspecting Aiden the same way I had the first time I saw him. But finally, she turned her wandering eyes away and went off to get our drinks started.

"So what happened out there today?" Aiden wasted no time getting down to the one question I dreaded answering.

"It's a long story and I'd rather not talk about."

Aiden just continued to stare at me expectantly, as if he would not take no for an answer. I sighed in defeat.

"I've been followed by some kind of creature in the forest for several weeks now. Jason and I went to hunt it down and, well I don't know how to explain it, but it wasn't human and it wasn't like any animal I've ever seen. It had great black, leathery wings and it was so fast and smart . . ." I trailed off trying to make sense of the day.

"Anyways, I remember seeing it once before, in my dream. It was the same creature that killed my parents."

"Was Jason there? The night your parents were—."

"Yeah. I mean, he never saw what killed my father. But it was the only one that had wings. Why?"

"Those are the memories Jason has been escaping," Aiden began to understand. "So did you get it? The creature?"

"No, not even close. It was just too fast. And I'm not sure if we can kill it or how."

"Weren't you afraid?"

It was the least expected question that I thought he would ask. It caught me off guard.

"Afraid of the creature? No. Now that you mention it, I remember being afraid the first time I encountered it. But not this time. Why would you ask something like that?"

"There's something about you. Something in your eyes . . ." he said, distant. "You intrigue me, confound me. There isn't much that you fear, is there?" His voice dimmed as his mind escaped to some faraway memory.

I stared into his beautiful eyes, lost and mesmerized. Inadvertently, I inhaled his sweet aroma. It made me dizzy and calm all at once.

"My fear is buried beneath grief and anger," I said shortly. "How do you do that? It's like you can see right through me, right into my thoughts and memories."

"I've been around a long time." His whisper was barely audible. It was as if he were talking to himself, as if he'd forgotten where he was.

"You never make any sense." I didn't understand how someone so young could see himself as having been around for a long time. Something just didn't fit about him. And he thought I was odd? "Why do I get the feeling you're not who you say you are?"

"I am everything that I have said, I do not lie."

"How old are you?" It was the one question that would shed light into all the muddy darkness.

"If I told you—you wouldn't believe me. And if you believed me, I'd have to kill you," he said with a sinister grin.

"You're impossible," I said dejected and irritated. My mind couldn't fathom what the hell he could possibly be referring to.

"And you, Lakota Avital, are not probable."

The waitress, Melissa, returned before I could process my racing thoughts. She gracefully set down the wine glasses, opened and poured the wine.

"Are we about ready?" she asked in her chipper voice.

"Ladies first," he said motioning to me as he sat back in his chair. He didn't stutter, didn't hesitate. It was as if the strange content of our conversation was inconsequential to him.

I fumbled around with the menu, scanning it and ordering quickly so that we could get back to our conversation.

"Top Sirloin, blood rare." He ordered without once taking his eyes away from mine. They just continued to burn a hole into my skull.

"Blood rare?" I asked as I raised an eyebrow in surprise.

He just shrugged his shoulders a bit, his gaze starting to feel slightly invasive.

I realized the server, Melissa, was still standing by our table. I looked up at her, warningly. I could tell she was mystified at his apparent lack of interest in her. She shifted away from my glare, hesitated for a moment, and then was off again.

"May the past not consume us, and the future not control us," Aiden said as he raised his glass to me, signaling a toast.

I lifted my glass to his, and the sweet chime it sang out as the two glasses touched reminded me of how I felt inside. We'd just met, really. Never in a million years did I think that I would be here, sitting down to dinner with him. It was all rather surreal.

"Jason's a quiet, private sort of man, isn't he?"

"He used to be so full of life, but after the massacre, he changed. He'd served in combat but it was nothing like what he witnessed with our people. That night changed a lot of people, it split our tribe and the people of Oakridge," I sighed, trying to maintain my composure.

"What happened here? Why will no one speak of it?" He was genuinely interested and disturbed.

"It feels like so long ago," I began. "My father moved here in his early twenties, became a skilled lumbar man and eventually became Timber Specialist for Region 6 Willamette Forest Services. Kyle Benson was the Fire Management Officer, so they worked together a lot. My father helped to build the community with Kyle, Jason and many other town leaders. All the people of Oakridge loved my father." I sat back in my chair, reflecting.

"Then he met and fell in love with my mother, Hot'ne, and they were married. My father left the town to live on the Reservation with my mother. If it had continued like that, my father working in town, married to a lovely native girl, life would have been a fairytale. Don't get me wrong, there was some prejudice, but the town loved my father and I think most people were content to see him happy. But there was no fairytale ending," I said sadness creeping into my voice.

"Around the same time that I was born, people started dying from bizarre animal attacks. My father became obsessed with finding and stopping the culprit and by the time I was one-year-old, he had abandoned his job as a Ranger. Before I was two, he had abandoned civilization altogether. He was withdrawn and angry, and he isolated himself in solitude in a tiny cabin in the forest."

"I remember the night he died, it was a full moon, and it was cold. They came, four of them, and they murdered and consumed my people until the fields ran thick with blood. Men, women, children . . . it didn't matter. They were so fast and merciless. Jason rallied a small group of men from town to try and fight them off, but most of them wouldn't see sunrise the next day."

"People from town blamed the Kalapuya for the deaths of the white men who had fought with us, and for polluting my father and stealing him away from the town. Those who chose to continue a relationship with the Kalapuya people have been forced to walk in the shadows of my parents death ever since. Jason became a recluse and has struggled to make a living for himself, haunted by the prejudice that followed. Kyle limits his interactions with my people to keep the peace."

"The Kalapuya believed that it was my conception that had brought the curse on the tribe, enraging the spirits and bringing death. The only surviving elder, Wakiza, took me as his own daughter as my father requested before he died. That act would cause a rift in the tribe so deep that we eventually split and those against Wakiza and myself moved north, creating the Three Sisters Kalapuya Tribe in Washington, near the border of Canada. Those who stayed thought of my father as a martyr of sorts, their savior and a being of higher power. To them my mother was a goddess, ultimately giving up her life in order to protect the lives of her people. Every year on the anniversary of the massacre we hold a sacred dance to honor their sacrifice."

"I am the spawn of their seed, the last remnant of their sacred blood line. But the townspeople only see me as the half-blood daughter of Trevor Avital and the native 'whore,' Hot'ne. The mud child whose parents brought so much pain and suffering. I am the living reminder of that horrible night."

"So you do fear . . ." he said almost in a whisper. "You fear them, the creatures that came that night."

"I used to. I was terrified that they would come back for me. But time has eluded me and I think I've forgotten who I am, or what I am or was meant to be. And now, I just feel, more or less, lost," I brooded, staring past him.

The waitress brought our entrees but this time she didn't wait around.

"Well I think that if they ever do return, you would be a force to be reckoned with," Aiden said as he began cutting his bloody steak.

"Your high opinion of me is disturbing," I retorted. "I'm not hero material."

After a few bites of dinner I was pleasantly surprised to find that with some food in my stomach, the butterflies began to subside. I noticed that Aiden ate slowly and looked almost as if he was having a hard time swallowing.

When we finished dinner, Aiden took the bill and put a neat stack of money into the check presenter and returned it quickly to Melissa's hand without a word.

I realized with disappointment how quickly the evening had gone by. I didn't want it to end. There was so much more I had hoped to uncover about him.

He held out his hand to me, and I could not refuse it. I longed for his comforting touch.

We walked through the parking lot slowly, lingering with each other.

"What is it you want most out of your life?" he asked.

I thought for several moments, as his question was not easy for me to answer.

"I don't know anymore," I said. It surprised me that I had never asked myself that question. "Once I just wanted to be normal, to live a normal life. Without fear, or grief, or loss, or this burning anger. But now, I just want to be at peace."

"What about you, my-Aiden-whom-I-know-practically-nothing-about?"

"I want to have a family, a wife who I'm desperately in love with me, and kids, and grandchildren. I want to die a peaceful death at a ripe old age," he said looking straight at me with a sadness I didn't understand.

"Is that dream so impossible?"

He did not answer me, but instead mounted his bike and started the engine, the purr of its motor breaking the silence between us. It was as if I had hit a sensitive chord in him, and I did not understand his quiet resolve.

"We should leave," he said abruptly. He looked up at the nearly full moon, now high in the dark night sky. I didn't understand his urgency.

A split second later I could feel a wave of pain course down my spine, an urgency in my bones.

"Yeah, I think that's a good idea," I agreed.

The ride back to the reservation was less horrifying, although I wondered if I could hold back the waves of pain until we set our feet on solid ground again. *Why now?* The agony couldn't have come at a worse time. Cautiously, I rested the side of my head on Aiden's broad, muscular upper back. The hum of the bike was comforting, and with my arms wrapped around his waist as tight as ever, I felt calm and safe.

We arrived back at the edge of the road a few miles out from the reservation. As I dismounted the bike, I realized that I had a fever.

Aiden sniffed the air intently, as if he were some kind of a dog. He looked up at the moon momentarily, almost expectant. His gaze turned to me as he cocked his head to one side.

Suddenly, I began to feel the familiar pains of the agony beginning again.

Panic set in. My ribs cracked and popped and I wrapped my arms tightly around my waist to try and hide the agony. My legs were throbbing and my arms were on fire.

"I have to go. I don't feel good," I stuttered as the pain enveloped me.

Aiden leaned in close to me and the excitement of the intimacy seemed to delay the agony for a few moments.

"Will you be alright?" he asked as he inhaled deeply.

"I'll . . . I'll be fine," I stammered as the pain returned.

He planted a lingering kiss on my forehead. His touch was icy cold on my skin, almost as if his lips had been frostbitten. For a moment I could feel my boiling blood attempting to warm the skin on my head where his touch had been.

I had so many questions but I couldn't think straight as a wave of agony writhed down my back. I turned in one swift motion and sprinted as fast as I could into the dark forest.

The sound of my painful screams echoed through the woods. My vision distorted horribly, my head rang with all the noises of the wilderness, my legs dragged like heavy iron.

I remember hearing the crunch of the leaves as my body hit the ground. I remember smelling the wet leaves near my face.

The reoccurring nightmare of my past years visited me that night with more intensity than ever before. It was as if I was actually there.

That night there was one thing that became painfully apparent to me. I was haunted by a past I would never escape.

7 Metamorphosis

When I came to, my body was cold and shivering uncontrollably. The only remnants of warmth that touched my skin were from the few areas where the sun's rays managed to penetrate the deep layers of the forest ceiling. Slowly, I pulled myself to my feet and headed home, dazed and confused.

As I broke through the edge of the woods I was stunned to see that *he* stood there on our porch in all his handsome glory, talking to someone in the doorway. I strained from the distance where I watched to try and hear what they were talking about.

"If you don't tell her, I will. There isn't much time. It's a full moon tonight," I heard Aiden say.

What happened next both insulted me, and shocked me.

"She is not yours to worry about. She never will be. You are not welcome here. You should leave," Wakiza said, his tone robotic and emotionless.

"Father!" I shouted in disbelief. I realized suddenly that I was at the base of the porch somehow, although I had no recollection of my legs carrying me there. It seemed an impossible distance to cover so fast. "He is my friend," I said as I met Aiden by the front door.

Wakiza eyed me in a way I had never seen before. He glanced at the forest where I had come from, and then back to where I was standing. The color in his face had drained and was horribly sullen and pale. He looked back and forth between Aiden and myself, his face locked in speechless shock.

I noticed that Aiden was inspecting me as well. Tentatively, I surveyed my body to find the tattered and torn remains of my clothes hanging in raggedy strips.

"I am not *them*. And my family may be the best thing you have right now," Aiden said to Wakiza. And with that he turned and walked off into the forest without so much as a glance at me.

"Aiden! Please wait," I called after him. He stopped but did not look back.

"Father, what's going on? What have you done?"

"He shouldn't be here. He isn't good for you." Although he seemed angry at me, his voice was devoid of emotion.

"I'm twenty-one! I think I can decide for myself what's good for me and what's not," I yelled angrily.

"Kota, please heed me. Trust me if just this once, I beg you," he pleaded with desperation as he looked at me through brooding eyes.

I felt myself inhale sharply with an anger that seemed inconceivable. "Why should I trust you? You have deceived me, father. You have been keeping secrets from me, haven't you?"

Wakiza stood there, silent and guilty.

"Your silence confirms it," I accused him with a hiss.

"I have only meant to protect you, but I fear the darkness has risen nonetheless. I am sorry Lakota. Please, calm yourself. We can discuss this civilly," he pleaded.

"Civilly?" I retorted. "We are way past civil. What have you been hiding from me? I want the truth," I demanded, stepping up onto the porch and slamming my hand against the wall.

"I have never lied to you. But . . ." he said as he sighed. He looked at me with loving eyes. The same loving eyes I had grown up with, grown to know as my father. "I have neglected to confide in you completely in order to protect you from your past. It was your father's wish," he admitted.

"I am haunted by my past, day after day and night after night, in a merciless cycle. I scarcely sleep, I barely function, and I am in constant agony. You cannot protect me from myself."

She was right, she warned me of my past I thought, remembering what the woman in the forest and the voice in my dreams had forewarned.

"Your father wanted so dearly for you to live a normal life . . . a life unaffected by that which tore his world apart. I will be breaking my vow to him," he said, genuinely torn.

"Don't you see? My life is an existence bordering on insanity. It's everything but normal. Tell me! Who am I? What am I?"

Wakiza stood there frozen in fear and thought for a moment. He looked at Aiden standing halfway between the house and the forest. Aiden nodded at him, as if giving him permission or encouragement. It was the longest moment of my life with the anger still brewing inside of me.

"Your father was a werewolf."

The silence that followed was deafening.

There were no words that would come to the front of my mind. There was no reaction that would come to a nerve in my body. There was only utter shock and several eternal moments of dreadful silence.

"That means that I'm . . ." I trailed off, trying to comprehend what it meant. "It's not possible."

My mind was racing with a thousand thoughts. "It's just not possible," I said as I stumbled a few steps backward until my foot touched the first step down from the porch.

My blood was coursing hard through my veins, and I felt my skin flush. And then there was a short, but agonizing wave of pain that coursed through my body like a tidal wave. I inhaled a sharp breath that burned my lungs.

"Your father hoped that if you survived and reached age, it would become only a repressed gene."

"*If* I survived?" I asked trying to contain the pain.

"We don't know of any like you that survived childhood, much less the change," he explained. "You are the offspring of a werewolf father and a human mother. You are a hybrid, a half blood."

A new wave of agony cascaded down my body and I was gasping for air now, my chest so heavy that it felt like it might shatter. I stumbled backwards down the steps and braced myself for the inevitable impact with the ground. But strong cool hands caught me just in time, and helped me regain my balance. I could smell his intoxicating scent and I could feel his imprisoning presence. I didn't understand how he had crossed the field so fast to save me from my fall.

"Are you all right Lakota? What's happening to her?" Wakiza looked to Aiden as if he would be able to answer the question. He proceeded down the steps to me and grabbed me gently around the shoulders. As he did, Aiden relinquished his heavenly hold on me. Wakiza's hands felt so warm against my already burning skin. I could feel his fast pulse in the palms of his hands, the blood that coursed like a river beneath his skin. His touch was not comforting, and I desperately missed Aiden's cool caress.

All this time—all these years, and all the agonizing nights. You knew and you never said a word," I said shaking off his steadying hands. I tried to stabilize my breathing, to calm the trembling that vibrated from every part of my body. And I tried to wrap my mind around the seemingly impossible truth.

"Please try to understand," Wakiza caught my gaze. "I never wanted this for you. Your father didn't want this for you. I have watched you as you have lost yourself slowly to this beast, but I had hoped that it would not consume you the way it did your father."

"This can't be happening," I said, my eyes distant. "Please tell me there is something I can do to stop it," I pleaded, my eyes refocusing on Wakiza.

"Your father experimented on himself with everything from Baneswolf to witchcraft. He wanted so desperately to undo his curse on you. But he never found a cure. I have been searching for the better part of your life for something, anything that could possibly reverse it," Wakiza said.

I waited, expectantly, for some hope in his face.

"It is part of your genetic makeup, it is part of who you are," he said with a great sadness in his eyes.

I felt empty and alone as the last remnant of hope escaped me. But in the absence of hope, many thoughts occurred to me at the same time. The shards of my life began to fall into a shape that made complete sense.

"When I was little, I played with the wolves."

"You've had a way with them since you were a baby. After your parents were murdered, I found you in that den sleeping with the pups."

I laughed. There was a heavy realization that was both satisfying and nauseating.

"All this time—the nightmare. It wasn't a dream," I said. "It was a memory. My memory of that night."

"I did not see your parents' murderer. It was a miracle that you survived," I muttered.

"I remember now! I remember everything," I said as I shut my eyes and for the first time invited the memory. I wanted to see now. My knees buckled as another wave of pain came over me, but *his* cold embrace again held me firm and steady.

"My mother put me in that den. She sacrificed herself to keep me safe. I watched her fall to the demon. The creature with great, black leathery wings and nails like talons. I remember his scent, and the scent of my mother's blood. I remember my father changing into a majestic creature, half wolf and half man. He rose up against the demon but he was no match for that—thing. When my father fell, there was silence and the black sky and blood.

"You carried me in your arms. I remember the meadow . . ." I said as the flashbacks broke against my closed eyelids. "The women, the children, the grandfathers, the grandmothers. They killed everyone they touched with no regard for human life," I said as the gaping hole inside my heart throbbed. "It was a massacre."

I felt my legs begin to give beneath me, but Aiden's hands steadied me. His touch was comforting, so I continued with the horror story playing in my mind's eye.

"There were four of them, inhumanly strong and unbelievably fast." My forehead was furrowed together as I frantically searched my mind for every fragment of the memory.

"Josiah!" I said suddenly. I felt Aiden's grip tighten a bit more when I mentioned the name. "His name was Josiah and he was the demon, the one who killed my father and my mother."

An indescribable rage began boiling inside of me, and it was all I could do to contain myself.

"He will pay," I said calmly, but resolutely as I opened my eyes.

"We have been dreading their return since that day. We have been waiting for them. But they never returned."

"They will . . . they will come," I repeated the words of the woman.

"Please don't do anything stupid Lakota. You are the only living half blood, an abomination in their eyes. They will hunt you down. Do not forget that you are the living legacy your mother and father left behind. You are Kalapuya, and you are my daughter. You have a destiny. Don't throw it away."

There was a deep hissing sound that came from somewhere inside Aiden, although I didn't understand how he could make such a sound. A moment later I picked up on their unmistakable scents. The warriors—Kotan, Yuri, and little Jesse—watched intently from a short distance away. Kotan stood proud and tall, but his face was deeply concerned. Yuri was thin, tall, and the oldest of the three. He stood in front of Kotan and Jesse, whispering some unheard words to them with authority in his gestures.

"They are . . . ." I couldn't finish the sentence but I knew they were not unlike what I was.

"Werewolves, by infection," Wakiza confirmed. "Your father's toxin runs in their veins. They have sacrificed all that they are to protect our people, and you."

"Werewolf," I repeated as if it would somehow help it sink in a little more. But it didn't. It still all seemed a fairy tale. Like I should be waking up at any moment now. But, then again, it made a whole lot of sense all of a sudden. I had always been curious as to why the warriors were always on nightshifts together and what they did out in the forest all night long.

"Even little Jesse?" He couldn't have been infected by my father. He was too young.

"When he was an infant, he became very ill and would have died had it not been for Yuri infecting him in small doses over time. It gave him the ability to heal and saved his life. He changed slower than the others, not completing his first full transformation until he was twelve years old."

"I am different though? Half blood," I whispered.

Another wave of pain coursed through my body, this one much worse than the last. I would have fallen to my knees had it not been for Aiden's ever-present hold on me. The agony was becoming unbearable and my vision began to blur. I looked up at Wakiza again, desperate. His eyes were filled with utter helplessness.

"This isn't right," he turned to Aiden for an explanation. "New werewolves are born on full moon and new moon nights, when the sun, moon, and earth align and the lunar pull is at its greatest."

"I don't think those rules apply to her."

I clutched desperately at my chest, my fingers digging into my skin until blood began to escape the fresh wounds. There was a shrieking scream that came from my vocal cords. An inhuman scream that was unrecognizable even to my own ears. I pushed Aiden away, terrified that I would hurt him. I was beginning to feel extremely volatile, as if I wanted to tear something apart. It was a primitive feeling that terrified me.

"Get away from me!" I screamed. "Please, stay—" I gasped. "Stay away from me."

My chest was heaving harder and harder, and my ribs felt like they were on fire. My skin burned hot, so hot.

The forest was suddenly awake with sounds that made my head spin. Every leaf that shifted, every creak of the trees. I could hear it, could hear all of the sounds at once. My eyes no longer saw in color, but instead in vivid hues of blacks, whites, and grays. My bones ached with anticipation. It seemed impossible to be in so much pain, and yet to be so numb.

I felt torment in my ribcage as if it was splitting in two down my sternum. My fists were clenched in tight balls, and they ached as if somebody had taken a torch to my hands. My legs throbbed as if they'd been broken. And then there was a new pain, an excruciating pain coming from my skull. I found myself holding my head, tossing it from side to side, back and forth.

I looked to the sky and screamed in anguish again, but this time it was not the sound of my voice that I heard echoing through the forest. It was the howl of a wolf. A heavy realization hit me then as I looked down into a pool of melted snow.

Metamorphosis. I no longer held human form. My ears were decidedly canine. My legs were that of a wolf, a strangely disproportionate face, and long claws where my short fingernails had been moments before. My shiny coat was white, with shades of grays, and blacks.

I looked up to see the stunned faces of Wakiza, my warrior brothers, and Aiden.

"Impossible," Wakiza whispered from the porch. But it sounded as if he had said it right into my ear.

I opened my mouth to say something, but my throat was scratchy and burned like fire. No words would come out. Frustrated, I turned, bounding for the forest as fast as I could.

The greenery of the woods wrapped me with the comfort of their familiar branches like a woolen blanket.

I ran . . . and ran . . . and ran, deep into the Willamette Wilderness until I was miles away from any human, and more importantly from anyone whom I might be capable of harming. When I finally stopped, I peered into a small lake and stared at my new form for hours. There was no acceptance, but there was no denial either. I felt an incarnation of emptiness, a complete void. I was lost . . . lost to the beast within.

My mind was a blank slate. There was numbness of mind, of body, of spirit. I did not know where to go, so I meandered in no particular direction for hours until the moon was high in the now black velvet sky.

Suddenly, there was a sharp twinge in the back of my mind and I froze still as ice. All my senses screamed at me. Standing there still and silent, I realized that I was not alone. There was someone behind me, I could feel it. It was a menacing presence, like in my nightmare.

I sniffed the air in that canine way, but this time it felt natural. There was a familiar scent in the air, but I couldn't make out what it was or where it came from. I turned over my shoulder in time to see a creature flying down from the canopy of the trees. It touch down gracefully onto the forest floor, resting on the earth about five hundred feet away. I realized how impossible it should have been to see that far out into the dark, thick forest.

When I opened my mouth to call to it my throat was so hoarse and dry that the sound was muffled and only echoed through my chest.

I squinted to try and see a little clearer. It was walking towards me, and there was something on its back. Huge, black, leathery things. But as it got closer, the wings impossibly disappeared.

"Lakota, I can help you."

The voice sounded vaguely familiar in my mind, but strangely foreign to my canine ears. My thoughts were racing as I tried to process hundreds of things all at once.

"Josiah?" I thought I recognized the creature as the one I had tried to find, to hunt, to kill. The demon that had killed my parents when I was a little girl. Now was my chance. Whatever this beast was, I would not let it get away this time. I would avenge my parents' death. I felt myself propelled forward before I realized that I was running towards the thing.

Then I heard a high pitched screech, like that of a hawk, coming from the creature. It stopped dead in its tracks when it realized I was attacking. I did not slow down. My blood was building to a boil again, and I caught myself growling under my breath with each stride.

The creatures' wings reappeared and began to flap and it lifted off the ground. It was a magnificent sight to see.

It looked to be the figure of a man, yet wearing the wings of a bat.

I ran faster, faster. Scaling the trunk of a tree, I jumped to the side of another, ricocheting back and forth between trees higher and higher each time in order to meet the elevation of the air-born creature. Our two bodies collided in midair with a magnificent clash.

A high-pitched yelp braised the horizon, like the cry of a dog that had just been hit. I felt a snap in my rib-cage and then I was falling to the ground.

I righted myself on all fours, a fierce growl escaping my vocal chords.

"Stop!" I heard a silvery voice.

I did not heed his command. With a snarl and a growl I was moving forward towards the creature again. I felt my jaw opening, ready to bite the creature and tear him to shreds.

But he was so fast and incredibly agile. I heard him yell something at me again, but my rage-filled fury blurred my understanding of what it was.

Suddenly I felt the weight of a thousand bricks hit me and I went hurling through the air. I landed with a hard thud against a tree. A yelp escaped my jaws. I was back up faster than I thought possible. He was standing there in front of me not three yards away.

I circled around him, snarling. I lurched forward to attack again, but he shifted to the side and easily redirected me.

How terribly clumsy I was in the new body with which I was horribly unfamiliar. I felt like a teenager experiencing all of adolescence in a single moment. I flew past him and tripped, rolling hard and finally landing with a painful thud into the bush at the base of a tree. A searing pain shot through my shoulder and collarbone, and with a slight turn of my head, I could see a shard of shattered tree protruding from my shoulder. Gripping the piece with my free hand I pulled it out. Blood trickled slowly from the wound.

I heard him yelling at me again, and I got back up onto all fours, straining to hear what he was saying, my canine ears turning in his direction.

"Stop!" There was something now terribly familiar about his voice, but I still couldn't place it. I was having a hard time differentiating between his voice and all the other sounds of the forest around me. My ears were ringing under the strain and my head spun as my brain desperately tried to adapt to the millions of stimuli bombarding me all at once.

"Please!" he begged. I could see his gleaming white teeth. Two were very pronounced. His wings were gone now, no sign of their existence or presence whatsoever. Most of him was shrouded in darkness and I couldn't make out his face.

I attacked again, unwilling to retreat and unable to control the incredible urge to attack. To kill. To tear the flesh from his body. The rage was intoxicating, like a drug. It sent rushes of adrenaline in horrible waves that made me sick to my stomach.

This time I bit into his arm with canine teeth. I regretted it instantaneously. I felt a burning sensation where my teeth and mouth had broken his skin . . . like acid. Before I released my grip though, I felt the palm of his hand hit the side of my skull. A sharp pain emanated through my eye into my jaw, and suddenly I was flying through the air again. And then he was on top of me, pinning my body into submission.

I struggled to get free, but he was so strong.

And then I caught a waft of something very familiar. I was close to vomiting when the recognition set in.

Honey and leather . . . .

Aiden!

My eyes cleared suddenly. I saw him. His pale, beautiful face.

I lay there limp, finally understanding.

He straddled me for a few more moments before jumping off of me in a very inhuman, but strangely graceful way.

"Stubborn ass of a new-lycan," he stood a few feet away from me now. "Shite! Calm down. It's me, love."

I flipped onto all fours and then onto my hind feet and up to my full height to face him. A thousand impossible thoughts flew through my head as I watched Aiden, standing there so still, as if he was frozen like ice. He could have passed for dead.

I approached him cautiously, my long hind legs increasing my normal height by several inches. A split second later, there was a loud slap in the air. And then his wings were there again, seeming to appear out of nowhere.

"This is what I am," he whispered as he, in turn, inspected my hybrid form.

I didn't think it was possible that he could be any more amazing, but I had been wrong.

"Please, don't look at me," I begged.

"Why? You are beautiful, just like my first memory of you in the forest. Do you remember?" His wings folded into his back and disappeared.

"That was you?" I thought back to that day in February when I had first sensed the creature. And then I thought of the day I'd tried to hunt and kill it. "It was you all along? And you weren't trying to kill me."

I wanted to be human again. I willed myself to be human again. A second later, a massive wave of pain coursed through my body and, indeed, I was human again just like that. I stumbled back a few feet as new pains made themselves present. This time, Aiden didn't come to my aid so I steadied myself by a tree trunk. He gazed at my broken body, and I watched as unearthly veins rippled in his face. I could see it in his eyes. He didn't want to be near me.

My ribcage burned and it hurt to breath; my shoulder throbbed, and my head ached. When I looked down to find the tattered remains of my clothing sticking to my blood and sweat soaked body, I was mortified.

"I may have had a little fun teasing you, and I have to admit the scent of your blood was very hard to resist. And when you told me you're an orphan, I wondered if anyone would miss you. But that's the beast in me," he inhaled as he edged a few steps closer to me. "I was mesmerized by you, your scent, your beauty, your lack of fear in the face of certain death. You confound me, and that is not an easy feat when you've been around for a couple hundred years."

With lightning fast speed he crossed the distance between us and he pinned me to the tree. I heard a hiss as his mouth came dangerously close to my neck. I froze, terrified but excited as well. He inhaled again and held his breath. Long seconds passed before he let out cold air on my collarbone and fixed his eyes on mine. He brushed strands of hair out of my face, his fingers lingering on my cheeks. My heart thumped wildly.

I stared off as the memories of our meeting and conversations flashed before my eyes. It was several moments before I was able to process and piece together all the parts to the puzzle.

"Pale, cold skin like that of the dead; speed and strength unimaginable; wings of a bat giving the gift of flight; an intoxicating scent to lure in your prey; the beauty of a god to hypnotize your victim; a presence not soon forgotten; and fangs meant for feeding," I trailed off. "The reason you will never grow old and die beside the wife you are madly in love with, the reason you will never have children, or grandchildren. The reason you have lost your hope and your humanity." I paused summoning the word to my tongue, but struggling to say it aloud.

"Vampire," I whispered under a raspy, forced breath. He nodded his head in confirmation, still struggling to reign himself in.

Another more sobering realization sent a crushing weight upon my chest.

"That's why Wakiza doesn't like you, it's what he's been warning me about all this time. He knew your kind killed our people, my mother, and my father. It was—" but I couldn't say the word again.

"Not me, but yes, it was *vampires*," he finished the sentence for me. "But didn't I already tell you that?"

I couldn't believe his honoree sarcasm and I waited for the anger to come to me. But his presence only brought an erotic excitement. Somehow his two-toned eyes held the universe, an eternity that only gods should know. I hated him . . . his beauty, his scent, his time-lessness.

And yet he unabatedly captured me.

"Our worlds are inevitably intertwined," he said. "And you are of destined purpose."

"I'm a monster, an abomination," I stuttered. "I don't belong in your world. Let me go." I tried to break free of his hold on me, but he was immovable.

"You're badly hurt and in need of medical attention," he pointed out. "Where will you go? Back to your father, your brother?"

"Please, just leave me alone," I said as I willed myself to turn back into my wolf-like form. A painful moment later, I had completed the transition. "I just want to be alone."

"You cannot run forever, love."

With a power that was new to me, I shoved him, breaking his bond over me. I turned and began running. I ran and ran and ran. At some point I realized that he wasn't following me, that he had let me go at least for the time being.

I wished that somehow I could just run away from my haunted past, the haunted presence, my haunted existence—all of it.

I ran until I could run no longer.

At some point, I blacked out.

The change I had anticipated for so long had finally come, but I never could have imagined that it would be so literal. I wasn't human anymore. I was cursed with this metamorphosis.

8 BROKEN

I WOKE THE NEXT MORNING IN A MEADOW by a river, but I wasn't sure exactly where I was. Throbbing pain racked every part of my body.

I lay there for several long moments, wishing I were dead. Wishing the whole revelation were some nightmare, but knowing in my gut, it was not.

When I tried to sit up, an excruciating distress in my side prevented me from doing so. In defeat, I looked down expecting to see those half-canine legs. But they weren't there and I let out a sigh of relief.

Somehow I managed to crawl on all fours to the mossy bank. Cautiously, I peered into the mirror of water to see what had become of me. To see if the beast had vanished along with the moon.

I gasped when I saw my human face. There were no traces of the beast ever having been there, but there was also no doubt that the events of the night before had actually happened.

The sight was horrible.

From the edge of my eyebrow, wrapping around my eye and down across my cheekbone, was a massive purple bruise. Dozens of tiny scratches caked with dried blood littered my once smooth face. There was a gaping wound on my right shoulder from which a stream of blood still trickled. I realized I must have broken a rib or two as well, as I couldn't take a deep breath without collapsing to the ground in pain.

My clothes were shreds of ribbon, leaving my body nearly naked except for the pieces of fabric that clung here and there. Almost every visible part of my skin was peppered with scratches, cuts, dried blood, sweat, or mud.

I barely recognized myself.

My throat burned and my stomach ached as if I hadn't had a thing to drink or eat in weeks. I scooped up handful after handful of water, forcing myself to swallow every drop as fast as it would go down.

Although my stomach was full of the liquid, my thirst was not satiated and the gnawing in the pit of my stomach grew stronger. I wanted more . . . .

More substance. More taste. More.

Flesh and blood.

I wanted flesh and blood.

Horrified by my new hunger and thirst, I collapsed into the riverbed in utter defeat. Terror filled my consciousness as I became aware of what I had become and what I might be capable of. My mind couldn't comprehend the nightmare that my life had suddenly become. I understood the burden that my father once carried. I was ashamed of the beast that lived within me. How could I possibly fathom an existence as a werewolf?

I was fatherless and motherless. An orphan, lost in a world where I simply didn't belong. I was broken and I was naked.

A blood curdling scream escaped my trembling lips. I wanted to tear out the beast inside of me.

I pulled my broken body off the ground and looked around trying to identify where I was. I began to walk, meandering in no particular direction. After a few miles of hiking, I reached a strange sense of familiarity.

I recognized the area from a place in my dream. Grief filled my soul. I turned around to find behind me, the opening to a cave that had once sheltered a four-year-old little girl from the vampire who took everyone she loved. My eyes followed the ground from the cave to the tree where that little girl watched her father and mother suffer the throes of their murder. I dug my hands into the dirt that had once been drenched with their blood.

It was the one place I had never returned to.

My right hand stung suddenly and I looked down to see that a cut on my hand had brushed against a plant growing there.

"Baneswolf," I whispered under my breath as I recognized it instantly. My father had done experiments with the poisonous plant. I remembered that it was deadly to most animals, and to humans when consumed in large quantities. But most importantly, it was said to be a death wish for a werewolf.

It was a beautiful plant. Little bell-like purple-blue flowers waving in the light breeze. "Strange . . . how such beautiful little flowers could cause so much death," I said quietly to myself. I wondered for several moments if it might kill the beast in me, if it might exorcise the werewolf out of me, or if it would kill me entirely.

My eyes reverted back to the place where my parents fell. I could almost feel the presence of their death and my chest was heaving hard. I relived that horrible day in my memories, but I couldn't bring myself to leave that place. It was as if it had some inexorable grasp on me.

A while later, I realized that my face was soaked in tears and there was a sour taste in my mouth. The world around me swirled and swayed.

I looked down to find little blue flowers in both my hands. In bewilderment, I looked a little closer to find that the roots appeared to have been bitten off. There was an increasing pain overtaking every cell in my body.

With horror, I realized that I had no recollection of what I had been doing for the last several minutes.

"What have I done?" I whispered as I looked down again at the rootless fistfuls of Baneswolf I held in both my hands.

I realized that I had just conducted the ultimate experiment on myself by inadvertently consuming the plant. My stomach ached and I started heaving, but nothing would come up. The herb had already gone too far into my bloodstream. I was sweating profusely and my skin was hot to the touch. Everything around me blurred, and my head began to spin.

I scooped up a handful of water and splashed my face trying to get a grip of myself. There was blood flowing freely from the wound in my shoulder and all my cuts had reopened. I tried wiping the blood off my face, but the wounds were flowing too fast. The deep gouge in my eyebrow and the bruise on my forehead pulsated as if someone hit me with a baseball bat.

I collapsed just outside the opening to the cave. My vision grew almost indistinguishable, my body felt icy cold, and I could hear my heart slowing pulse . . . .

By pulse . . . .

By pulse . . . .

The world around me grew dark and black as my consciousness slipped away.

"Lakota!" A voice in the distance called as if from a dream. That melodic, angelic voice.

Aiden. My dark angel.

And then the darkness took me.

It would have been easier if I had just died that day. But no, death would not take me.

I tried once to lift my eyelids, but they were so heavy. I heard myself moaning, as if I was suspended somewhere outside my body, the sound of my own voice, distant and unattached.

I was uncertain where I was, but I could tell that it was a dark, damp place. There was a musty smell in the air mixed with the smell of my own blood.

Someone was pushing at my body here and there and every touch stung like a thousand bees. Pressure curdled the wound on my shoulder, and then the smell of rubbing alcohol wakened me slightly. Shortly after, I felt crunching bone on bone as my ribs were reset. A horrendous ache in my side seemed to go on forever and I could hear my whimpering attempts at a scream break the silence.

"Shhhh—" he put a finger to my lips "—be still."

"It hurts." My voice was barely audible.

"I know, just stay with me." His voice whispered back.

The already dim light in the room grew dimmer and dimmer. For a fleeting moment before unconsciousness took me again, I wished that death's hands would take me.

I woke from my dreamless sleep in a faintly lit room with no light except that of the moon streaming in from a small window above my head. I touched my hands to my face and felt bandages on my brow. My face felt human, no trace of canine. The bruises around my eyes were tender, but not throbbing so much. I touched my shoulder, and found bandages there too. My stomach was still tied in a knot, my vision not quite clear so I shut my eyes again. I felt like a truck had run me over.

I tried to sit up, but something cold and hard pushed me back down into the bed. Aiden's hand? I sniffed the air trying to pick up his heavenly scent. But I could only smell the scent of my own blood.

No one answered.

I tried hard to focus my eyes, alternating between blinking and squinting. Slowly my vision cleared and I scanned the room. It was dark and damp, like a basement, or a dungeon.

No one was there. Even though I was sure someone had been next to me just seconds before. I heard no footsteps either. My heart was racing and I sat up, regretting it instantly. The pain started at the top of my skull and coursed down through every cell in my body. The room went dark again as I realized I was slipping away. I fought it hard this time as two cold and hard things gently eased me to lay back down. They felt like hands. I felt a pinch in my right arm, like a needle. And then darkness swallowed me.

No peace in my dreamless sleep. Horrible nightmares. Nightmares of the vampires devouring my mother and my father. And then they took me. The last thing I remembered were those cold, hard hands taking me. Cold as ice, hard as stone.

When I woke, the room was lit by sunlight streaming through the tiny window. I scrutinized my surroundings. I was in some type of underground quarters, the walls were made of brick and smelled of earth.

I sat up gingerly, felt for my face, my shoulder, my ribcage. Felt bandages everywhere, though the bruises didn't hurt quite as bad as before. Slowly, I swung my feet to the cold floor. The change in temperature felt good. I cautiously pushed myself into a standing position and paused for a minute to reset my equilibrium. I wasn't sure how long I had been in the bed unable to move, or speak, or function.

Clothes were laid out neatly on the back of a chair. They weren't mine, but they were definitely meant for a female. A light blue blouse with a lace trim, and a pair of basic jeans with a bit of floral embroidery along the bottom. There was nothing else in the tiny room. No desk, table, lamp, dresser, not even a closet. Only the bed, a chair, the window, and a full length narrow mirror on the back of the door facing me.

I tentatively made my way to the mirror, my heart pounding fast and hard. I gasped, barely recognizing the girl I saw reflected in the mirror.

My entire left side, from the bone of my brow to the line of my jaw, was several different shades of black, blue, and dark red. Upon closer inspection I could see several very neat stitches just below my eyebrow and underneath my eye. Coagulated blood clung to the left side of the bridge of my nose.

My god, I thought to myself.

I let the white cloth robe that hung loosely drop to the floor, wincing at the pain in my ribs and shoulder as I moved.

Carefully, I pulled back the bandages on my shoulder, revealing a row of stitches along my collarbone, the clear thread flashed against my discolored skin. The once smooth, bronze casing that covered my ribs was now vivid hues of black and lavender and I could see the broken blood vessels where my ribs pressed close to the skin.

I smiled as I traced over the shadow of a hand in the bruises across my ribs. I was so stupid, so naïve. He was so strong—like some indestructible creature. He could have easily killed me. There was no way I could possibly ever match what he was.

Disgruntled, I stared at my naked disfigured body and face. My dark coloring only minimally hid the extensive bruising, the several scattered hematomas, and the discoloration from the deep tissue damage. I was angry at myself for being so consumed by the beast within me that I hadn't recognize him sooner.

With calculated caution, I managed to dress myself. One step at a time, I willed my achy, broken body out of the tiny room. The next room had the same stone walls and floor but it was massive. There was a medical bed and equipment in one corner, and in another what looked like laboratory supplies. There was light in this room, but it was a strange dim light. Some type of material coated the tiny windows of this room, filtering the sunlight in a mysterious blue glow that sufficed as a light source.

It worked perfectly for a vampire.

A vampire with cold, hard hands. Incredible speed and strength. The reality was sinking in fast.

A truth I had already confronted once, even admitted. And yet the denial of it was still so powerful.

Several agonizing steps later I found another door. Beyond it lay the expanse of the forest and the bright light from the sun made me stop for a minute to allow my eyes to adjust. I stepped out into the woods and inhaled as deeply as my broken ribcage would allow. The forest smelled so good.

I turned to scrutinize the door I had come from. It was set in a hillside, hidden by the foliage around it. The only hint of its existence and the secret rooms within was that door. A door to a secret world.

I stumbled through the forest, every step as painful as the last. My mind was only partially aware of the fact that I was searching for *him*. I sniffed the air cautiously. It felt like fire was coursing through my ribcage as my lungs expanded. He wasn't far. I could smell him.

Staggering farther and farther, closer and closer to him, I suddenly sensed that I was not alone. The sixth sense thing was becoming very familiar, almost second nature.

He was standing about ten yards away with his back turned to me. His head jerked up as if he was surprised, and he turned his head just slightly over his shoulder. He inhaled the air around him as if he was smelling a rose, but he did not turn to fully face me.

He was with someone else . . . a female. They looked like they were arguing. I hesitantly continued walking forward, uncertain as to what to expect next.

The girl stopped and sent an intense glare in my direction. Her deathly stare morphed into a contempt-filled chuckle and I could hear her whisper "that's what you're fighting for? You should have killed her when you had the chance, put her out of her misery."

She was thin and no taller than I. Her hair was jet black with streaks of pure white that highlighted her pale, beautiful face. She looked of Asian descent, her almond eyes angelic, yet strong and fierce. Her lips were as red and luscious as the petals of a red rose. Her beauty was intimidating.

Now that I was no more than five or six yards from the pair, I could see that she had the same two-toned glowing eyes that Aiden had. The intensity of her stare made me shy away, my gaze sinking to the ground.

She said something in a foreign language. Japanese, or maybe Chinese, and her tone had the timbre of a curse. She turned suddenly and was gone. She moved with the same speed as Aiden, practically disappearing in front of my eyes.

I realized that she was, like him, a vampire.

Aiden turned to me then, a concerned look on his face as our eyes met. Faster than I could blink, he closed the gap between us. And then I realized that I had been falling, although a moment before, I was hardly aware of it.

I looked down to see his arms wrapped around my waist, and cried out in torment as his touch on my broken ribs resonated through my body. Dizziness hit me a split second later, and my head bobbed as I blinked several times to regain my perception of the world around me.

"You shouldn't be out. You need time to heal," he said as he repositioned my body so that his arms weren't near my ribs. He gently pulled the bandage from my shoulder, checking my wound. His delicate touch, and the cold sensation of his skin eased the ache of the wounds.

"I'm fine."

"You have three broken ribs, a shattered collar bone, and internal bleeding and bruising. And that burning inside of you, that's the Baneswolf. You poisoned yourself."

"Who was that?" I asked curiously.

"In a way, I suppose she is my sister," he said second-handedly. "You need to feed. Your wounds will heal faster," he said, not allowing me to change the subject. He scooped me up into his arms, careful not to disturb my ribcage.

"I'm fine, let me down," I said with defiance as I pushed away from him. I tried to fight his hold, but it was as strong and secure as stone and mortar and I was very weak.

"Don't waste your energy, love."

He was right. I didn't have the energy to fight him so I was quiet for a while as he carried me back to the door in the hill.

"She doesn't look like your sister," I returned to my earlier inquiries. I didn't know who she was, but I realized, to my dismay, I was jealous.

"Her name is Yuki Rin. She was seventeen when she was turned, two hundred and eighty years ago. She is an ex-ninja assassin geisha from the 17th century, the newest addition to our coven."

"Do you—care for her?" I asked, hesitantly. I wasn't sure that I wanted to hear his answer.

"In a romantic way?" he asked, with a sly smile. "No, only as a sister. I'm not attracted to my kind," he said, satisfied with his explanation.

"Your kind," I reiterated. "Vampires," I stated, trying to wrap my mind around the idea.

"I miss the warmth of a human body, the flow of blood and life. I thirst for it to survive, and I hunger for it to satiate my innermost desires. But it is the one thing I can never have," he said sadly.

"Because we humans are so fragile to your kind," I said, as I realized what he was getting at. "She doesn't like me, does she?" I blurted out. I realized that if Yuki and Aiden had no romantic interest, then her aggression towards me seemed suddenly misplaced.

"She is very particular about the company we keep," he said. "Deep-seeded trust issues, you know what I mean now?"

"Do vampires associate with werewolves?"

"Rarely. There have been times in history when vampires and werewolves worked together. But it is rare that that relationship continues for any length of time without hostility. You're not entirely of their kind though. You are different, the likes of which we have not seen in centuries," he trailed off into distant memories. "Your very existence is both an anomaly to your kind, and an abomination to mine."

"So vampires will hate me in particular," I said with a touch of dry sarcasm. "Is that why you are here? Were you sent here to kill me?" I asked, half joking, half serious.

I watched Aiden furrow his eyebrows together, deep in thought as he avoided my question. My head was spinning again and I felt sick to my stomach.

"Please let me down, I think I'm going to be sick," I begged him.

Reluctantly, he gave in this time, gently letting me take on my own weight. I leaned against a tree nearby for support, clutching at my nauseated stomach.

"You need to feed." Aiden placed his cool hands gently on my temples and leaned in dangerously close to my trembling body. "Take a deep breath," he instructed.

I did the best I could and grimaced as I inhaled until my broken ribcage would not allow any more expansion. My queasy stomach somehow subsided and my nerves calmed.

"How do you do that? It feels like you drugged me."

"Vampires emit unique pheromones that cause a deep sense of relaxation and euphoria."

"So you can feed without an audience." The idea should have frightened me.

"For most of us, a blood meal tastes best when it isn't tainted with adrenaline. And the ability to hunt with stealth helps keep our existence invisible, which is how vampires have survived without persecution for thousands of years."

"Do you want my blood?" I leaned closer to him, taunting.

"You have no idea how much." He inhaled sharply and held his breath as he cocked his head to one side and inched his lips perilously close to my neck. "Go back and wait for me, I will bring you what you need," he whispered in my ear, his voice calm and authoritative.

"Where are you going?"

"To hunt with Yuki."

"Take me with you."

"You are weak, you should rest. I don't want you to see us feed." His voice left no room for argument, and it made me feel cold and shut out.

"I'm not afraid," I stated firmly. "Of you, or her."

I realized with disgust that my mouth was watering suddenly. The thought of raw flesh would not leave my mind. There was a burning in my stomach, in my throat, that I realized was a hunger and thirst all at once. It felt insatiable.

Abruptly, I found myself standing on my tippy toes sniffing the air intently. There was something there, something ravenously tantalizing.

Blood.

I could smell it as if it were right in front of me.

I took a step forward, swallowing hard as I tried to grasp the gravity of what I wanted. Involuntarily, I shivered as stabbing pains coursed down my legs, my arms, my ribs, my back, and my skull. I was losing to the beast within me. My eyes burned horribly, and my ears rang miserably. My legs moved me forward towards the scent.

Spirits of the earth and sky, how my throat burned and ached. Oh my throat—it was so dry, so sore, and so scratchy. As if I hadn't had a drink in weeks.

The pains of my previous injuries roared to life as I ran through the forest half-morphed. But with one last wave of pain that felt as if it would shred my body to pieces I made the complete metamorphosis. I was my hybrid werewolf-self.

"I underestimated you," his voice seemed to echo in my strange canine ears as we both stopped. "Your hunger drives you."

"What is she doing here?" came Yuki's angry voice from a short distance away. I couldn't see her, but I realized that when I focused, I could smell her beautiful scent, and I could sense her presence. Aiden pushed a bush to the side and stepped forward into a small clearing in the middle of the forest. I followed shortly behind him and with utter shock saw that not one hundred feet away, was Yuki and a huge mountain lion. They circled as if they were playing some game of cat and mouse. The lion had a large gash in its side from which that scent of blood I'd picked up on originated.

Yuki looked over in my direction, taking a double take at my morphed form, her crimson red eyes burning with an angry lust.

"Abomination!" Her words dripped with disdain. "And midday? Really?"

I looked to Aiden, trying to understand what she was talking about. Without a word or even the slightest look of surprise, he pointed to the sky.

It was the middle of the day. I understood then. I had taken my werewolf form in the middle of the day. That wasn't supposed to be possible.

"She is what she was born to be," he said as his eyes caught mine, and he gazed at me with admiration.

There was a loud growl from the mountain lion which reminded us that he was still there, waiting to take down the rather frail looking Yuki with one fell swoop.

"Stop playing with the prey and make the kill, Yuki," Aiden said, his eyes never straying from mine, but his voice firm and commanding.

I could not help but watch as Yuki wordlessly obeyed Aiden's command and leapt an impossible distance towards the lion, colliding with it in mid-air. The beast and the vampire fell to the forest floor with a resounding thud. Yuki was back on her feet faster than my eyes could see or my brain could comprehend.

The mountain lion tried to get up, but his body would not move. It was as if he had been paralyzed. There was that smell wafting through the air.

Blood.

Beautiful, succulent blood.

Then I saw it streaming from a bite mark in the beast's neck. It sizzled and smelled of seared flesh.

Yuki was on top of the beast. In one swift motion she lifted its paralyzed head and twisted as if crinkling a paper. The snap of its neck was undeniable and made me shudder.

Although I hadn't seen her move, Yuki was in front of me now, no more than a few inches from my face. Her fangs and lips dripping from her kill, her frozen face as beautiful as an angel.

"I smell another beast, brother," she hissed in my face in the most inhuman way.

"I wonder what she tastes like," she said as she licked her lips. She was inches away from my face, and I could smell the blood from the mountain lion on her breath. The smell made me want to tear her face off.

I began to fidget trying to contain what beastly manners I had. Looking past her at the lion, I could almost taste its flesh in my mouth. The scent was tormenting. I was so hungry and thirsty at the same time. I craved to feed like I had never craved anything in my life. I needed it almost as much as I needed the oxygen in the air.

Flesh and blood.

I couldn't bear it anymore. I bounded forward towards the animal with an incredible speed and strength that felt foreign to me. With a ravenous appetite, my half-canine teeth tore into its thick furry skin. I tore at the flesh until the muscle underneath was visible. The raw flesh was everything I thought it would be and more, the blood that drained down my throat quenched my dry esophagus.

"You had to go and find the only living half-blood on the planet as your playmate?" Yuki's impatient angry voice echoed in my ears. "Aiden, what do you intend to do with her? She'll be the end of us. They'll find out about her. They'll kill us all," she yelled with sincere fear in her every word.

Momentarily, I paused to look up at them but my hunger was intense and I could only be an eavesdropper on their conversation as I fed my own needs.

"You ever wonder why we ended up here, Yuki?" Aiden asked her.

"What are you talking about?"

There was silence for several moments.

"Are you insinuating that Draigon and Enya knew about her?" she queried in disbelief.

"Think about it," he said, now vehement. "Every other place we have been for the last century has been nearer to a coven. This move was oddly secretive, abrupt, and much more permanent."

Again, uncomfortable silence.

My hunger finally satisfied, I took a few steps back from the beast.

"Let's drink before it gets cold," Yuki said quickly, avoiding Aiden's implications.

Without having seen them move to the dead beast, I heard the snap as Aiden sank his fangs deep into the jugular vein. He pulled the head of the beast close to him, and you could hear the sucking sound of his mouth as he drank the blood.

With a watchful, careful eye always on me, Yuki followed suit on a vein in the hind leg.

Stepping back from the animal, I saw that there was little left of the once majestic creature. The beast was deflated to skin and bones. Sadness filled my heart, as I realized what I had done. What we had done.

Without thinking, I swiftly hefted the lion onto my back. With large canine strides, I headed towards the reservation while Aiden and Yuki looked on in surprise.

"What is she doing?" came Yuki's voice from behind me as the two proceeded to follow me.

Aiden didn't respond.

Running on all fours, I focused on the simplicity of existing in that canine state, with both its shame and glory.

I felt very strong. Very powerful. It was an addictive feeling. And I was surprised I liked it.

The speed with which my hybrid legs carried me was blinding. The strength I felt was immeasurable. All my senses were strong, and the forest looked bright and hopeful through my colorless vision.

I left the corpse of the lion on the outskirts of the reservation.

"She is seriously going to be the final death of us," I heard Yuki whisper angrily.

"It is sacred to the Kalapuya, to honor the creatures they bring death to," he said.

And with my deed complete, I felt the aches in my body cascade down from my head as I made the transformation back to my human form. The pain from my wounds rebounded, and it took me a few minutes to catch my breath.

"You did a real number on her, didn't you Aiden?" Yuki eyed my broken human body.

"You would be wise not to say another word," he said with a strange hiss under his breath. The scowl he shot towards Yuki was decidedly warning.

I said nothing as I pushed past Yuki, but I did not hide the animosity in my facial expression.

"Wait—" Yuki stalled, thoughtful for a moment. "Do your people know . . . about us?"

I kept walking as a certain repressed anger boiled inside of me. Desperately, I prayed that she would drop the subject.

"Answer me, you half-blood mutt," she screamed as she shoved me hard from behind.

I don't remember moving towards her, but the next thing I knew my bruised, discolored forearm was pinning Yuki against a tree and my eyes burned with an insatiable fire.

"Your kind murdered my people," I hissed, in disdain. "My world is broken because of vampires like you. You have no right to ask me that question."

There was a sudden hatred I felt burning inside me that I had been unaware of. I hated them. Vampires. It was so utterly unfair that they could be so invincible, so strong, and so perfect. Then, there was an abysmal anger that rose from my gut.

Josiah! I hated him, I loathed him with a rage that seemed inconceivable. He was the reason that my parents were dead, that my tribe had split, that I was left with only the shattered remains of what once was whole. My heart sank as both the grief and rage consumed me.

It couldn't get any worse. My body was broken, my spirit was broken, my world was broken, and my heart was broken.

I was helplessly broken.

9 Collisions

In the next instant, I felt myself being slammed into the dirt and my body went skidding across the forest floor, a sharp spasm shooting through my abdomen. I felt a heavy weight pulled off of me, and realized quickly that it was Yuki. I righted myself to a full stand as quickly as my feeble human body would allow.

"Get out of here, or I'll be the final death of you myself," I heard Aiden command Yuki in a calculated monotone. It was as if he was trying to control something inside himself.

Yuki stepped back a few feet, alternating her eye contact between Aiden and myself. Her eyes were livid with a vicious thirst.

It was then that I recognized the pungent odor in the air.

Blood! It was a vampire's calling card.

I righted myself on two feet and looked down at my broken body to find a stick protruding from my abdomen, blood slowly beginning to trickle from the wound.

With horror, I looked back at Yuki. This time, it was a begging, terrified gaze I sent her way. I knew I was no match for her prowess or her strength. And my blood was drawing her to me.

I saw Yuki attempt to lunge and felt the air move around me. I saw massive black wings envelope the air above me—and then I saw Aiden's wings pinning Yuki to a tree.

"Leave! Now!" he hissed, the words barely audible, but sinister and threatening nonetheless.

In a split second, Yuki was gone.

Aiden turned to me as he stretched his wings to their magnificent full width, and then they disappeared into his back as if they had never existed.

The threat of Yuki tearing me to shreds gone, the adrenaline in my system rapidly dissipated only to be replaced with a new agony. I could feel myself hyperventilating and the world around me seemed to fade. I felt my body collapse to the ground.

But before I made impact with the earthen floor, his strong careful arms caught me and eased me down.

"Be still," I heard Aiden's whisper. I looked up at him with desperate eyes.

"I can't breathe," I gasped.

"I can't hurt you, I won't hurt you," Aiden said as he watched the blood stream from my side. I knew he was trying to reassure himself. I knew he was just as tempted as Yuki had been by my fresh blood, and terror gripped me for but an instant. I found his stony hands and placed them around the stick protruding from my body.

"I trust you," I breathed, as I put my trembling hands over his.

With reluctance he took hold and quickly yanked the stick out of my body. A scream escaped my lips.

Through weary eyes I looked up to find Aiden with his eyes shut tightly, concentrating hard, his jaw clenched into a tight square and his face impossibly pale. Looking down, I could see blood pouring from my wound.

Aiden placed his trembling hands on my bleeding side, applying pressure. I gritted my teeth, forcing myself to take shallow breaths to avoid passing out from the pain and loss of blood.

"Breathe," he instructed me between his tightly clasped jaw.

With immense effort, I inhaled as deeply as I could, and then exhaled. I tried to stay as still as possible so as not to break his concentration. I knew that if he lost control, it would be the end of me.

"Aiden, talk to me. Don't think about it," I whispered.

"I can almost taste you," he whispered as he released his hands from my side and sat back a bit. He was staring at his hands, covered in my blood.

Slowly, I covered his hands with mine pulling myself up to my knees and catching his lost gaze. I was starting to feel a little better now. I looked down to find the flow of blood had slowed to a trickle, and then a moment later it had stopped altogether. The skin slowly began to close around it.

I leaned in close to Aiden, my hands still on his.

"Aiden, listen to me. Look at me," I whispered, as I got his full attention. "You won't hurt me. I trust you."

A few short moments later, he seemed to snap out of his stupor.

"You're healing much faster now. That's good," he said as if talking about the weather.

"I guess it's one of the perks of being a monster," I mocked as my eyes sank to the ground.

"The ability to heal rapidly is the only reason your kind survive the change. After the first feed your abilities begin to multiply," he explained.

I inspected the new wound to find it almost completely closed.

"Not this fast though, not this soon," he commented. "You are more advanced than your brother werewolves. Most new werewolves can't heal this effectively until after their second or third lunar pull and several feeds. And none of them can change during the day. Werewolves are and always have been slaves to the moon."

"But I'm different—because I'm a half blood." I tried to wrap my mind around it.

"When a human is infected with the lupine parvovirus it mutates part of the human genetic code. Gravitational changes from the lunar pull awakens the virus. But you . . . ."

He paused again, thoughtful.

"The earth's forces seem to have no bearing on your abilities. I believe that your mutation is so complete that the virus is living in symbiosis with your human DNA, rather than as a parasite."

He leaned in close to me again, gently touching my abdomen where I should have had a gaping, bleeding hole.

"So why haven't my other wounds healed yet?" I asked as I touch my collarbone, still tender and raw and caked in blood.

"I think the virus only recognizes the wounds following your first feed, the preexisting being more immune to it at this stage. The lycanthrope virus is made up of a protein shell that attaches itself to the human cells, using it as its manufacturing site to slowly take over and alter human DNA. This process can take weeks until your DNA is fully integrated, at which time it will recognize all your cells and proceed to heal them as its own. It's the adolescence of the werewolf state. And in your case, the process doesn't seem to turn on and off like the others, it just stays on waiting for your command," he explained.

"Baneswolf isn't a cure then?"

"There is no cure," he said with an agitation in his voice. "It should have been the death of you though. I've never seen anyone, human or not, survive ingestion of such high quantities of that stuff."

"I don't know what came over me," I paused, trying to remember what had happened that day. "I didn't want to be this monster, and I was hurting. I just wanted it to end," I said as I remembered my parents' faces in my minds' eye.

"You are not a monster," he said firmly. "You are what you were born to be. Never forget that."

"There's no turning back, is there?" I asked as my eyes grew distant and the feeling of hopelessness crept back into my consciousness.

"No," he said shortly.

"Was there any hope for you, of turning back?" I asked.

"No. Vampires can only be created when the human host is close to death. The venom overtakes the host just before death."

"How did you get through it—the change?" I asked as I looked into his two-toned eyes.

He thought for a minute, sadness in his eyes.

"Time . . . mostly," he mumbled. "That's all vampires really have, an abundance of time."

"How did it happen?" I wanted to know him. I wanted to know the real Aiden.

He looked off into the forest with distant eyes as if he was trying to remember something he had hidden away.

"It was 1752, and a particularly evil coven, with a very powerful leader was feeding on the people of our village," he said trailing off, lost in horrible memories. "My father locked my stepmother and myself in a cellar and fought to protect us. But they were smart and it wasn't long before they found us. They mortally wounded my father and infected him, condemning him to eternal life in their service instead of death. They left him to make the transition alone, with us as his first meal."

"My step-mother loved him dearly, I remember her mournful cries. We had been raised Catholic, like most in Ireland at the time. If he turned, our belief was that he would be condemned to hell. I couldn't bear to let my father be damned, so I sucked the venom out of his veins, I drank his blood till it was clean. He died in my arms, but at least he never turned."

"The venom began to kill me, it should have killed me. But somehow instead of dying it infected me from the inside out. It bonded with my DNA in a way that should not have been possible. After I turned, I had an insatiable thirst. I killed many people. Innocent people."

He paused as the unmistakable look of regret spread across his face.

"Not long after, Enya begged me to turn her, so that I would not be alone and so that she could continue to be my mother. Eventually, I consented and stabbed her and then infected her. For decades we tracked the coven that destroyed our lives. We learned that they are part of a huge organization of vampires who we dared not challenge. The Untouchables. And since then, we have been plotting our revenge and strategizing ways to take them down."

"So wait—how old are you?"

"I'm twenty five. I've been twenty five for two-hundred and sixty-three years."

It should have bothered me, what he said. He was a vampire and I was a half blood werewolf. My whole world had been turned upside down. But somehow with Aiden, my existence ceased to be broken. I was finally finding my rightful place in life.

"Why do you have wings? Are you different, like me?" I prodded with still more questions.

"When you are infected with the venom of a vampire, if you survive, you inherit some of the traits of the one that infected you. Yuki and I were both infected by very powerful vampires, alpha coven leaders. And we inherited some of their unique evolutionary changes. My satanic wings are from the one that infected my father, and by default, me," he said with a sad smile. "Enya has the ability to commune with the spirits world and to cause other supernatural creatures to see hallucinations and visions. Yuki is a shape shifter. And Draigon has the ability of hypnosis. Our level of thirst for blood, and the type of blood, is from our creators. My insatiable thirst is a mirror of my creators' thirst."

"But don't all vampires want human blood more than anything?" I asked, confused.

"All vampires thirst for human blood to some extent, but the intensity of the thirst varies considerably depending on many factors. There is a hierarchy in the vampire world, the alphas and the omegas. The omegas are usually those who were infected against their will at death or who were infected by weaker vampires, and their thirst is not particularly specialized. Their connection to their human selves is strong, and so is their respect for human life. They sustain themselves on animal blood, donor blood, or clone blood, and most are able to blend in to some extent with the human world."

"And then there are the alphas. Those who are infected by powerful vampires, or sacrifice their human lives in order to be turned. These vampires lose all connection with their human resemblance, and once they embrace their cannibalistic tendencies, they can only survive off the blood of humans. Over time, alphas evolve, becoming even more powerful and strong as they feed off humans. They relinquish all of their humanity, and their every desire is more sinister than humanly imaginable."

"And you? Where do you fit in?"

"I am neither, and I am both. The one that infected my father was very powerful, one of the strongest. He was an Untouchable. Because of my willingness to sacrifice my life for my father, I inadvertently welcomed whatever consequences might come. I didn't know then what I know now, but I also can't say I'd change what I did. Enya and I believe that because I ingested the venom instead of it entering my blood stream first, my human blood was better able to assimilate with the infection. I need at least some human blood to survive, my thirst rivals that of the alphas. But I also have a strong connection with humanity, for as long as I can control my thirst," he explained.

"How do you control it, your thirst?" I asked.

"I don't." He stared at me as his words sank in.

"You drink human blood," I said mostly to confirm what I already knew was true. "But, the mountain lion. Why?"

"I had no part in that mountain lion, that was Enya. She hates drinking human blood. For me, animal blood is like a light snack," he said with a sinister smile at the edge of his lips. He brought his hands, covered in my blood, up to his face and breathed in. "It helps me tolerate being around you, but you don't make it any easier for me."

"Oh, I'm sorry. I didn't know," I said as guilt weighed me down. "How often do vampires need to feed?"

"The highest level alphas, usually the Untouchables, need to feed every day. They don't, however, need to kill their victims. Willing human donors are able to feed their needs. They simply enjoy killing. On the other hand, our oldest omegas have sustained themselves for hundreds of years off animal blood just a few times a month," he said.

"And you?" I asked. A chill went down my spine. Although I had recognized the thought before, it was then that the reality of his life sank into my soul. I was in the presence of a killer, a murderer.

"I need blood every day. Enya is the same, although she can go much longer on animal blood than I can. Most of the time I use a donor bag, sometimes a willing donor, a wayward homeless person, and for the rest I fill in the blanks with animal blood. Yuki is able to get away with more animal blood then human and less often for both. She was turned by an alpha vampire, but against her will. And then there's Draigon," he paused as a proud look came over his face. "He is one of the oldest living true Omegas. He has never taken a human life, which is extremely rare. He has survived for over four hundred years almost entirely on animal sustenance."

My mind spun with all the impossible things he was telling me. And although I could not deny that it was all true, neither could I fully accept it.

"We are both cursed, in our own ways," I mumbled. Another thought occurred to me. "If being around me is so difficult for you, why do you do it? Why did you help me?"

"I have been wandering around for the last century trying to find any reason to hope, to exist, to go on. You rekindled life in me," he whispered as he leaned in and brushed a hair out of my face. "I've never felt this way about anyone in all my hundreds of years."

I felt my face flush with hot blood as my eyes turned down to the ground in embarrassment. My head spun and I felt my lungs lose the little air I had left there.

"How can you see me that way? I am fragile and imperfect and broken compared to you," I said looking down at my broken body.

"You are everything you should be."

"In your time, have you ever met another one like me?"

"Werewolf, yes. Half blood, no. Not living, anyway. I heard rumors once of a hybrid that survived the pregnancy and birth, but the boy died in his childhood. He wasn't strong enough to endure the change. You have to be strong in spirit and body to survive."

"Strong? I don't feel strong."

"But you are. You have the ability to change, to morph into only that which you want or need to become at any given time. You never entirely lose your human identity, and you never become full wolf. Your metamorphosis is symbiotic with what your mind wants. You're strength makes all that possible."

There was a long uncomfortable silence as his words sank in. I was some sort of anomaly, it seemed. Maybe destiny did have a plan for me, although I could not imagine what use I would be to anyone.

"I never had the chance to say thank you—" I said, pausing for a minute "—for saving my life."

"You don't owe me anything," he mumbled with disdain. "You wouldn't be in this condition if it wasn't for my following you. I should have just let you be alone." His voice was heavy with shame.

"Then I would have died of poison from the Baneswolf if you hadn't helped me," I reminded him.

He stood up and helped me to my feet without a response. With his steadying hold on me, we began walking back to the door in the mountain.

When we arrived back in the little room, Aiden checked my bandages once more and then lay me down to rest and heal.

As the sun began to set, I suddenly awoke with all my senses tingling as if I had been electrocuted. Anxious, I jumped up and out my little door and then through the door in the mountain to a sky littered with stars that looked like thousands of fireflies.

But it wasn't the night that pulled at my attention. It was something else. Something distant, but important.

There were several familiar scents in the air and I couldn't explain how I knew exactly to whom they belonged. I just knew.

The scents were of Aiden, Wakiza, and three inexplicably disproportionate looking wolves. Hissing and growling sounds permeated my ears. I felt tension enter Aiden's body, and anticipation filling the air.

"Lakota!" I heard a familiar call from nearby.

Abruptly the singular hissing sound ceased, and the growls quieted down.

"Father."

It hurt me to see the shock in my father's eyes. I knew he would blame himself for what had happened to me. And I knew there was no hiding how horrible my battle wounds looked.

But my mind did not have time to dwell on my father's concerns. There were three figures behind him that captivated my attention. Three figures I should have recognized, but did not.

They stood upright like humans, but had the resemblance of wolves. I knew it was Kotan, Yuri, and Jesse.

My werewolf brothers.

I heard a hiss emanating from just behind me, and turned to see that it was Aiden. Simultaneously, I heard the growls of three angry beasts increasing in intensity. Stepping forward a few steps, I put myself in between the two rivaling sides. A grimace spread slowly across my face as shooting pains emanated from everywhere all at once.

"Stop! Don't do this," I demanded in the direction of my father.

"What has he done to you?" Wakiza demanded back angrily.

"*He* saved my life and stopped me from hurting any-one," I yelled with conviction. "He is not one of them, one of those who took our family."

Wakiza took a step back, a look of horror in his face.

"Please Lakota . . . don't be so naïve. You don't know what they are capable of," he begged.

"No! It's you who doesn't know what I am capable of, father. And you cannot judge the Kathel's for crimes that they did not commit. They are not like the ghosts that haunt us. If you want to blame someone for what happened to us, then blame Josiah. He is the vampire responsible for the massacre."

Wakiza was silent for a long moment.

"I will not lose you to *them*," Wakiza stated. "You have to come home with us Lakota!"

There was hatred in his voice that was difficult for me to understand, or comprehend. It was hatred that seemed distant, but very real nonetheless.

A smile crept across my face as a new feeling came over me. The sound of my laughter filled the air. Wakiza was not amused.

"Or what?" I challenged. "It is not your place to make my decisions anymore father."

Appalled by my sudden outburst, I was shocked with how outspoken I was.

"Lakota," his voice beckoned to me softly. "Be care-ful—the change," Aiden warned.

I knew he was referring to the metamorphosis. I looked up to see the silhouette of the moon over head against a backdrop of a billion stars. I could feel the pull of the lunar cycle on every cell in my body, coaxing me into the change. I knew already that I did not need the moon, but still, its pull was undeniable.

"Lakota, please," Wakiza begged. I could see then that he knew he had lost all control over me.

"No father," I stood firm. "I am not one of them," I said referring to the three creatures that stood behind him.

"I know," he admitted. "But you do not belong with the likes of him either," Wakiza said as he nodded towards Aiden.

I stepped back, next to Aiden. My feet dug firmly into the ground next to him.

Wakiza's face lit up with an anger I had never seen before. An anger that scared me. He nodded his head, as if signaling to the werewolves.

Their collective snarls filled the air with a thunderous roar and they jumped towards me.

I could feel Aiden's body tensed for action. Quickly, I looked to him.

"No," I demanded of him. "This is not your battle. They are my brothers, I will let no harm come to them. Stay here!" My command left no room for discussion. He stood there content to watch for the time being. Although I knew he would step in if the situation necessitated.

"Kotan, Yuri, Jesse," I commanded, recognizing the three warriors by their individual scents. "Step down!"

The three hesitated for a split second, sniffing the air. But with another nod from Wakiza, they continued to proceed.

I stepped forward, my body ripping with an incredible pain. A horrid scream escaped my trembling lips. And then it was done. I had made the transformation and the pull I had felt before from the moon wrapped me in its power. Wakiza's face was frozen in awe.

With a loud crash I met Kotan mid-air, sending him into the tree behind him. I pinned him to the ground there and growled my intent for him to stay there. He let out a whimper as Yuri ran into me head on, and Jesse's teeth barely missed my right arm. I turned with blinding speed and my head hit Yuri hard, sending him sprawling across the ground. Jesse stood there unsure as to what he should do.

"Jesse, stop. You may win at cards, but this is one game you won't win. Just go home brother," I commanded.

"Kotan, Yuri. Go home," I said as I turned back to the other two. They were getting up slowly from where I had thrown them. But this time I knew I had their attention.

Together, they backed up in submission, as if they had just remembered who their master was. It was as if I was suddenly the alpha. But that couldn't be possible. Females were never the alpha if there was a male option.

Kotan hesitated and looked back over his shoulder.

I turned back to Wakiza, irritation written all over my face. "The tribe will be in danger if I come home. I don't know what I'm capable of. You must do what is right for the people."

"She is safe with me," Aiden tried to reassure my father.

"And I'm just supposed to trust you? A vampire?" Wakiza snarled.

"You don't need to trust him . . . you need to trust me. Please go home before someone gets hurt," I interjected.

I could see the turmoil in my father's face. It was as if I had broken his heart.

Wakiza stepped closer to Aiden, hesitantly.

"Take care of her," Wakiza told Aiden shooting him a deathly glare.

"You have my word," Aiden promised, holding his gaze.

Wakiza nodded and relinquished any further argument, turning to leave. Moments later, Aiden and I were alone.

I turned back to face him, the speed of my movement made me dizzy. He had a decidedly worried look on his already pale face and I felt suddenly very weak.

"That's enough excitement for you. You need to rest," he steadied my shifting balance before I lost my footing. And as usual, I welcomed his touch.

A split second later, my vision grew dim and dark.

The weight of the collisions in my world sank to the bottom of my heart.

The last thing I remember were his cold arms cradling my fragile body.

Our two worlds had collided and the course that destiny chose for me as a half blood was as unclear as it was unnerving. But in his arms I felt safe and loved. With him by my side, there were no collisions. Only a dawning clarity. For the first time in my life, I felt like I was where I belonged. And I belonged with him, in his world.

10 Beauty and Beast

A sweet, calming melody gently pulled my consciousness back to reality. I could hear a dozen stringed instruments, most notably was that of a harp. I wasn't sure where it was coming from, but I didn't care. It calmed my mind and soothed my spirit so much that I did not want to open my eyes.

I could feel the warm rays of the sun on my skin, the way they warmed my blood and burned where my wounds were exposed. Reluctantly, I forced my eyes open, lying there for several moments taking in the sounds that enveloped me. Gingerly, I sat up and realized that I was on a massive bed in the center of an equally massive room. One wall was, quite literally, a wall of books: Floor to ceiling bookshelves set into the wall and filled with hundreds of books. There was a small, ornate nightstand next to the bed with an equally ornate antique lamp. At the base of the bed, there was a chest, the kind that had been popular a century earlier. I think they called them "Hope Chests."

"Greensleeves . . ." I whispered under my breath as I recognized the melody. It was an old Irish tune I remembered from my last year of music in high school and the most beautiful orchestra was playing it.

"You know your music," came a sultry voice from one corner of the room.

"Aiden," I croaked. I realized that I missed his touch, his scent, his presence.

"Good morning, love," came his melodic voice from beside me.

My beautiful. My dark angel. My Aiden.

I turned to find him shrouded by the shadows of the corner, hidden from the rays of the sun that were streaming onto the bed.

"Why do you have such large windows when you can't bear the sun?" I asked, suddenly curious.

He reached up to a switch on the wall and adjusted it. The rays from the sun disappeared from the room as the windows seemed to magically grow a tint. You could still see out of the windows into the green of the forest, but the sun no longer made its presence so blatantly known.

"I like to see the world," he said as he stood up and walked to two large doors that reached from the floor to the ceiling. He swung them open and the smells of the forest came rushing in like a flood. He beckoned for me to come to him.

I tried to stand up. I began to collapse as my legs could not bear my weight, but Aiden was beside me in the blink of an eye. He caught me before I fell. Delicately, as if I was made of glass, he guided me back to the edge of the bed.

I realized that I wasn't fully healed yet; my wounds still stung and throbbed. I flinched as I touched my shoulder where the massive gouge had been a few days before. It was healing faster than humanly possible, but not fast enough for me.

"I want to show you something," Aiden said as he helped me to my feet. Slowly, we made our way through the double doors that led out onto a massive porch. There was a thick mesh to shield the porch from the harmful sun.

The view was spectacular, timeless, and awe-inspiring. His porch looked down upon a little creek, its rippling waters seemed to resonate perfectly with the classical music coming from the room. Douglas firs and other conifer trees stretched high into the heavens, and the fog dancing around the dense foliage made the scene surreal and unearthly.

"It's beautiful," I said, inhaling the sweet forest air that I missed so much. It was my home, the only thing in the world that I always felt comfortable and confident with.

"Many of these trees are older than I am," he said with sadness. "These forests protect us from one of the few things that can destroy us."

"The sun," I said.

"For a long time, I always thought of myself as a tree; an inanimate living thing existing in life simply as a spectator to all the world's mysteries and horrors . . ." he trailed off in a sorrowful tone.

"You're not the only one that feels that way," I said thoughtfully.

He looked at me, raising his brow.

"I anticipated my change. I felt as if I was frozen in a timeless existence. Never moving forward, but neither regressing backwards either. And now I am cursed, unable to escape the existence that destiny has given me—but neither wanting to accept it either," I confided.

We stood in a long silence as both of us accepted our fateful feelings.

"But . . ." I said as I realized something, "I guess there is another way of looking at it, another point of view."

"What would that be?" he asked.

"Well . . . through the centuries, against winds, rains, and snow, they are still here. They still stand united, strong, and alive. Their change is so slow to human eyes that it would seem they are frozen in time. But they still grow, and adapt, and change at a pace that is their own," I thought out loud. "Are we not both like these trees?"

Aiden was thoughtful, and the way he furrowed his eyebrows together when he was pondering something made me smile.

"So . . . would we not be stronger together, in a circle of those like us? Shouldn't all supernatural creatures band together in unity?"

"That is what I love about you . . ." he said with a smile.

I looked at him, curious.

"You remind me of what it is to hope," he said as our eyes met.

For moments eternal we stood, eyes locked, simply mesmerized in each other's company.

We inadvertently leaned closer, and closer, as the moment became utterly undeniable. For the first time, I anticipated his kiss.

But before our lips could meet, I felt my breath leave me, and the world spun around me as I lost balance again.

He caught me again, and we gazed at each other for a few more silent moments.

"I'm so sorry," I said, embarrassed. "I just feel so weak."

"I know," he said. "You need to hunt soon."

My silence was my agreement to his suggestion.

"But first, there is someone here to see you. Your brother followed the warriors yesterday. He refused to leave until he spoke to you. He is down in the basement waiting for you."

My heart jumped for joy at the thought of seeing my brother, of sharing with him everything that had happened to me.

Aiden wrapped my left arm around his neck to stabilize my stance. Every bone in my body ached, and again, the previous wounds hurt as bad as before. I was thirsty and hungry again. I knew I would soon need nourishment.

He led me down a beautiful oak spiral staircase, down into what looked to be some sort of a living room. The furniture was very ornate, and everything in the room was pristine in its proper place. It was as if the room had never been touched.

We went through a glass sliding door that was tinted the same way his room windows had been. I stepped outside into the bright sunlight, and my eyes took several minutes to adjust. Instead of moving quickly to the shadows, Aiden stood there under the sun, and beneath the rays. He looked like a god from the heavens. His skin was a pale opaque color. And a vapor seemed to rise from his exposed skin. I realized that the smell in the air was that of his skin burning, but it was mysteriously sweet and aromatic. All he was missing was a pair of white wings to complete the image of an angel.

"What are you doing? The sun!" I exclaimed.

He pushed his arm towards me. His skin, where it had been exposed the longest had started to peel like a snake's skin. When I touched it, it fell to the ground revealing bone and black veins filled with coagulating blood and venom, like something from a horror movie.

"In case you had any doubts," he said. "This—thing that I am, is real."

I swallowed hard as the gruesome sight of his disintegrating arm burned into my mind along with my dark realization about the gravity of the situation.

Aiden pulled me into the shadows again and led me down a slope around a side yard and down to the back of a hill. And there, set into the mountainside, was the familiar small door.

He pushed the door open and motioned for me to enter.

"I'll leave you two to talk," Aiden whispered, and then he was gone.

I rounded the corner to the room where I had been broken and waiting for change just a short while before.

There, sitting on the edge of the bed, looking as anxious as ever, was my big brother, Notak. I let out a sigh of relief as I ran to him and we embraced like long lost best friends. I grimaced as his strong arms squeezed me tight, and my ribcage screamed its vehement disapproval.

"My god, Kota! You look horrible." The smile he had greeted me with quickly disintegrated into a frown. "Did *he* do this to you? I'll kill that son of a bitch."

"Calm down, brother. I'm fine. It's not his fault," I reassured him.

"Jesse said he is a—vampire. And you're a were-wolf?" he carefully inspected my broken body. "Father told me the most unbelievable story about your parents. Is it true?"

"Um, sort of," I admitted. "I'm a half blood, because Hot'ne was not infected, but my father was."

"I go out hunting for a few days and come home to a wolf sister," he said nodding his head. "I wish I didn't believe you, but it explains all your problems over the last couple of years, doesn't it?"

"It explains everything, even the agony. I can't see any purpose in existing like this. Everything is upside down now; my world is a mess . . . I mean, werewolves and vampires? This is the stuff of myth and storytelling. I'm a monster, brother," I mumbled.

"You're not a monster. You're the living legacy your father left behind. You are fulfilling your destiny."

"Legacy? Destiny?" I mocked as I stepped away from him.

"It feels more like a curse, Notak. I am a beast," I said, angrily.

"That's what your father thought too, and yet we are both alive today because of him," he reminded me.

"I don't want to become what my father was," I said with determination.

"You won't. You will become something far greater," he said. "Lakota, you have to admit that maybe the spirits chose you, chose your father, chose your mother . . . for a purpose, even if you can't see that purpose now," he said ever so calmly. "Listen, Lakota. I am not claiming to understand what you are going through, because I don't. But you have been waiting for change for a long time, of that I am sure. Embrace it. Do not deny your destiny. Be who you were born to be."

There was silence as I contemplated his wise words.

"I wanted you to know that even if you have lost yours, I still have faith in you," he said with sincerity. "You will always be my best friend, my sister, no matter what you are or what form you take."

"I know, brother," I said, as a tear threatened angrily at the edge of my eye.

He grabbed my hand and pulled me closer to him. I tried to pull away, but he just gripped me harder.

"We are Kalapuya. You are my sister, and I have lived with you, loved you—" he paused as he pulled my chin up, forcing my eyes to meet his. "I would die for you."

"You're more than I deserve," I hugged him tight, resting my head against his bronzed-toned chest.

"I know you can't come home right now, and I understand why. You know where to find me if you need me. I wanted you to know that I am still here for you. I always will be," he reminded me as we shared the equal sadness of a mutual goodbye. "Take care of yourself sister."

He left the room, my steps shortly behind him. Aiden was standing just outside the exit from the basement, in the safe shade of a large tree.

"If you let anything happen to her, I will find a way to kill you," Notak warned Aiden as he stepped out into the sunlight.

"You're a good brother, and a good man. I will do everything in my power to keep Lakota safe. You have my word," Aiden promised.

Then Notak disappeared into the forest.

I realized a morbid insight as I watched Notak walk away and I crumbled to the ground, pulling my knees into my chest. A knot in my throat threatened to break into sobs and tears.

"I'll outlive them all, won't I? I'll watch them grow old and die, while I continue to live." My heart was heavy.

"Yes, with immortal life or near immortal, there are consequences," Aiden confirmed as he made his way slowly to my side. His cool, strong arms pulled me towards his even cooler body. I gasped when I saw his mutilated arm, still raw from the damage of the sun. And yet, his embrace felt perfect to me.

Somehow I felt less burdened when he was there. With his presence, the pieces of my broken world stopped falling around me. Instead, they just hung there, suspended in time.

I wasn't so scared, so terrified, so alone, when he was beside me. He held me for as long as I needed, and longer.

We hunted together, united in our search for blood and flesh. And after our thirst and hunger had been quenched, we gave the rest of the day to each other. Time seemed to have no place in his life. It appeared to slow or stop altogether. And it was in those moments that I wondered if we could just exist like that forever.

Forever lost in each other.

"There is something I have been meaning to ask you, but the right time had not presented itself," he said. We were walking in the gardens adjacent to Draigon and Enya's mansion. The house was a blend of Victorian architecture with a twist of the modern woven into the design here and there. It was built of logs and steel and the woodwork of the porches was exquisite. The whole house seamlessly blended with—almost disappeared—into the mountain behind. The gardens surrounding the house were serene despite the nippy air from the cold evening breeze.

"Remember the note I left for you . . . I asked for the pleasure of your presence again?" he asked.

"Yes?"

"If you had known then what you know now . . ." he trailed off as if he was ashamed. "Would it have changed anything?"

I bit my lower lip, perturbed at the heaviness in his voice.

"The truth?" I looked to him. "The truth is that I've been infatuated with you since the first day I met you in Marcus's bookstore. I was drawn to you immediately and I didn't care who you were or what you were then. And that hasn't changed," I told him.

He took my hand into his, as if I were a princess.

"Then my heart is yours," he said as he kissed my hand.

His devotion shocked me. I did not feel worthy of his desire.

"I don't understand why I am so special to you," I said, my voice cracking. "I mean, look at me."

"You are perfect and beautiful, and I desire you in more ways than you can even imagine." His words were a little bit creepy, but I had grown accustomed to his accent, his voice, and the old ways of his verbiage.

"When did you know . . . that I was different?"

"After a couple decades, humans start looking rather petty to us. It is easy to look at them as just cattle. You see them be born, live, have children, and then die. It's a cycle that repeats itself, and they all seem to blend into one another until you don't really notice their uniqueness or differences any more than you would the spots on one cow or another. So you must understand the gravity of the situation when I say that . . . the first time I saw you, I was mesmerized."

My breath left me and I willed myself to take a step back, but my feet wouldn't move. My legs felt so heavy. I felt so utterly naked and vulnerable.

He took another step forward and inhaled deeply as if he was smelling me. "There was always something unique about you—your strength, your loyalty, your beauty. It could not have been a coincidence that we met," he said as he took a step closer to me, backing me against a tree trunk. Now he was but a few inches away. I could feel his cold breath on my face as he leaned in even closer.

"You are the most beautiful creature I have ever seen." He said each word slowly and with intense care. "You are intoxicating and infectious to me." His hands caressed my cheek. The cold of his skin was soothing on my bruise. "Your skin glows like some goddess of the earth, so full of color and life." He traced his fingers gently down my jawline, and over my collarbone.

"And your scent is . . ." he put his head to my neck, inhaling the scent of my skin and then gently kissing my neckline. He clenched his jaw and froze for a split second as if trying to restrain himself from saying something—or doing something. I wasn't sure which it was. For an instant he did not look like himself.

"I find you both arousing and mouthwatering at the same time." He released me from his heavenly captivation suddenly, staring into my eyes with an intimate intensity that scared me.

"You're eyes . . . so angelic. As if they hold the entire universe in them." He seemed to look into my soul.

"You have made me believe that our meeting was destined and so our fate shall be equally tangled in destiny's arms." His voice was poetic.

I felt an overwhelming sense of sadness as I realized that our future together would truly be left to fate.

What future could a half blood werewolf and a vampire possible have?

He took both of my hands into his and there was that strained look in his face again. And then I understood why. My skin was warm, my veins ran thick with blood. Blood that was much warmer, much hotter than normal.

"How do you bear it? Being so close to me?" I pulled my hands away from him, not so much out of fear, but out of an incredible need to make things easier on him.

But he grabbed my hands and slowly brought them up to his stone-smooth chest. He pulled me closer, wrapping one arm around to the small of my back. I could feel his coldness through the thin white shirt he wore. Yet despite his lack of body heat, his silky smooth embrace made me feel warm inside.

"Not easily. It's nice to feel a warmth that I cannot produce, but tempting to smell the blood that courses through your veins," he said with a steady, controlled voice.

To think that my blood was so desirable made me feel a little sick, but I imagined the blood of a hybrid would be quite the commodity for him. Especially if I truly was the only one in existence.

"With you I feel complete, whole in a way I have never felt before, Lakota." The words made my heart ache. They made my heart bleed.

His eyes smoldered with suffering.

Entwined in a timeless embrace that I wanted to last an eternity, I could not think of wanting to be any other place but there, with him. I wasn't sure anymore who was beauty and who was the beast, but none of that mattered.

The winds of change had come, the monotony did not exist here. The sense of longing for something more was gone.

I was content here with him. The emptiness that I had been trying to fill for so long was gone.

He made me feel complete.

His chin tilted slightly and he eased in closer and closer to my face, still cautiously restraining himself from his blood lust.

I could feel my face flushing with the liquid, the blood getting warm and then hot. It was a human response exacerbated by canine traits, and I was sure that it wasn't helping his attempted restraint. Attempted restraint in not consuming me.

Cold, but gentle lips gently brushed mine. I was terrified that I might move the wrong way—that I might make him snap. So I stood very still and I let my lips linger until I felt his anxiety melt a little.

His right hand gently brushed my left cheek, and I cringed at the sharp pain that it sent through my face. The bruises became more sensitive as my blood became increasingly warmer.

Gently, he pressed the palm of his cool hand against my black and blue face. His cold touch was like ice, both soothing and relaxing against the pain.

I was instantly grateful for his touch, for the way he cared for me, for the way he made me feel. I pushed my lips hard against his, as a ferocious appetite for his taste took over me. Our tongues met, and he tasted like honeysuckle and cloves.

I melted into his touch, embracing his cold passionate kiss. I found myself clawing at his back, desperately trying to get closer to him, although our bodies were already meshed together in one tangled mess. It wasn't enough. I wanted all of him. Now and forever.

It felt natural. It felt right.

It felt as if time stood still as we shared in that passionate kiss, that intimate embrace.

I could feel my skin getting warmer and warmer. Too warm . . . .

I winced every now and then, as certain movements made my ribs hurt, or my shoulder throb. His hands moved from one bruised area to the next, and I knew he was attempting to soothe my agony.

But the longer we lingered close to each other, the hotter I got, and the more everything hurt. My blood felt like it was boiling.

Abruptly he pulled himself from me, and then I saw two sharp white knives thrust towards me.

Fangs.

His fangs.

I threw myself out of his path faster than humanly possible and a horrible growl escaped from somewhere inside of me. I realized I was on all fours and the pains of an impending transformation were biting at the edge of my every nerve.

He stopped short and his face drained pale as a ghost.

"I'm so sorry love. I want you in so many ways. I cannot lose control." There was a horrible look of pain in his now crimson-red eyes.

"I must go—"

And then he was gone.

I stood up onto my rightful two legs, the transformation pains melting away with each heartbeat. The pain of my battered body did not subside, but instead, flared full force.

I sank to the ground with a thud and I felt a heavy breath escape my trembling lips. I shuddered from the wave of pain that crashed down on me then.

There were two types of pain now. One was physical and bearable. The other was emotional and psychological.

I was alone again. He was gone.

And in his absence I realized how much my desire for him tore at my gut. When I was with him, it was like a dream. But when we were apart, it was a black void.

Sitting there on the cool forest floor, I pulled my knees into my chest and wrapped my arms around my legs. I wondered how we could possibly exist together when we were such opposites. Being with him felt so right, so natural, but I knew it was horribly abnormal.

His world and my world had never existed in unity before, so how could we expect to live, to exist in one or the other. Was there even an in-between?

I sat there for hours, until fatigue overtook me and I lay down on the forest floor. As dozens of unanswered questions and concerns roamed my thoughts, unconsciousness eventually came to me.

But even in my dreams I stood there across from him, wanting to run to him so that I might feel whole again. But then I realized that there was a dark abyss separating us. And so we stood there staring longingly at each other, with a fall to certain death dividing us. My heart ached with desire to feel his touch, his skin, his kiss again.

How peculiar, that we both thought of ourselves as beasts, yet we saw each other as beautiful. We were each *beauty* and *beast*, mirrored images of what we hated and what we loved.

11   FORBIDDEN

WHEN CONSCIOUSNESS RETURNED TO ME, I EXPECTED to be cold and damp from the moisture of the forest floor. But I was strangely warm, and comfortable. I thought for a moment that I was dreaming about being back in *his* bed, in *his* room, with *him*.

And then I realized that there was a familiar light from tinted windows that came through in a hazy glow. I blinked several times as my eyes adjusted to the light.

I realized that it wasn't a dream.

I winced in pain as I tried to turn over, but something held me tight and secure. I gasped when I craned my neck to look down at what was securing me, realizing that *his* arms held my achy, broken body. My heart thudded wildly at the thought of his embrace.

I was in *his* room, in *his* bed, and in *his* embrace.

Contorting myself, I managed to turn myself over to see him. I was surprised to find him awake.

"You were so still, I thought you were sleeping," I said.

"I'm sorry. I didn't mean to startle you," he said with that melodic Irish accent and a sly smile.

"I'm just glad you're here," I said pausing. "Did you sleep with me all night? I hope one of my episodes didn't keep you up."

"You slept like a baby, not even a sound. Vampires don't really sleep much. When we do it is a very deep sleep, but usually for very short periods of time. We only need sleep to clear our minds or to heal our wounds," he said as he showed me his perfectly healed arm. I remembered how horrible it had looked the day before after his demonstration in the sun.

I thought momentarily how odd it was that I had slept so soundly, so quietly, and so peacefully. But a thousand questions picked at my brain.

"So no coffins or graveyards?" I was curious.

"Some of the old-fashioned vampires still prefer a coffin. Our most effective slumber is in complete darkness, and for centuries it was a great place to hide from vampire hunters. For centuries, most mortals dared not touch the dead, or anything having to do with the dead."

"Sometimes we take to hibernating . . . to pass time. Coffins became a favorite hiding and resting place, out of necessity."

"Vampire hunters?" I asked, intrigued.

"They have been around in one form or another since the beginning of our existence. Witches, sorcerers, werewolves, even humans."

"What match could a human possibly be to your kind?"

"They have used everything from black magic to chemical warfare to defeat the covens," he said with a sadness in his voice. "There have been times in the not so distant past when humans coerced werewolves to do their bidding, to make war against us, in exchange for a *cure*."

"What?" I was shocked. Why hadn't he said anything about a cure before?

"Except that there never was a cure. There never has been. And instead, the werewolves would be executed when their deeds were complete."

"That's horrible . . ." I trailed off, appalled. "Do vampires use werewolves as slaves?"

Aiden looked at me inquisitively.

"Not often. Most covens, especially the Untouchables, view themselves as superior beings of the earth. And they hold no regard for any life, be it human, animal, or beast. They see no need for such inferior beings, except for food and pleasure."

"But you, you're different?"

"We believe in balance between all things living, dead, and undead. When the balance is disturbed, nature has a way of correcting itself. The balance is always returned. We honor that balance in life."

His eyes were sad and brooding, and his face looked as if it held the weight of a thousand worlds.

"Greed drives all of us, no matter our state of existence," he continued. "And ultimately it is the fruition of that greed that brings about our destruction, and returns balance to the universe."

I knew he was referring to things that had happened, to events that had passed, but I had no way of knowing *exactly* what he was referring to.

"We think of ourselves as peace keepers. We seek to preserve the human existence and therefore retain our connection with our humanity. To coexist . . ." he trailed off. He was sad again.

"But—" I began to understand. "Coexisting in a world that cannot accept you is a calamity in itself. You must feed on the very beings you seek to protect."

"A sad reality of our world, but a part of life none-the-less. There are a few like us," he continued. "We feed on the scourge of your society. The murderers, the rapists, the drug lords and death dealers, but in feeding on such tainted blood, we too become more like those whose blood we consume."

"You are trapped—" I said with a sad realization "—in an existence that you have not chosen, that dooms you to a certain fate, and that brings the potential end to the humanity in you. But still you fight." My heart ached for him, for the suffering he must have endured in the name of what is right and noble for humanity.

"What choice do we have? If we value what we once were, we cannot give in. If we do, the human in us will cease to exist and we will become lifeless, heartless creatures," he said. "We have to fight for every ounce, every shred of humanity that we have left in us. Until there is none left," he said thoughtful.

I could not console him, for there was no comfort to give. There was no happy ending to his story. Being neither dead nor alive was a curse for which there was no resolve.

"You are more than human. You have the heart of a lamb and the strength of a bear. You are more human than many can ever hope to become," I said as I gently touched my fingers to his face.

I looked at him and an extraordinary feeling came over me. It was as if my eyes had suddenly been opened, or a light had turned on.

"You will be a very powerful vampire one day. Covens will bow at your presence in terrified fear. You will own the vampire world. That is your destiny." I said the words as if they were not my own. It was as if I had been possessed.

Aiden was silent, contemplative.

"Impossible. That can never be. They will only ever bow to an Untouchable. I may have been infected by an alpha, but I should never have survived. If the alpha covens found out about my method of conversion, they would kill me," he said.

His argument did not sway my resolve. I could never know how I could possibly be so certain about such a thing. But I had never been so convinced about anything else in all my life.

"You will see. It will happen," I said, just as convinced as I had been before.

"There is something we need to do today," he said changing the subject. "But I must warn you, just the idea of it is truly terrifying," he said with sarcasm.

"More terrifying than turning into a hybrid? Or dating a blood-sucking vampire?" I mocked playfully.

"My family has been asking about you, and now that I have brought you into our home—" he smiled, amused. "It would only be proper to make formal introductions."

"But I'm not healed yet," I said as I made my way to a full-length mirror on the back of his door. My wounds were almost healed by all outside appearances, but the pain I felt when I moved reminded me that all was not quite right. And I worried about a single drop of blood that might have escaped. I worried that his family might not share the same restraint that *he* so carefully practiced when he was around me.

"The pain you feel is internal. You are healing from the outside in. It's an odd reaction to werewolf infection. We think that it is because skin cells are the easiest and fastest to regenerate," he explained. "And don't worry, my family can handle it. They don't want to wait any longer. My ma won't stop bugging me till I bring you down," he said with a little chuckle.

"Well it definitely sounds terrifying and insane," I thought about what might happen if things went badly for a half-blood werewolf in a house of vampires. "So—let's go. Crazy-insane is my middle name."

Aiden's room exited into a large hallway with several doors on either side. The walls were painted a navy blue, creating a dark corridor through the house even in the day.

We went down a flight of dark wood stairs that came out into a huge room with the same dark wood floors. The walls here were a rich burgundy, like the earthy color of the rocks I pulled from the creek. It made the room feel very warm and homely, despite its vast size.

Three figures entered the room from a large arched doorway on the other end. They were all pale and very angelic looking. And there was their scent, which I couldn't help but deeply inhale. Each one was slightly different, but I recognized Yuki's instantly.

"This is Lakota," he introduced me to his family. "Lakota, this is Draigon and Enya Kathel. And, you know my sister, Yuki Rin," he said pushing me gently towards them.

The one called Draigon stepped forward holding out his hand to me. I shook it after hesitating for a moment. I hadn't expected them to be so friendly. His hand was cold like Aiden's, but his smile was warm. He was a handsome man with long brown hair, perhaps about thirty-five in human years.

"Very nice to finally meet you," he said in a familiar liquid voice. He had a different accent than Aiden's though and it sounded English perhaps. "You have been quite the preoccupation for Aiden in the last couple of months," he said with a casual chuckle in his voice. I saw Aiden shift uncomfortably in the corner of my eye.

"Draigon is over four hundred years old, his family was lost in war in the late 1500s," Aiden said as a matter of fact.

I gasped a little, the reality of the presences I was witness to beginning to sink in.

The one called Enya stepped forward with a regal demeanor. There was a familiar scent that I recognized.

"I know you . . ." I said hesitantly. "You were in the forest that day, and in my dreams. You were warning me of something." I was shocked with my own vocalized realizations.

She eyed me cautiously and everyone in the room stood still as stone, waiting for her response.

"We have much to talk about, young one," she said coldly in her Irish-accented voice. I realized that she had neither confirmed nor denied my accusations.

"It is done, her fate is sealed," I heard her whisper to her husband, Draigon. There was a fear that came into her eyes that I did not understand.

"Please, excuse us," Draigon said as he guided the woman out of the room.

"Don't mind her, she's a little crazy," Yuki said. "She can see things . . . supernatural things."

"It's alright," was all I could manage. My thoughts had wandered to what she had said. *Her fate is sealed.* What did that mean?

"And for the record, my brother is stupid for dating a werewolf, or a half blood, or whatever you are," she said as she got off the couch and stomped up to me. "I guess insanity runs in his family." She spoke with obvious distaste, only a few inches from my face.

"Invite her to dinner for us, won't you brother?" Yuki said to Aiden with a smart smirk. "She smells delicious."

Aiden threw Yuki an angry look.

"Yuki is almost three hundred years old and the sole survivor of her clan. Her family were, for many decades, the most powerful ninja assassins in Japan. She's always hostile to newcomers," Aiden gave Yuki a stern warning look.

Yuki turned up her nose and stormed out of the room, but not before giving me an evil glare.

The room was empty again, with only Aiden, myself, and a sultry silence.

"Well," he said with a sigh, "That went just great." I detected the sarcasm in his voice.

"It was as terrifying as you promised," I commented. "Terrifyingly sad."

Aiden led me out of the room.

"Come on love, I have something for you," he said, beckoning for me to follow him. We went down another hallway to a door at the end of the house and out into the forest. He led me through the brush and I realized that their huge house was quite literally built into the mountain.

We were headed for the back of the house, and there, hidden by foliage and trees so thick you could barely see it, was two large wooden double doors set into the mountain. He unlocked the doors, and motioned for me to enter first.

I walked through the big doorway into a small foyer of what looked like another house. It was dim in this room though, unlike the bright cheeriness of the main house. And I didn't see a single window.

We went down a staircase carpeted in velvet red. At the end there were two more huge doors, flanked by two small doors on either side.

He walked over to the small door on the right and swung it open, motioning for me to follow.

I looked at him in surprise. There were a few candles illuminating the small room with a large free-standing mirror at the back of it. Hanging from it was a gorgeous blue and white gown that looked like it belonged to a world long forgotten.

"Oh my god, it's beautiful," I said as my jaw dropped. I didn't own a dress—there was no need for one on the reservation. They were rather impractical, and a luxury none of us could afford.

I slowly entered the small room, delicately tracing my fingers over the simple lace and beading that embellished the gown. It looked absolutely exquisite, like something that a princess might wear.

I looked to Aiden for an explanation.

"It was my mother's dress, on her wedding day," he said with a distant sadness in his voice. "I want you to have it."

"I couldn't possibly take such a gift," I said as a sudden wave of guilt took me.

"I won't be taking no for an answer," he insisted. "Amuse me, put it on," he said.

I sighed in defeat and nodded.

Aiden motioned towards a room off to the side with red velvet drapes covering it. Reluctantly, I agreed and took the dress to change.

I had no problem taking off my jeans, but after several attempts, I realized that I wasn't making any headway with my shirt. My ribs ached and the healing hole in my abdomen screamed at me to cease moving.

Irritated, I let out a sigh. I didn't want to disappoint Aiden though.

"Um, I can't," I stuttered, uncomfortable. But before I could finish asking Aiden to help me, he was in front of me. I bit my lower lip and took a timid step back into the wall.

"I—" I stuttered as my heart raced with his presence. I was sure he could see the goose bumps covering my half-undressed body.

"Please, don't be embarrassed," he whispered as he gently helped me pull my shirt over my head. I gasped as the movement sent pain through my ribcage and abdomen. My knees buckled underneath me, but his strong arms steadied me.

I stood there for a few moments, my eyes closed as I forcibly made myself catch my breath. I felt his cold palm against my body. Relief filled my body, as his cold touch eased the pain and made it a little easier to breath.

"How do you do that?" I asked as I opened my eyes, catching his gaze.

"Do what?" he asked, innocently.

"Make me feel this way?" I breathed. "It's as if you already know what I need, and what I want."

He didn't answer, but only smiled.

I inhaled sharply, trying to quell my deep-seeded desires.

Aiden placed one hand on the wall behind me, leaning into my near naked body with a closeness I was unaccustomed to. His other hand slid from my now calmed wounds to the small of my back, and he pulled me even closer to him.

My heart beat faster, and I felt as if I was hyperventilating.

"I can hear your heart," he said in a sensual whisper.

I hoped he hadn't notice the blood rushing to my cheeks. Uncomfortably, I tried to push back against his grip. But his hold did not budge.

"I can feel your blood beneath your skin, I can hear your every breath. I love how human you are, how alive you are."

I felt my breath escape me for a moment.

"You know what you do to me?" I demanded, somewhat violated. "And still you continue?"

"I feel your exhilaration," he said. "Do you deny that you enjoy this?" he asked as he took one of my hands and placed it on his chest.

The air around me didn't satisfy my burning lungs, and I felt as if I would pass out. His chest was hard as stone, and refreshingly cool under his thin tank top. My desire for him was insatiable.

"It's not right, being able to know everything about my chemistry when I know nothing about yours," I said, with irritation.

"Is that what you think?" he asked. "Can you not see what you do to me?" he asked, as he released his hold on me and began helping me into the dress.

I thought for several silent moments as he loosely tied the corset for me. And when he finished, he placed a kiss on the side of my neck. I could hear him as he inhaled my scent deeply.

"I only see that you enjoy my primitive reactions to your intoxication," I said, turning to him.

"It is you that intoxicate me," he said. "How is it that I cannot detect adrenaline in your blood? It's as if you have never feared me, not even for a moment."

"I only fear that which is a threat to what I cherish most, and my life is not that."

"Your people, you fear only for them—" he said realizing what I had meant. "It's that selflessness, that complete disregard for your own safety and the rawness of your honesty that I am drawn to. It thrills me with an excitement that I haven't felt in a very long time." He pulled me close to him and leaned in, hovering just above my lips. My heart thrashed in my chest, my blood grew dangerously hot and my skin crawled with anticipation. I yearned for his touch.

"I've never encountered another human like you. You don't make any sense," he whispered, as he leaned in just centimeters from my lips.

I closed my eyes waiting desperately for his lips to meet with mine. But he suddenly released his hold on me.

He opened the curtain to reveal a full-size free standing mirror.

"You are everything that I want," he said as he stepped out of the frame in the mirror.

The blue and white glowed next to my bronze skin, making me look like a fairy from some long-forgotten land. I was shocked at the image in the mirror and I barely recognized myself.

Aiden took my hand and led me through massive double doors to an equally massive circular chamber. He let me wander forward in awe. The ceiling must have been at least three stories high, and it was a dome etched in gold. In the large chamber there was a grand piano in one corner, glistening black ebony. In another corner there was a cello, several violins neatly organized on special displays, and flutes, clarinets, and piccolos. To the right of the piano there was a golden harp.

"It's incredible," I said, taking it all in.

Aiden made his way to a dark corner of the room, and fiddled with something there. I meandered around the room, inspecting the shiny instruments.

Suddenly music began to fill the air, as I realized he had been setting up a CD in a player. He was next to me then, although I hadn't seen or heard him approach. He held his hand out to me.

The music was calm, beautiful music that began with chimes and flutes, and then transitioned into a chorus of angelic voices and the sweet plucking of a harp. It wasn't classical, but it wasn't entirely modern. It echoed the sounds of another world or time. It floated and flickered around the room with its angelic melody.

"Dance with me?" he invited in his equally melodious voice.

But before I could explain that I didn't know how to dance, he pulled me close and wrapped his hand around my waist.

I relented, resting my left hand on his right shoulder. We twirled and glided across the huge chamber, which I suddenly realized was obviously designed for music and dancing.

It was strangely easy, dancing with him. He led and I simply glided with his footsteps, our eyes eternally locked in each other's souls.

It was strange how easy everything was with him. How natural it was to be with him, and how content I felt.

"I've missed this dearly," he told me as he pulled me still closer to him.

"Missed what?"

"Companionship, conversation, feeling human," he lamented.

"Haven't you had other girlfriends in your two-hundred years?" I asked.

"A few . . . but not human. Vampire companions are more often than not very cold, calculated, and emotionless. There are few that remember how to love or be loved. Fewer hold on to love if they find it, rarely will you find a married couple. Draigon and Enya are one of those rare couples."

"And we humans are weak and fragile to your kind, so not exactly good long-term relationship material, I suppose," I said. We were still gliding across the floor, seamlessly.

"Vampire-human relationships are more or less forbidden. Our perpetual blood lust makes it very difficult to be with a human, and our inordinate strength makes us dangerous to be around. You have, unfortunately, had first-hand experience with that." He touched me gently around my ribcage where the bones were healing but still sensitive.

"And of course, there is the inevitable; humans grow old and die, but we continue locked in time forever . . ." he trailed off, lost in dark thoughts.

"Not the best mating choice," I agreed. "But won't I get old and die?"

"Human DNA combined with the mutated werewolf gene to regenerate tissue triples your life expectancy."

"So I'll live longer than the average human, and I'm a little more resilient to your strength, but you still want my blood."

"Yes, but I can't control the way I feel about you. I'm drawn to you in a way I didn't even know was possible."

I had no words to respond with, the music was almost as intoxicating as his scent. I was certain by now that it was Irish in influence. I let it waft through my every cell as he led me gliding across the floor.

My gown swayed this way and that, and I had to admit that I felt rather pretty in the dress. It somehow made me feel graceful and ladylike, unlike the clumsy oaf I always saw myself as. It was refreshing. I felt like a princess in some fairytale, dancing with my prince.

I didn't want it to end. Every moment with him became more and more intoxicating, addicting.

Our symbiotic steps began to steadily slow, until we both stopped and gazed longingly into each others' eyes. The music continued to fill the air with its magic.

"A gra mo chroi," he whispered in his native language as he leaned daringly close to me. "My heart is yours," he translated as he took my right hand and held my ring finger.

I looked down at my finger to find a ring that he held just above it. It was silver inlaid with black, with an ornate interwoven band coming together to form two hands holding a heart with a crown on top of it.

"An old Irish tradition of ours is to gift our beloved with an Irish Claddagh ring. The hands represent friendship, the heart love, and the crown loyalty. When you wear the crown closest to you on your right hand, it symbolizes friendship. If you reverse it on the right with the heart closest to you, it means love. If you wear it on your left with the crown near you, it symbolizes engagement. And with the heart closest . . . marriage."

I took the ring and turned it so that the heart was facing me, and the crown was facing out. I pushed it onto my finger.

A smile crept into the corner of Aiden's lips as he accepted my gesture of love. We had begun to lean in closer to each other, and then everything went black. I realized I had closed my eyes a moment later.

I felt cold lips against my hot lips. This time I didn't linger on the strangeness of his touch. His skin was very cool, as if he had just come in from a snowy, winters' night. I was getting strangely accustomed to the feel of his skin.

He pulled me closer to him and I found myself wrapping my right hand around his back up to his neck and head, desperately trying to get closer to him. His neck was just as cold as his lips.

What had started as a cautious kiss turned into a passionate and unbridled kiss. It was sensual, violent, and nurturing all at the same time.

I wanted him so badly.

He pulled away from me abruptly, resting his forehead against mine, the fingers of his one hand still intertwined in the strands of my hair and the other one tightly wrapped around my waist. I opened my eyes to find his eyes tightly shut.

"My apologies love, I don't want to hurt you," he said. When he opened his eyes, they were crimson red with lust for blood. Dark veins under his skin rippled as if they had a life of their own.

I knew he was fighting his natural desire to feed.

"You want my blood," I said shortly.

"I want your blood, your body, your soul," he said. "I can smell the way your werewolf blood is bonded to your human blood, and when you are close to me, it is all I can do to contain myself." He gritted his teeth.

"Will it always be this difficult?" I asked.

"I don't know," he confided.

"Could we ever be . . . you know," I hesitated, uncomfortable with the personal question. "Is it possible to be physically intimate?"

"I'm terrified of hurting you. The closer we are—the harder it is," he said, troubled.

I contemplated our predicament. It was disheartening. How could such a perfect love face so many obstacles?

"If I were a human, and only human, could you turn me? Then we could be together in every way . . . forever," I said entertaining the fantasy.

"You wouldn't be the same," he said. "It is your intricacies, your unique state of existence that makes you who you are."

"I will never be an immortal. I will die one day . . . I will always be just this," I said, slightly embarrassed. "And we may never be able to, you know, be anything but this."

"I know. But I'm lifeless without you." He shut his eyes again, controlling his lust.

"Then our fate will be its own," I said. "My world is complete when you are in it."

There was a long silence as we both contemplated our future together.

Something overtook me, that canine feeling again. My bones ached and I shut my eyes against the pain. It felt as if a metamorphosis was imminent. The instincts of my werewolf existence came in waves; the sight, the smell, the hot blood beneath my skin. They were all magnified now. It was only an internal change though, and I somehow maintained my human form. I had somehow blended with the creature. There was a crazy idea that came to me then.

An idea only defined as absolutely insane by any normal standards.

I couldn't possibly—

Oh, but I could.

No normal person in their right mind would do what I was about to do. But then again, I wasn't entirely human, now was I? And I certainly wasn't normal. For the first time, I completely embraced the creature, the beast that lived within me. I embraced the power, the strength, and the life of my half blood existence.

I brought my wrist to my mouth, willing my canine incisors to emerge. I bit hard and the blood started flowing with a trickle at first and then a light flow.

"No! What have you done?" Aiden stumbled backwards, appalled. I knew he could smell the blood. I knew he wanted my blood.

"I love you, Aiden Kathel, and I will bind myself to you in every possible way. I want you to have me." I was holding my wrist out to him, insistently.

"I could kill you," he stuttered as he stumbled backwards a few more steps.

"But you won't. I trust you," I said as I moved twice as quickly forward towards him. I thrust my bleeding arm into his face.

"I am yours, and you will have me," I said with a dedicated strength in my voice.

I was prepared for the consequences, but I knew he wouldn't kill me.

Well, I felt almost certain that he wouldn't kill me.

He looked lost and I saw his eyes glaze over into that mesmerizing shade of crimson red. He glared at me with what I could only imagine was the most intense lust he had ever felt.

His eyes shifted from mine to the blood that was escaping my veins in a flow like a river now, and he took a hesitant step forward.

And then with a speed and strength I knew but still couldn't comprehend, he grabbed me and took my wrist into his mouth like a ravenous animal. His eyes burned hot red as he tasted and drank the hot liquid.

I closed my eyes in ecstasy. There was a thrill I felt, the thrill of pleasuring him. I tilted my head back and laughed as I began to feel lightheaded from the loss of blood. It should have scared me, it should have terrified me, but I felt no fear.

Losing control—or rather giving it up—was somehow erotic and exciting.

He gazed at me with those predatorily glowing-red eyes. I matched his intense thirsty glare. He wanted to stop, I could see the struggle in his eyes. But it was as if he was hooked on some drug that he simply couldn't pull away from.

I tried to pull my arm away from the fangs that sunk deep into my veins, but he wouldn't let me go. I felt a fleeting moment of panic, realizing at the same time that the world around me was spinning. He was slowly starting to kill me.

Suddenly, I felt something different enter my blood. Slight pains rippled down my spine and I realized the werewolf in me was surfacing. I yanked my arm out of his greedy grip with a strength I knew wasn't entirely my own. Stumbling backwards, I put my wrist to my mouth and licked and sucked the wound clean like a dog.

The world was still spinning around me, and I blinked several times to try and clear away the hundreds of tiny stars that blurred my vision. I pulled my wrist away from my mouth, inspecting it. The blood had already coagulated and the skin around the wound had neatly reconnected itself and begun to heal.

That could really come in handy, I thought to myself.

I felt my legs crumple underneath me, and I heard my body hit the ground before I felt the floor against my body.

"Lakota, I'm so sorry!" I heard a familiar voice. "What have I done?"

Aiden knelt down beside me, concern etched in his face.

I looked down at my arm to inspect the damage. But there was now only a mostly-healed, silvery tissue where the gaping wound had been.

I smiled, content and amused at my abilities, and their obvious perks.

"I'm so sorry love," he said with a deep pain in his voice.

"I'm fine," I reminded him. "Look, it's healed."

"You shouldn't have done that," he said looking away.

I ignored his scolding.

"So how do I taste?" I asked with a wide grin on my face.

He looked at me and sighed. "Like the most enticing cocktail I have ever had the privilege of tasting. You must have a death wish. Now that I've tasted you, I will always want what you have," he said, as he stared at me in bewilderment.

"Then you shall have it."

There was another short silence, as Aiden nodded his head in disbelief.

I attempted to stand up, Aiden was quickly there to help me to my feet. I brushed the dress off, inspecting it to see if I had stained it with blood. But I didn't see a drop.

Aiden gently took one of my hands into his as his other hand traced gently from the top of my ear down my jaw line to my chin.

"Aiden, I love you," I said. "So maybe love is stupid, or blind . . . or both. But I don't care. I feel complete with you," I whispered. I gently placed the palms of my hands around his face, framing his angelic beauty with my earthen skin.

"I would die for you," I breathed as I deeply inhaled his scent. Our lips inched slowly closer and closer, as the anticipation of his touch tore me apart inside.

"I wouldn't let you," he said.

Gently, he planted his cold lips on mine. I could taste the residual blood on his lips and in his mouth. And in some sick, twisted way, it excited me. I wrapped one arm around the small of his icy back as my other hand meandered through his messy brown hair.

We groped at each other with ferocious intensity, my hands securing his body against mine, and his holding my body in a steely grip. I could feel my skin burning fiery hot, my desire smoldering like the lava from a volcanic eruption. He would pause momentarily here and there so that I could take a breath, a basic need that I seemed to forget to do on my own, but then our lips meshed together as one again.

It was a timeless moment. It felt like time had evaporated or even ceased to exist at all. It lingered. Yet I knew it would end and it wouldn't have been long enough. It was never long enough. To be both timeless and short-lived at the same time.

Such a contradiction . . . .

He pulled away just as slowly as it had all began, his jaw clenched in a hard line. He rested his forehead on mine, eyes still tightly shut.

We stood there lost in each other. I didn't feel like I had a care in the world. I had never felt connected in this way to another being in all my life. I was whole with him. And sane in otherwise insane circumstances.

Ironic, that one who survives by taking lives . . . had given me mine back.

Although our union felt so utterly perfect, the idea of us together was still so terribly wrong. Vampire and Half Blood werewolf—forbidden.

But we were unreservedly in love, and in our world there was no room for the forbidden.

12 DARKNESS

WE RETURNED TO AIDEN'S BEDROOM, and I fell asleep in his cool embrace. The crickets chirped softly outside, the creek serenading us with its gentle *swish-swoosh*, and the light breeze rustled the leaves every now and then.

I felt peace that night. When I was with him, there were no nightmares, no voices, no fears, no haunting. Aiden informed me the next day that Enya and Draigon had gone to Europe on business. And Yuki had gone away to visit an old vampire friend.

Aiden and I had the Kathel house to ourselves, and the forests were unreserved at our feet. The nights came and went, and we became tangled in each other's lives. We spent the days taking long walks in the Kathels' expansive gardens or the abundant forests, talking and enjoying one another's company. At night we ran and frolicked together under the moonlight. The whole world was our backyard, and our happiness together held no boundaries. In unison we hunted, we fed, we laughed, and we danced together.

It was like the most beautiful dream. The kind of dream you never want to wake up from. When I was in his world, it was difficult to see anything outside of it. Nothing seemed to matter and time blurred into a single, extended moment.

I didn't understand how he could bear to be around me, how he controlled the lust I saw in his eyes. He drank from blood bags most days, but my veins constantly called to him. I tried to ease his burden by letting him feed on my blood every now and then.

I trusted him.

Yet in the pit of my stomach there was an unnerving feeling that told me that my perfect dream would not last forever. I knew I would eventually have to go back to town and face real life again.

"I should probably go and see my father," I told Aiden one morning as he sucked on a bag of blood.

"He will want to know when you will be coming home. What will you tell him?" Aiden's question was one I had worried about the entire time since I'd left.

"I don't know. I would never forgive myself if I ever hurt anyone. But I can't just run away forever either," I told him. "And then there is us—I don't ever want this to end."

Aiden was quiet for a few moments, thoughtful.

"It doesn't have to," he said locking eyes with mine. "Stay with me."

My heart thudded wildly in my chest. The very idea of staying with him was exciting.

"Stay with you, in your house? But your family, won't they disapprove?" I was concerned about our differences.

"They'll grow to like you more over time. Vampires take a while to adapt to change."

"You're serious?"

"You don't belong in their world. And you don't trust yourself. And, to be honest, I don't want to live a day without you."

"Oh thank you, Aiden," I said as I fell into his embrace. It was impossible to hide my happiness.

"I'll be right back, I have to tell father," I said.

"Be careful, stay calm and control yourself," he advised me.

When I arrived at my old house, Notak was in the front, splitting wood.

"Kota!" he said as he threw his arms around me in a big bear hug. "You look good, you look great," he said, scrutinizing where my battle wounds had once been.

"Being a werewolf has its perks. So . . . how is father?" I asked, concerned that I hadn't seen him since our last disagreement.

"He went to the northern reservation, some kind of business," he said. "He'll be back in a few days."

"I see." I wondered if it had anything to do with me. Father only went to the Three Sisters Reservation if he needed something. And he had to need it pretty badly. I was instantly concerned about his business there.

"How have you been brother?"

"No complaints. Just the usual. It's hunting season so we're all busy. You know how it is."

"Yeah, I'm sorry I'm not here to help." I felt guilty that I wasn't acting as a member of the tribe.

"Actually, the animals you leave for us have been a big help. Not a whole lot of meat left, but it all adds up. You've been keeping the sisters busy using the carcasses. They have been able to double their normal production of the things we sell."

"That's amazing. I'm so happy their deaths are not for nothing." I was a little embarrassed that I had been leaving the leftovers of our meals to the tribe. But it was simply a sad part of my current existence.

"So how are handling the whole werewolf thing?" he asked.

"It's been a rocky adjustment, but I'm managing."

"When will you be coming home?" I could see the anticipation in his eyes, and I felt suddenly guilty that I would disappoint him.

"Actually, that's what I came to talk to you and father about," I said as my eyes dropped to the ground.

"You're not coming home are you? You're going to stay with him." Notak couldn't hide his frustration and sadness.

"I don't want to hurt anyone and I don't trust myself. I don't belong here anymore brother," I said with sadness in my voice. "I trust him to protect me from myself. And . . . I'm in love with him."

Notak was quiet for some time as he processed everything that I had told him. I could tell he was attempting to quell his sadness and his anger.

"I miss you, sister, it's lonely around here without you. Father worries about you constantly, and Jesse doesn't understand why you don't just join the pack. I wish you would come home. But—" he stopped as he carefully chose his words. "I always knew your destiny would be unique, that your path would be much different than any of ours. I don't know this Aiden fellow much, but I see how he looks at you. I can tell he cares a great deal about you. And I see that you are happy now," he said. "I can't stop you from becoming who you are meant to be."

"Thank you for being so understanding. And you know where to find me, I'm not far and I'll be around," I said as I hugged Notak again. "Will you tell father I came by?"

"I'll tell him everything," he said with sadness in his voice. "You just stay safe and come back and see me soon."

"I will brother, thank you so much. I love you."

"I love you too. And remember, you will always have a home here," he said, as he gently brushed a strand of hair out of my face.

"I know. I'll come back soon," I promised Notak, before I headed back into the thick of the forest.

"You'd better, I know where to find you," he called out to me as I headed back to the Kathel house.

That night, there was a new dream that haunted me. It was of my brother and Wakiza fighting the dark spirits—the vampires. I realized that the woman's voice in my dream hadn't been warning me about vampires in general. She had been warning about the vampire's from our past. Josiah in particular.

Enya.

I woke up in a heavy sweat, relieved as I came to the realization that I'd been dreaming.

"What is it?" I heard Aiden's concerned voice.

I did not answer him. I inhaled the air deeply, trying to pick up on the scent of my desire. I got up and walked to the doorway, inhaling again.

Down the hallway, I could pick it up much better. She was back.

In my infatuation with my love, my Aiden, I had almost forgotten about my connection with the woman.

We had unfinished business.

"Lakota, what are you looking for?" Aiden asked, mystified.

"Draigon and Enya. They're back. I have to speak with her," I answered simply as I headed down the staircase. I knew Aiden was following just behind me.

There in the grand living room she sat on the massive Victorian couch, shrouded in a dark burgundy cape like I had seen her in before.

"Enya," I greeted her.

"Lakota," she returned and beckoned for me to sit beside her.

I could tell that she knew why I had approached her at this hour, although for a vampire it was no odd time at all. There was a certain formality in her posture that told me she had already accepted my unspoken questions.

"I think you already know what questions I have for you," I began. "You owe me some answers," I said as I sat beside her.

She gently took my right hand into hers and began inspecting it. I remembered then the ring I wore. She looked to Aiden with a horrible look of sadness in her eyes, before letting go of my hand.

I did not understand her sadness, but I knew she understood my relationship with Aiden. The tradition in the Celtic Claddagh ring Aiden had given me could not have made it any clearer for her.

"I am sorry that I cannot save you from the sadness that is sure to come," she said shortly in her melodic

Irish accent. "Yes, I was the one who left the mountain lion. I wanted you to find me, I wanted you to learn about your past. I have been following you for years—watching you, protecting you," she confirmed my suspicions.

"I knew it," Aiden exclaimed. "This move was far too permanent not to have a secret agenda behind it."

I realized that Aiden might not know much more than I did about Enya's secrets.

"Why?" I was stunned and felt slightly violated.

"It was a business arrangement with the Xavier Coven. I have been building trust with them so that one day we might be able to get close enough to Xavier himself, the most powerful and notorious vampire alive. The origin of the venom that runs in our veins . . ." she trailed off as she shared a sad expression with Aiden.

"The Untouchables," I said, beginning to understand. "There's a reason they are called that. They are untouchable. And you wanted vengeance."

"They murdered our family, they took my sister, and they infected Aiden's father. They are the reason that we are what we are. Aiden didn't want this, and I didn't want Aiden to be alone. At first, we only wanted revenge on the ones that were responsible for our last human days. But when I met him, Xavier, I saw the darkness in his soul . . . so much innocent blood on his hands, so much evil in his heart. Vengeance wasn't enough. We made it our mission to find a way to destroy the entire coven. But our mission is not without great sacrifice. I swore an oath to serve their coven. I have done many things that I am not proud of in the hopes that one day I might find a way to destroy them." She shared a sorrowful look with Aiden.

"Remember I told you Enya has the ability to commune with the other side?" Aiden asked.

I nodded my head, recalling our conversation.

"They tell her things about this world, about humans and supernatural creatures with special gifts. She made herself an indispensable asset to Xavier because she can hone in on these gifted people, including vampires and werewolves. She informs the coven of new talent, and they recruit the strongest ones to join them. They kill those who will not convert. They call her the Seer," he explained to me. But then he turned to his mother with an anger in his eyes.

"What have you done ma? What have you told them? I won't let anything happen to Lakota. I will die to protect her," he warned as he took a few steps closer to us.

"You saw me? You knew I was different, a half blood, and it was your duty to tell Xavier," I said with a heavy realization.

"No, I never foresaw your existence. Somehow you have eluded my abilities. Your life is known only to a handful of supernatural creatures. It was Josiah that sent me to spy on you. Thirty years ago, he fell out of favor with Xavier, but was promised one chance at redemption. If he could find and capture 'a single gifted creature whose value is priceless', then he would earn his rank as an Untouchable."

"That's vampire code for a half blood," Aiden elaborated.

"You are the key to Josiah's redemption. He knew that your mother and father had a daughter when he killed them. He knew you were in that cave and he let you live. Few vampires know about his history with your people, and with you. He has been waiting all this time to see if you would survive the change. He needs you alive, as a half blood."

Enya let the reality of her words sink into my consciousness.

"I thought my existence is an abomination to your kind. What aren't you telling me?" I demanded as irritation gnawed at the edge of my mind.

"You have been feeding on her blood, have you not son?"

Aiden was shocked at the question, but he reluctantly nodded his head in confirmation. Enya sat silent for several moments.

"You are not an abomination to our kind, or your own. You are a rare gift. Only the Untouchables know the truth," she said, turning back to me. "Do you know how to kill a vampire Lakota? Do you know our weaknesses?"

"The sun." I was trying so hard to understand how it all made sense, how it all fit. And what I had to do with it all.

"That isn't our only weakness. A werewolf's blood is toxic to vampires," Aiden added.

"What?" I was shocked. "But Aiden, you've been drinking my blood for days now." I was instantly concerned for Aiden.

"You aren't a werewolf, not entirely. I assumed that your unique existence allowed you to somehow suppress the werewolf blood, but to be honest I have wondered since the first time I tasted you how and why your blood is so . . ." Aiden trailed off unable to find the right word. There was a blood lust in his eyes that I had long ago come to recognize.

"*Exquisite* might be the word you're looking for son. It is the rarest blood a vampire can drink. You must have wondered at some point why our two worlds have always been rivals, why we hate each other so deeply," she said to both Aiden and myself.

"Do tell, mother. That part always seems to be left out of the story of our history," Aiden prodded with an impatience I had never seen from him before. I realized that I wasn't the only one with secrets I didn't understand. Aiden had his own too.

"It is the reason that we are forbidden to hunt werewolves into extinction, although that would be easy to accomplish and the war between our worlds would end. But we have codes and rules laid out by the oldest of the Untouchables. We are allowed to control the werewolf population, so that they will never be strong enough to rise up against us. But we must always let some survive," she explained.

"A half blood is the key to making us nearly invincible," Enya began. "Lakota, your kind, your blood, it accentuates a vampires abilities and makes him stronger, more resilient to the sun. It allows us to connect with our once human existence, to feel, to be warm again. The coven leaders would never allow that kind of power to be in any other hands but their own. Half bloods are hunted in order to harvest their blood to make vampires stronger."

"My god! Are there others like me?" I began to realize that my existence had always been destined to be intertwined with their world.

"Not living. Not anymore. I'm sure you are well aware that it takes a strong human to survive the change of becoming a half blood. That kind of strength can't be reproduced, or pre-planned. A half blood must be born and they have to survive. It is an extremely rare phenomenon," she said.

"So the Untouchables let nature take its course in hopes that every couple decades, a half blood will survive," Aiden said as he began to understand as well. Enya nodded her head in agreement.

"But if we aren't supposed to know this, than how do you know?" Aiden's tone was filled with fear and worry.

"We have our ways," came a deep voice from a dark corner of the room. "If they find you, if they take you, we will never be able to kill Xavier. With your blood in his veins, he will be indestructible. They cannot know that you are alive, that you survived," Draigon said as he emerged from the shadows of a corner.

"Listen to me, both of you. And listen very carefully," her words were desperate. "Aiden, you know the power of her blood. You've felt it. It hasn't gone unnoticed. And Lakota, to willingly give your blood is one of the most powerful gifts a vampire can receive. Your love for each other has no bounds, it's timeless and eternal. It is like the ripples in a pond. When you are together, it sets off a chain reaction that is simply impossible to ignore. It emits a powerful energy," she paused, her eyes gloomy. "There is another like me. She is with Xavier and she is stronger than I am. I fear that it will not be long before she realizes what you two share, how strong you make each when you are together."

"What are you saying?" I felt a heavy weight on my chest, threatening to crush me.

"I told Josiah that you died, that you didn't survive the change. I've bought you some time but I cannot protect you forever," she warned. "The longer you two are together, the stronger you both will grow, united and as individuals. With that increased strength will come a power within both of you. A power the likes of which we have not seen in centuries. The ripples will spread and their Seer will find both of you. If they discover what I've done, that you are alive . . . Josiah will return with a coven to claim his redemption, to kill your people, to end us, and to capture you, Lakota. He will redeem himself by giving you to Xavier, and you will be forced to serve them for the remainder of your life. With your blood, they will become gods."

I was speechless, tears threatening at the corner of my eyes. This couldn't be happening to me. I looked to Aiden, but his face was not comforting this time. He wore an equally shocked and saddened expression. We both knew what this meant, but neither of us wanted to speak of it.

"I am so sorry," Enya said, gently touching my hand to comfort me. "I did everything I could."

My heart fell to pieces, the dream had ended. And now the harsh darkness of reality fell upon me like a tidal wave.

I stood up. I was crushed.

"I understand. We can't be together," I finally worked up the courage to speak the words we both dreaded as I gazed at Aiden. I couldn't breathe, it was as if the walls were closing in on me. "I need some air," I said as I turned and walked out into the dark forest. A bitter, cold wind nipped at my skin, but my blood boiled hot.

Alone, I changed and ran. Alone, I hunted and fed. And alone, I cried.

He found me the next day. I was human, and I was broken again.

We stood in the midst of the greenery, so beautiful on any other day. But not today.

Today felt heavy, dark, lingering with a bleak emptiness that I couldn't fully grasp.

"Tell me it's not true. Tell me this isn't happening," I said with tears already welling up in my eyes. He just stared beyond where I stood, as if there was something out in the distance that held his gaze.

His eyes meandered finally to me. They were cold and felt void of emotion. "This isn't your fault." His eyes bore into mine with a painful intensity.

Something was caught in my throat, and I wasn't sure if I would be able to speak. "There must be a way," the words came out sharp and violent. "There has to be a way," I whispered as the last remnants of any hope escaped my entity. I knew there wasn't any other way.

He stepped closer to me, his eyes lingering on my heaving chest. He pressed the palm of his hand atop my chest. The coolness of his touch calmed me a bit.

"I will hunt Josiah down before he ever gets the chance to come back for you. And I will find a way to kill Xavier. He can't stay untouchable forever, and without him the vampire world will fall into chaos and they will all forget about you. If it is our destiny to be together, then we will." I could see the pain in his eyes then.

I bit my lower lip, trying to quell the tears. But one escaped. Aiden's finger caught it, and he wiped it away.

"I hate him. I've never met him, and already he has destroyed my life, just the way Josiah did. My people don't stand a chance against any of them, but as long as I play by Xavier's rules, my people are safe." The anger boiled underneath my skin. "I can't do this alone, without you. I can't breathe without you. I am broken without you," I said as I fell to my knees with a full realization that I would lose him.

"Our love will always be our own, forever. No one can take that away from us," he said.

I broke down, as the reality of the end, the end of us, crashed down on me with the weight of hundreds of boulders. I felt as if my very essence was torn apart. Tears flowed in an uncontrollable stream down my trembling face. He was everything to me, I would rather die than lose him.

"I can't live without you." My words were nearly unrecognizable now.

"I have wanted a life with you for my own selfish reasons. But you have given me new life. Because of you, I know what my destiny is—I must see our mission through, I must find a way to kill Xavier. And then we will be free. It ends with him. I'm sorry I didn't understand earlier why our kind and your kind just can't . . . be, can't exist together. I'm sorry I did this to you, pulled you into this godforsaken world. But none of that matters now, this isn't about us anymore, Lakota."

"I know," I admitted.

"You belong here. You were born to protect your people, as your father did before you. You must never give up, never stop fighting. Promise me, you will fight," he demanded as he grabbed me and pulled me into his embrace.

"I promise," I said. "Where will you go? And your family?" I asked.

"We'll split up for a while, I'll go back to Ireland. The covens have to believe what my mother told them. Our being apart should confuse Xavier's Seer. I will not let them take you, I will find a way to keep you safe," he said as he looked deeply into my eyes. "If I kill Xavier in your lifetime, I will come back for you."

I wrapped my arms around his waist, embracing him. My heart pounded and throbbed, and my blood coursed fast and hot through my vessels and veins.

Our eyes met and we stayed locked in each other's gaze for timeless moments as we both absorbed all that it was that we loved about each other.

"Don't forget me," I begged him, my head still buried in his chest.

"My heart will always be in your captivity, for eternity. You will always be my Lakota," he said as he took my right ring finger into his hand. He gently adjusted the ring so that it sat square on my finger.

"I love you, Aiden," I said between sobs.

"Lakota," he said.

"Yes?"

"If I fail, or if time eludes us and you find someone who can give you what I cannot; intimacy, children, a life. You have to let me go and give yourself a chance at a normal life," he said, still holding my ring finger.

"No, I will always be yours, forever," I said as I violently took my hand from his.

He grabbed me by the shoulders. "You must!"

"I cannot," I said with tears in my eyes. "Please don't make me," I begged. "I will honor my people, I will protect them. And you must destroy Xavier and the Untouchables, but I will not promise my heart to anyone but you," I said firmly. I took the ring off my right hand and put it into Aiden's hand. "I am yours in life and death, or I will belong to no one," I whispered as I shut his hand over the ring.

Aiden turned his back to me, agitated.

I could not speak anymore. I wasn't breathing anymore, and I could hear my gasps for air.

He turned back to me slowly, taking my left hand gently and putting the ring on my left ring finger. I looked down to see the crown close to me and the heart facing out. It symbolized my heart being taken.

"Keep this, to remember me by. I will kill him, if it's the last thing I do. If we find each other again in your lifetime, I will return for you and I will make you my wife."

Our lips met, ever so gently at first. And then more intimate, more desperate. It would be our last kiss.

I became lost in his embrace. I tried to take in everything I loved about him. His scent, his touch, his skin, his voice.

I didn't want it to end.

He pulled away, with great effort.

"I will always love you, Lakota Avital."

I was so choked up on my own tears, I couldn't say the words. They came out as a mumbled whisper. "I love you."

And then he was gone.

And I was alone.

I fell to the ground with a new agony. There was a part of my world that had been ripped away from me.

I fell apart. My sobs filling the forest around me and my screams of agony echoed through their branches. I found myself hyperventilating, unable to get enough oxygen into my lungs. I was lightheaded, and dizzy, and numb.

My screams of grief, of pain, of heartbreak continued through the night. I felt as if someone had ripped my heart out, blended it into a fine pulp and then put it back into my chest still throbbing with blood.

I heard a loud thud and realized it was the sound my body made as it collapsed to the ground.

I don't remember my eyelids closing, but somehow the darkness took me.

And I didn't care.

There were no dreams, no nightmares.

Nothing.

Only an emptiness that paired perfectly with my empty heart.

Complete and utter darkness.

13 Murderer

When I awoke, the sun was high in the sky and it filtered through the dense tree cover in trickles of light. I should have felt the warmth on my skin, but I felt only coldness. I should have felt the earth beneath my crumpled body, but every limb felt numb. I tried to focus on the simplicity of my breathing, as I gazed at the ring on my left hand.

Love and engagement was supposed to be a happy time. But it held no such emotion for me. Instead, I realized that I was betrothed to a man whom I was forbidden to love, and with whom I was forbidden to share an existence. And I knew than even with my extended lifespan, it might take several centuries for Aiden to find a way to kill Xavier and free us all from his reign.

I lay there on the forest floor and fiddled with the ring on my left ring finger hour after hour. My thoughts were of everything and nothing at the same time. But there was no mistaking the horrible feeling of loss that coursed through my body like a great tidal wave crashing down on me with all its ferocity. Once one wave relinquished back to the ocean, another one hit me head on and I felt as if I could never fully catch my breath. I felt as if I was drowning. I was drowning in my own emotions.

In his absence, I felt a horrible inability to function, to breathe, to live. I tried to shove the feelings of abandonment and isolation deep into the bleak darkness that consumed my heart.

I eventually willed myself to my two rightful feet, and I wandered and meandered for some indefinite period of time, eventually, collapsing to the forest floor from both the mental and physical exhaustion as the sun began to make its descent.

The crickets began their serenade, welcoming the coming of nightfall. I was numb and achy from the cold, from the lack of feeding, and from the pain that gnawed at the edge of my bleeding heart.

I don't remember when the darkness took me, but I remember that it was a dreamless sleep. Where my heart should have been, there was only a black chasm.

When I came to, all my senses were screaming. I came to life in that unnatural state that I always felt before I made the change.

The metamorphosis—I embraced it this time, full heartedly. It was all I was . . . nothing more than a beast, a freak of nature, and the horror of mankind.

The physical pain was a refreshing change from the emotional abyss my soul had been sent to.

But it didn't last long enough.

When the change was complete, I felt the rush of hormones flooding my system along with the incessant emotional anguish that refused to let me rest.

I made my way to a nearby creek and peeked into it with only the moonlight to show my reflection. I was half-human and half-wolf, and suddenly there was nothing about it I could even pretend to like. Aiden always made me feel so good about myself, so beautiful, so . . . whole. But without him there, I could not see a shred of beauty or hope.

I saw only the bestial side of myself.

I stared, disgusted, until the moon was high in the sky. My stomach hurt as if my intestines were bunched into a horrible tight knot. My mouth was wet from salivation, and I was inadvertently sniffing the air like a predator. I realized then that I was craving flesh.

There was nothing that I smelled in the nearby air that satiated my senses. Nothing of substance that appealed to me.

Eventually I found myself wandering in the forests for hours. And thinking about *him*. I missed his touch, his scent, his eyes, his voice, his very presence.

There was a boiling anger that roared inside of me, threatening to explode at any moment. It was an anger directed at no one in particular, but still just as charged as ever.

I had been raised to believe in destiny and fate all my life. But I felt no hope, no comfort—no sense of destiny that night.

I jerked my head around suddenly, surprising myself at the speed in which I moved towards the noise.

The noise! I realized they were screams coming from a distance, female screams. I found myself running with an urgency that I could neither explain nor fathom. I came to a screeching halt at the end of an alleyway, listening for the source of the panicked scream. I realized then that I was on the outskirts of the town of Eugene, more than forty miles from the reservation.

Then I saw him, a rough looking man pushing a woman hard against a wall. I felt an overwhelming power inside me telling me to run, to capture, to kill, and to feed.

Unable to contain it any longer, the culmination of my sadness, my anger, my hunger, and my rage exploded in a merciless frenzy.

I tore the man apart with one move, the girl screaming as she witnessed the awesome power of my hybrid form. I bit into his warm flesh, swallowing the first bite with a ravenous appetite. I froze as I saw his thoughts through his eyes.

Through his blood memories I saw him rape and kill a woman, a pretty young blond girl. And then I saw the broadcast on the TV of the missing woman's image. I saw how he had followed the brunette-headed girl behind me from her ballet lessons. How he had stalked her, and shoved the young girl around, beating her, and then thrashing her against the wall until blood gushed from her head. I saw the panic in her face. And I felt his lack of empathy for her.

And then I saw his intent to take her, to strip her, to rape her, and then to kill her. He had planned on stabbing her with a knife he had in his right boot.

Her screams still filled the air, but when I looked at her, she instantly stopped. She clasped her trembling hands to her mouth and stared at me, terrified.

I looked down at the man's right boot, my heart thudded wildly at the thought that what I had seen might have come true. Slowly, I reached down inside the boot.

I pulled out the knife. My heart skipped a beat.

Impossible.

Through his blood memories, I had seen the horrible crimes he'd already committed as well as the actions he was intending.

My hybrid wolf hand trembled at the reality of the truth and the blade slipped from my hand to the ground, clinking as it hit the pavement.

I looked at the girl again. She stood there frozen. Our eyes locked for a minute, and the horror, and sadness, and fear that I saw in her eyes made my heart sink.

Slowly, her hands slid off her mouth.

"He was really going to kill me . . ." she mumbled.

"Get out of here," I screamed at her.

She did not argue, and slowly edged away from the man and myself.

"Thank you," she said as she looked back at me once. And then she ran.

I watched her leave, wishing I could run away from my monster. But I could not. It lived within me, and there was no escape.

I fed on the man as if I was starving. I consumed all that I could of his flesh until I heard police sirens in the background. I ran back towards the Kathel grounds with renewed and invigorated strength.

Quickly and easily I transformed back to my human form. All night, I cried as I wandered the forests. There was no going back from what I had done. The taste of his flesh and the strength of his blood coursed through my system, reminding me of the beast I had become. I became sickeningly aware of how strong and powerful I was as a hybrid—and guilty, because I could not escape the fact that I had killed a man.

I was a murderer.

But there was a part of me that didn't feel so bad for the man and his fate—the young blond whose face was now etched in my mind, her life taken in such a horrible way. And the intent he had for the girl in the alleyway made me sick to my stomach. I knew that if I had not intervened, the girl would have met a terrible fate.

It disgusted me that certain humans could prey on their own kind in such a repulsive way. There was nothing natural or necessary about it.

I wondered if it was chance, coincidence, or fate that had brought me to save the girl in that alley that night, by murdering a man.

But eventually my mind began to wander back to Aiden. As the only living half blood known to the world, I felt as if I was condemned in hell. Alone. My worst version of hell was one of isolation.

The one thing I feared most. Being alone.

He was gone.

In every sense of the word.

I felt utterly lost again, as if the blackness was swallowing me up whole.

My world was broken, smashed to bits and pieces. I didn't know if there would be any way to put the pieces back together. I was cursed, haunted, and condemned to an existence that I did not choose and I could not escape. The horrible agony of loss and grief, and it an entirely new definition to pain. I wondered how long I would be able to bear it, collapsing as the weight of the utter truth sank in. It took my breath away. I gasped for air, my chest heaving hard from the stress of the effort.

This is all just a bad dream, I heard my mind whisper in desperation. I kept trying to convince myself of that statement, so it wouldn't hurt so badly, so that my heart didn't feel so terribly shredded to pieces.

I returned to the Kathel house, knowing full well that Aiden's family was long gone. It was unusual, how the house had come to embody everything that I loved about his family. Their unique scents lingered, although in the faintest way. I closed my eyes and remembered Draigon's stern, but calm eyes. I could hear Enya's voice echo in my head as if in a dream. And Yuki seemed to glow in my mind's eye like the perfect, beautiful angel I had first seen her to be.

After a while, I stopped trying to run away from the memories. Instead, I embraced them for what they were, beautiful bitter-sweet memories of my heaven on earth. With all their memories still ingrained so vividly in my mind, the empty house was a sad reminder of the equally empty heart they had left me with.

I hadn't put any thought into the attachment to his family that had grown on me. The Kathel house had become my haven from the world. A safe place where I could be myself. It had become my home.

I took a shower in the bathroom that had once been Aiden's. I dressed slowly in some simple blue jeans and a blouse, made a cup of tea, and sat on Aiden's porch watching the sun rise over the trees. I sipped the tea and twisted the Celtic ring around my finger, deep in thought.

I had not been a very socially outgoing person before, but now, I was even less so. I was somehow content to sit on that porch, in the Kathel house, alone.

It was like my own private sanctuary.

My heart still ached and throbbed, but here I was content to let it throb and ache.

One week went by, then two, and then a month. I lost track of the day, of the hours, of time all together. In a desperate attempt to entertain myself, I read books from Aiden's massive collection, I tended to the Kathel gardens, and I taught myself to play the piano. I did anything I could really, to tame the volatile, unstable emotions that brewed inside of me.

Eventually, I worked up the nerve to go back to work. I hoped that it would help me resume some amount of normalcy in my mundane life.

Kyle welcomed me back happily, and for the first month, he didn't ask too many questions. But I knew that it wouldn't last.

He watched as time crept by, first a day, then a week, then a month, and it became sadly apparent that I was not myself.

"It was an animal of some type, like a wolf. It just jumped out of nowhere and attacked him." It was a familiar voice. I looked up and realized that it was coming from a TV. It was the girl whose life was inadvertently spared when I had taken her predator.

I was a little surprised that she hadn't sold me out. I was grateful she hadn't said more, and I was appalled at my mistake. If she told anyone what she really saw, the covens would catch wind and my parting with Aiden would have been for nothing.

"The remains of the man that was slaughtered on Theresa Young's behalf have been positively identified through both blood DNA and fingerprints as Noah Baker. He was wanted in association with several missing women in Oregon, Washington, Utah, Nevada, and New Mexico. He was considered one of the most dangerous serial rapists and murderers at large. Authorities are baffled by the remains of Noah. It appears that this 'wolf' literally ate him."

"I had no idea who he was. And I know his death was really gruesome, but maybe it was a fitting end to his filthy life. My heart goes out to all the girls and women who were not as lucky as I am," Theresa said.

"We asked District Ranger Kyle Benson of the Willamette Forest Ranger Services what continuing threat this 'wolf' might have here in Eugene and the surrounding towns. He said that while this attack was most likely a singular incident, it wouldn't hurt to keep your doors locked, and stay out of the streets after nightfall."

And then the TV froze. I realized that it was a recording that Kyle had been playing. I also realized that he was staring right at me.

"Would you have anything to do with this?" he asked. I could hear the weight of the question in his voice.

"I have no idea what you're talking about," I tried to sound dismissive.

"Uh huh," Kyle mused unconvinced. His eyes did not stray from me. "Do I look that stupid to you?"

I was a little taken back by his forward question, and I just nodded my head in disbelief and denial. His intense eyes bore down on me.

"I've known you since you were a baby and I have watched you change as you've grown up. You started acting weird, and then you go A-wall on me, and now you're an entirely different person," he said, thoughtful.

"I've seen it before . . ." he said trailing off.

I waited for him to finish his sentence as my mind panicked. What did he know? How did he know? How much did he know?

"You're not the only one with dark secrets in this town, Lakota. I knew your father before the change, during the change, and until the day he was murdered," he confessed.

"Well, I guess I'm just following in my fathers' footsteps, aren't I?" I remarked angrily. I thought that maybe that wouldn't be so bad. If I could be murdered like my father, at least I wouldn't be miserable anymore.

"Your father was a great man. His death was a tragedy. The people will look to you to find the same strength they found in your father," he said with purpose. "You should be proud to be your fathers' daughter."

"Yeah, it's a real gift he passed on to me," I said with dry sarcasm as I stormed towards the door to leave the Station.

"Lakota."

I turned back to Kyle on my way out.

"The next time you kill a serial killer, get rid of the body. It'll draw less attention."

I nodded in agreement, a little surprised at his advice and apparent support. Maybe he would be more understanding than I had originally thought.

As the months ticked by, my demeanor became increasingly more dark and withdrawn despite my best attempts to mask my emotions. I resorted to working solo most of the time, and Kyle and I grew more and more distant. I visited the reservation as often as I could emotionally bear. Notak and I grew distant from my lack of openness. I couldn't expect him to understand my plight.

The truth was so painful I could barely admit it to myself. Even if Aiden did kill Xavier in my lifetime, if he did come back for me—it didn't change the fact that our two worlds would always be at odds with each other and neither side would tolerate our existence together. The union of a hybrid and a vampire was and always would be forbidden. We could never be together. Engaged, married or otherwise. We would be forced to suffer an empty life apart in order to preserve mankind and our two rival worlds.

It was all so inconsequentially unfair. I hated being half blood. I hated existing this way, somewhat living yet somehow dead. Walking through life aimlessly, unwhole, and alone.

My only hope was that the passing of time would ease my broken heart. A month passed, but it did not help. Then another month, and another. I should have been able to let go, to move on. But I could not. And instead, a year later, I found myself stuck in yet another state of perpetual suspension. Again, I was neither moving forward nor backward.

I took eight human lives during that time. All of them corrupt murderers, lost souls with no hope of redemption. I dealt with a new emotion—disgust. The tainted flesh of my victims made me strong, but it disgusted me.

I made the Kathel house my own, although I barely changed a thing. Dedicated to my people with a fervor I had never known, I kept constant vigil over them.

Strange how I thought of them as my people now.

I was disgusted that I was a murderer, but somehow knowing that I was protecting my people, made it a little easier. The human meals made me momentarily forget about my broken heart and kept me strong as I waited and watched over my people.

14 RESURRECTION

I SAT ON AIDEN'S PORCH SIPPING TEA on yet another endless day, contemplating my useless existence. It was Sunday, and I had meandered most of the day reading, walking, and brooding as I always did on my days off.

I wondered if this was how it felt to be a vampire, to be haunted by your victims while trapped in a world where you are neither fully alive nor dead. It felt as if time itself had forgotten me and I was simply a spectator watching the rest of the world pass by.

Nothing satisfied me anymore. Even the simple things that used to make me happy—a rose in full bloom, the sound the wind made as it passed through the branches of the trees, the way the sky looked like an oil painting of crimsons, and blues, and purples when the sun set—it all felt somehow distant, and out of reach without his life intertwined with mine.

I sniffed the air around me. There was something different in the air today, but I couldn't quite put my finger on it.

There was a feeling in the pit of my stomach that had once been very familiar to me.

Suddenly I recognized it. Change was in the air.

A cool breeze hit me in the face and with it came an acute sense of danger. Birds, squirrels, and deer alike suddenly scampered this way and that as if startled.

All my senses came to life in one instant and the fever of an impending change set in automatically. The sun was still high in the sky, but the clouds had begun to drop to below the tips of the trees in a dense fog that made the forest floor dark.

Despite a lack of the visible moon, I could still feel its omnipresent lunar pull on my consciousness. Its strength felt almost magnetic. It was much stronger than I'd remembered previously.

Something was terribly wrong.

I jumped over the rail of Aiden's porch down two stories to the forest floor, landing adeptly on my two feet. I sniffed the air again in a completely canine way.

There was a scent of the most terrifying kind in the air. A scent whose properties I would never be able to escape, forget, or deny.

Blood.

Human blood.

Panic lapped at the edge of my mind as I feared the worst for my brother and father. The moon would not rise for another couple of hours and the pack would be unable to change until then. I would be my people's only defense against any threat. And there was but one threat in the back of my mind that I feared.

With a ferocious intensity, I let out a mind-shattering howl before I burst into a sprint for the reservation.

Even in my human form, I could feel the werewolf cells in me merging with my human cells. It was an in-toxicating, and invigorating feeling, like a drug. I had never so entirely accepted what I was. Never so fully let my two identities mesh together in such a symbiotic pattern.

I was Lakota Avital, half blood werewolf of the Kalapuya tribe pack.

It was as if I had been resurrected.

The hormones that flooded my veins and coursed through my heart made me run faster and faster. The strength that I felt was incredible, and my resolve had never been stronger.

The closer I got to the reservation, the more I became entirely convinced of the one thing I dreaded most.

They were here . . . vampires. I could sense it.

Of one other thing I was certain—I would not let them be the demise of my people.

The smell, the scent of fresh blood was now unmis-takable in the air. The blood of my people. An intense anger and hatred made my blood boil as I came to an abrupt halt on the outskirts of the dark forest surrounding the Communal area of the reservation.

"Where is he? Where is Aiden Kathel?" I heard a resonating sound roar.

I peered from behind the brush at the source of the unfamiliar voice. A dark caped figure yanked back on Jesse's hair, our youngest warrior. He had a deep cut across his forehead and one arm, but his blood was not the only one I smelled.

I could smell the blood escaping the wounds of Kotan and Yuri as well. Three dark figures herded a group of my brothers and sisters against the wall of the Communal building. Notak and the warriors were there in front them, pushing them back away from the strangers, using their bodies as a barrier between the vampires.

"I swear, I don't know who you're talking about," he gasped.

The dark figure lifted Jesse off the ground by his neck and then threw him fifteen feet across the ground where he lay limp. In a flash of movement the vampire bounded on top of the boy and then off just as swiftly to a full stand.

I could smell the blood before anyone saw it begin to escape the new gash across his chest. And then I heard a horrified shriek of a woman's voice . . . Jesse's mother. The gasps of my people followed as they absorbed what had just happened. The fury within me burned crimson red, and I could feel the guttural snarls starting to escape my throat.

I inhaled deeply inviting the beast within me to roar to life. There was no moon and no nightfall yet, but I let the magnetic pull from the lunar cycle seep into my every cell of every bone in my body.

"Are you looking for me?" I hissed as I stepped out from the brush and bushes. Out of the corner of my eye, I caught the surprised look on the faces of my people. I could feel the pains of the change coming on, the adrenalin coursing through my veins.

The dark caped man quickly jerked around in my direction. He tilted his head to one side in a feline demeanor. "Do not play games with me stupid girl," he said with a laugh as he turned back to Jesse, preparing to deliver the blow of death.

"Let my brother go!" I commanded in a deep voice. My eyes bore into his soulless existence with an intensity that made them burn.

I heard the shocked gasps of my people underneath the hideous laugh of the vampire. His three accomplices joined him with their chuckles.

The metamorphosis came, in all its awesome power. My canine howl welcomed its presence as I bowed down to the earth and changed. Their hideous laughs ceased.

My legs and arms changed along with my torso, then my canine ears and half-snout morphed with my human face. As usual, much of my midsection remained human morphing at the extremities into the dog-like resemblances I had grown accustomed to. The silence in the air was harrowing, and I rose on my two hind hybrid legs to my full height.

"You're supposed to be dead, little girl," the man in the black cape said as he stepped backwards away from Jesse in shock and horror. The young boy crawled to the safety of his mothers' arms.

I strode forward towards the vampire with a burning, primitive feeling to attack. My senses were honed, my eyes focused, my muscles tensed and ready. I saw the warriors nodding their heads for me to retreat. I knew they felt helpless to assist at their full potential.

But I knew there would be no time to wait for their help. And if I had to stand alone, I would be one god-damn force to be reckoned with.

"Jonathan, how can this be? It is only dusk," said one of the other vampires.

"She isn't werewolf. She's a half blood," the one called Jonathan breathed. His black eyes were devoid of any real life as he stared at my hybrid form.

My snout was pulled up in a snarl, showing my ca-nine teeth. I did not stop, I continued one slow step forward at a time, inviting the vampires to take me on. I had no plan other than to lead them away from my people. To distract them in any way possible. I also had no idea what I might be capable of. I had never tested the full strength of my powers.

"Lakota! NO! You won't stand a chance," I heard Notak's frantic voice scream at me. I did not heed his command.

Jonathan motioned to his three accomplices. "Take her! Alive!" He commanded calmly. "We came to harvest your lovers' blood. Through him, we were told, your blood runs pure. But this is truly better. Josiah will be very pleased that you are alive," he hissed with a disturbing excitement as he took a step closer to me.

I didn't see him move, but suddenly he was behind me and I could smell a new scent.

My own blood.

His fangs sank deep into my neck, as he drank my blood. I turned away from him with a deep growl, shoving him hard. He fell to the ground. The other vampires were by their leaders' side now.

I felt the flow of blood from my neck slow to a drip until it coagulated.

Jonathon let out a sinister laugh, stepping into the rays of the sun that filtered through the trees here and there. His skin burned at first, but then stopped and he seemed unharmed by the warm light.

"It's true. Your blood is the key." The glare in his eyes was intimidating and sinister.

One of the subservient vampires strode towards me, with fangs exposed and a menacing look in his murderous eyes. His hair was blond with streaks of gold in it. He was young—maybe twenty-seven or so by human standards—but I had no way of telling how long he had been frozen at that age.

Then the other two followed, engaging me as well. One looked to be about twenty years older than the first one, his thinning dark black hair permanently giving away his age for all time. He had the same menacing approach.

I braced myself for the attack, looking back over my shoulder for a split second to be sure that Notak and the others were at a safe distance. They looked on, speechless from the horror and wonder of what they were witnessing.

Two vampires were on top of me in less time than it took to blink, their arms entangling me as if they were trying to crush me. Their strength was incredible, and the pressure from their force threatened to break me. But the harder they tried, the harder I fought.

I tossed my body this way and that, eventually throwing my weight hard enough to buck them off. I sidestepped once and turned to face the pair. They regrouped, but now there were the four.

"Enough with play time. Take her!" Jonathon commanded as his black cape fell from his head revealing long grey and brown hair that was ruffled and haywire. His appearance reminded me of a crazy old loon.

They came at me once again, but this time I anticipated the speed of their approach. I threw my right shoulder out with exact timing, hitting the first vampire so hard that I sent him through the air at least ten feet. With incredible speed and precision I swiped my paw through the air, my extended sharp claws just catching the vampire across the face and chest. The impact sent him hurling through the air back towards his master, and he fell to Jonathan's feet with gaping, bloody wounds.

I roared a deafening growl filled with both anger and territorial poise.

"Get up you fool, get up," Jonathan yelled at the one at his feet. He was up in a blur of movement and then attacking me again, but this time he was able to anticipate my moves.

His fists flew, meeting my solid sternum or canine jaw every once in a while. I let out a yelp every now and then with sensitivity to the blows.

My sharp claws were just as relentless though, and the threat of the menacing mouth of teeth I was gnashing in his direction proved to be a good distraction.

I fought valiantly, but it was to no avail. They were strong, stronger than one hundred humans put together and Jonathan was relentless in his assault. Together, they hit me again and again and again with fists that felt like rocks.

Eventually, I lost my strength and collapsed to the ground motionless. I breathed deeply trying to regain my strength and heal my wounds, but I needed more time.

I remembered my promise to Aiden. I promised him I would fight, that I wouldn't let them take me. But then, I realized that if I stopped resisting, they might leave my people alone. If it was only me that they wanted, then they could have me.

"And take some of the little ones for Xavier," Jonathan said as he approached the group still hovering against the wall.

NO! I was horrified.

With sudden and ferocious intensity I threw my head back, stunning the vampire that mounted me. Then I jumped up with insane speed to my full height as I let out a massive guttural growl. In the same instant, I threw my right paw forward and straight through the chest of the vampire in front of me.

He looked down at my paw through his cracking torso as the blood of his last feed began spewing out and running down his icy body creating a stark contrast. I swiped my left paw through the air with so much speed that you could hear the wind that it created. I knocked his pale head clear off his shoulders and sent it flying until it landed with a resounding thud against a tree in the near distance.

The next instant, I was sent sliding in the dirt twenty or thirty feet. I shook my head, and looked up to find that Jonathan was on top of me. I had royally pissed him off now and there was no hiding the anger in his face.

I tried to move, but I realized quickly that the other vampires were assisting in pinning me down. I thrashed around, but their combined strength was simply no match for my newborn werewolf form. I was strong, agile, and fast—but I lacked the experience and finesse with which these creatures moved.

"Calm down little one. It's useless to resist," he said but I barely heard his words over my screams of pain. He had slowly begun to force his razor sharp nails into my chest cavity as if he intended to tear my still beating heart from my chest. I could smell my own blood. I shut my eyes against the excruciating pain and pictured Aiden's angelic face against my eyelids.

Time seemed to slow down to an intolerable speed, it lingered for what seemed like an eternity. I waited for him to tear my chest cavity to shreds, but I knew he wouldn't. I was too important to him, to his master, my immortal enemy, Josiah.

Suddenly, the heavy weight of the vampires pinning me down was lifted off of me. I opened my eyes to see what had happened. To my utter surprise there were four incredibly fast figures attempting to overtake the vampires. I flipped to my rightful upright position, prepped for another counterattack, but I collapsed from my wounds. I blinked my eyes to clear them and be sure I was seeing what my brain thought it was registering.

Draigon, Enya, Yuki, and . . .

Aiden.

The four of them fought valiantly, but they were no match for Jonathan and his followers. I began to understand how and why the Untouchables were so untouchable. Their forces were old, wise, and stronger than most vampires from centuries of human blood consumption. The evil in them from years of ravaging humans made them merciless, intolerable demons.

"You lied to us Enya," Jonathon said. "Xavier will be very displeased," he laughed.

"You don't deserve her," Enya hissed. "There is no end to the horrors your coven is responsible for."

Jonathon angrily threw his hand into her chest, reaching for her heart.

Enya seemed unaffected by her impending doom and smiled at him with satisfaction. "You will die by the hands of my son tonight. The have spirits have spoken," she cackled.

He continued deeper into her chest, and I knew he would rip her heart out.

"Please, leave her alone. I'll go with you," I begged.

"You'll do no such thing," came the whisper of a voice to my right. It was *his* voice. My Aiden. "I'm sorry for this," he said. But I didn't understand until a moment later what he was apologizing for. He gently tilted my head away from him, and leaned into my neck. I felt the sting of a thousand knives as his fangs sank deep into my carotid artery, the blood spilling into his mouth with every beat of my heart.

"Aiden, stop. You're hurting me," I pleaded. And then he let me go. I clasped my hand over my neck, willing my werewolf blood to heal me.

In a blur, he left my side and pinned Jonathan to a tree in the suns' rays. I realized suddenly that it was my blood that had given him the strength to retaliate against their leader.

"Feeding on arterial blood is a death wish to most. You have great trust in her to be able to heal a wound of that magnitude," he hissed. "If you kill me, Josiah will hunt you down, and he will kill you. All of you," Jonathon warned with a hideous laugh, but I could see in his eyes how he feared Aiden.

"He won't kill her, that's all that matters," Aiden said with a hiss. And then he snapped Jonathon's head off his shoulders, the blood from his last several victim's spewed for a few seconds, and then stopped. His body disintegrated to ashes in the rays from the sun.

A split second later, Yuki, Enya, and Draigon literally bit the neck off the last two vampires, severing their heads as well.

I heard the gasps in the background, but then there was utter silence. And I knew all eyes were on the Kathel coven and myself.

In a split second, Aiden was by my side. A moment later, Notak was there as well.

"Start a fire," Yuki commanded with a power that almost frightened me. "NOW!"

I heard the scurrying of my brothers and sisters as they hurried to obey Yuki's command. I felt pressure as Aiden pressed hard against my chest to stop the bleeding, his cool hands moving quickly to assess the damage. He tilted my neck to one side, inspecting the damage he had caused moments before.

"How bad is it?" I asked.

"What I did to you—it's healed. That's amazing," he said as I winced here and there from his poking and prodding. "The rest seems to be mending, but much slower. You must have used most of your abilities to heal the most fatal wound first. Otherwise, two broken ribs, but the rest is just muscle damage and torn tissue. I need to set your ribs," he said. And without any warning my screams of agony filled the air as he did so. As quickly as it had begun, it ended. I felt the broken pieces of my body beginning to reunite themselves. I knew I would need to feed in order to fully heal.

"She'll be alright. Just needs time to heal," Aiden said and I realized that he was talking to a worried Notak. I opened my eyes to a shirtless Aiden and Notak, who had both used their clothes to cover and wrap my bleeding wounds.

I felt myself swooped up into Aiden's embrace. His scent was as intoxicating and comforting as I remembered. A short distance away, he propped me up against a tree stump.

Aiden helped his family gather the four vampires' body parts and throw them into the blazing fire. I realized with surprise that I hadn't even noticed when I'd returned to my human form. The transitions were getting easier.

I felt a presence behind me and had no need to turn to know who it was. I inhaled the sorely missed scent and it seemed to heal the raw edges around my bleeding heart. A cool hand caressed my soft shoulder, and the touch seemed to sew the pieces of my broken heart back together in an instant. His lips brushed gently against the broad part of my back, up the crease in my neck, to my ears. I shut my eyes to savor and revel in the stolen kisses he laid on my back.

I was whole again. But there was still an incessant ache.

This ache was different then the ache of loss. It was the ache you feel when you love someone so truly . . . so exclusively . . . so entirely . . . that it hurts.

"You came back," I muttered between trembling lips. My body had gone cold and limp from physical exertion and the emotional stress.

"I never should have left you," his angelic voice sang in my ringing ears. "Seems our absence alone was not enough to stop the ripples. The rumor of your existence has caused quite the stir in the covens. Apparently, it wasn't more than a few months after we left that Xavier's Seer had a vision of you. So Enya planted a hallucination in her mind, one where you died. We didn't find out until later that the Seer also knew that I had been drinking your blood, so they sent Jonathan after me," he said as he pulled me into his embrace. His fingertips gently held my chin so that our eyes met. His eyes seemed to hold the universe in them, there was no limit to what was there.

"It's my fault. I never should have given in to my temptation. I came back because I could not let them have you," he whispered.

"What's done is done. I have no regrets. I tried to fight them, but they were impossible."

"I know. But they are not impossible. You just haven't fought our kind before. I knew you and the Kalapuya people didn't stand a chance against them alone," he said. "Lakota, I will never leave you again. I will stand by you, I will protect you for as long you live. And if you spend your entire life protecting your people, then I'll spend all of eternity protecting them when you are gone," he said with solemnness. He leaned in ever so slowly, cautiously calculating—the way it had to be when the one thing you want in life more than anything, was blood.

His lips were cool as usual, but they were more passionate than they had been before. I matched his passionate kiss with my urgency. It wasn't enough. I wanted more . . . I wanted him forever.

If I could stay frozen in the ecstasy of the love and lust we felt for each other, I would have been in heaven.

We groped and clawed at each other as if there would be no tomorrow. I heard his skin crackling from where my hybrid fingernails tore into him. I could feel the heat from my blood spilling out of the tissues from my wounds, as my heart beat hard and fast.

"Slow down, you need to heal," Aiden commanded as he pulled away from our embrace, forcing me to slow down as I tried to catch my breath. I rested my head against his hard chest. I listened for the beat of a heart, the beat that could only be awakened by a short list of things. Myself, as one of them. I listened hard . . . .

And there it was! Ever so faint and almost inaudible. I wondered for a moment if maybe I was just hearing the echo of my own heartbeat through his stony breastplate.

"You give my undead existence a life that I never knew could exist," he said.

"I don't know what our future holds but you have to know that our existence together will be condemned by both our kind," I said. My eyes sank to the ground with a familiar sadness. "How can something that feels so right, be so wrong?" I whispered.

"The covens know, about you and about us. It's too late to hide. Your very existence will make you the most hunted creature alive. Our life will never be easy, but we will face it together. When they come for us, we will fight," he said as he caught my eyes again. "Whatever time we can steal away from them, I choose to spend it with you," he said with an unbreakable gaze into the depths of my soul.

It still stung, knowing that my hybrid existence was the fuel for inevitable war. And even if I survived, if we survived, I would always be mortal and he would always be immortal. Perhaps that is part of what made our love so special . . . we knew that our time together would eventually have to end. It was simply a necessity.

Maybe that is what made him so human when he was with me—together, we were living the closest thing we each would ever have to a human existence. But it was the one thing that was completely out of reach for both of us.

I melted into his embrace. His arms held me firmly against his cool, soothing chest. I clasped my hands together firmly at the small of his back.

As the flames lapped about viscously, the last remnants of the vampires' bodies smoldered to ashes. The rising of the moon brought with it an increased ability for me to heal.

I dozed into a dreamless sleep in his heavenly embrace.

I embraced the night, the moon, and my abilities.

I knew not what the future held, but I knew that my state of perpetual darkness had ended. I knew now and accepted who and what I was.

It was my resurrection.

15 ECSTASY

When I came to, I realized that I was in the familiar bedroom in which I had spent the last year. I realized that in that time, I never once thought of it as "my" room. It was and always would be *his* room and *their* house. I was simply a temporary occupant.

I blinked several times before my vision cleared and I gingerly attempted to sit up. Inspecting my torso where Jonathan's hand had ripped through, I saw that I had almost completely healed. There were only a few silvery lines in my skin, and when I moved they ached only a little.

The sun was high in the sky and when I looked at the clock on the wall, it read half past three. Panic set in quickly as I realized I had been comatose for almost twenty-four hours.

"Where is Notak?" I demanded, as I began hyperventilating. "Is Jesse alright? Where is my father?" My voice was desperate and anxious. I frantically looked around for Aiden, whom I knew was in the room somewhere. His scent was unmistakable.

And then my eye caught him, sitting still as the dead in a chair shrouded by darkness in a corner of the room.

Aiden.

"Calm down love. Don't worry, your people are safe. Enya is tending to the little one . . . Jesse. Your werewolf brothers are healing fast, but you probably already knew that. And Notak, Wakiza, and Draigon are discussing an alliance for protection," he said.

"An alliance?" I repeated, curious.

"It's only a matter of time before Xavier catches wind of what we've done. The vision Enya planted in the Seer will wear off soon, and she will know that you are alive," he said as he made his way to where I sat on the bed. Gently, he touched the wounds on my abdomen.

"The one that did this to you—Jonathan," he said with slight hesitation in his voice. "Josiah will be expecting his return. When he doesn't, our fate will be sealed and he will come."

It took me a few moments for it all to sink in. And when it did, it felt like a one hundred pound stone had been placed on my chest.

"This is all my fault. I wish I had never been born. I'm going to be the end of my people," I said with disgust. "Unless . . ." I trailed off, thoughtful.

"Unless you run away, or turn yourself in to the coven like you tried to do yesterday?" Aiden finished the thoughts that floated through my mind.

I nodded my head in confirmation.

"The Untouchables are soulless, blood-thirsty beings and they will not be content to simply take you. They will want you to suffer in the worst humanly possible way. They will make you watch as they murder your people. They will destroy everything and everyone you love. Then they will torture you until you agree to servitude and they will feed on you again and again and again. Your blood will make them so powerful that no one will ever be able to destroy them. That is their way," he said with obvious disdain in his voice.

I could not respond. I just sat there in disbelief.

"What am I supposed to do?" I said, frantic. "I won't let them take my people . . . not this time, not again! I know our chances are slim but we have to fight."

"And fight we will," he said. "Xavier knows how desperately Josiah wants to become an Untouchable. His promise still stands and he will give Josiah his chance at redemption. Josiah's return is a kind of blessing. It's better than one of the Untouchables coming for you. If we prepare and combine our strengths with your werewolf pack, we can defeat Josiah. Like Jonathon, he is old and very strong, but he isn't an Untouchable yet. He can be defeated."

"It's time we faced the ghosts from our past. He destroyed our people, he murdered my parents, and now we live in fear . . . this is our chance for redemption."

"You need to understand that if we defeat Josiah," he hesitated, "if we kill him, we will begin a war against Xavier and his covens. Vampires have attempted to overthrow him before, but none have lived to tell the tale. I still don't know how to kill an Untouchable."

"When the time comes, we will figure it out. We will find a way to destroy Xavier and the Untouchables. All of this is because of me. I won't runaway and watch Josiah or any of the Untouchables kill everyone I love. What has been done to the Kalapuya people is unforgivable. Enya is as good as dead for lying to them to protect me. And you are marked for being with me, for drinking my blood. There is no escape now, war is inevitable," I said sadly. "Someone has to stop them, someone has to end their reign. And my blood is the one thing they want most."

"This isn't your fault. If I'd never met you, if we'd never fallen in love, then maybe none of this would be happening," he said as he sat down beside me on the bed.

"It isn't your fault and it isn't my fault. Don't you see? This is what we were born for. You shouldn't have turned the way you did. And I shouldn't have survived.

Our union was fate. This is our purpose, this is our destiny." The conviction in my voice was sure and strong.

I lay my head on his shoulder, a sigh escaping my lips as I shut my eyes to a darkness that only intensified. I felt suddenly weak as the reality of the burden made its full weight known.

"Come on, we need to hunt. You'll need to completely heal and regain your strength if we're going to teach you how to fight vampires," Aiden said, with the slightest hint of a smile at the edge of his perfect lips.

"I know, I will go. Stay here, wait for me." I stood up and turned to him.

His look of surprise and confusion amused me.

"You will feed, but no more blood bags or mediocre animal blood. I know what you want. I know what you need," I said.

"No!" He stood, towering over me, shock and horror in his face. "Don't even speak of it."

"If we're going to be together, then we will have to embrace everything that we are," I said as I took his hands into mine. "I am half blood werewolf and I will hunt and feed like one. And you are a vampire who thirsts for my blood above all others. They fear what we could become if we realize what we are capable of. I saw it in Jonathon's eyes before you killed him. You need to practice just as much as I do, become accustomed to the way my blood feels inside of you."

"I don't want to hurt you. I don't need it." He gripped my right arm tightly, begging me to stop my persistence.

"I trust you. You don't need it, but you are stronger with it than without it. And I will give it to you," I said as I locked eyes with him.

There was a sadness in his eyes, and guilt. I didn't doubt that he probably hated what he was.

"A year ago, I didn't think I would see you again. I was lost without you because I was never meant to be without you. Embrace your destiny. My blood is the key to everything, Aiden. It is the one thing the Untouchables covet, but it will never be more powerful than when I willing give it to you," I said as I cupped my hands around his cheekbones.

He reluctantly agreed as he turned his head into my wrist, deeply inhaling my scent.

"I will hunt, and I will be back, and then you will feed," I told him as I headed for the window. I jumped over the banister of his porch, changing in a split second before I touched the forest floor. I knew Aiden watched. I caught his smile as I looked back over my shoulder.

It was strange how comfortable I was in the skin of the beast I once held so much disdain for. But now it almost felt like my safe haven. The strength and power I felt in this form somehow helped me cope with the impossible situation that I, that we, were destined to endure.

When I returned to the Kathel house it was dark and the moon was just below the tips of the trees. Draigon, Enya, Yuki, and the three warriors in werewolf form were in front of the house. The pack welcomed me quickly, although I'm sure that my half-werewolf and half-human form against their fully werewolf bodies was quite a contrast.

"It is decided. To be free of Josiah's hold on Lakota and your people, we will defend and fight together until death or victory. We will finish the battle that began here almost twenty years ago and this will be either the end of our chapter or the beginning of a new one," Enya said with purpose as she stepped closer to me. She gently touched my arms with her icy cold skin. "There is no turning back now without irrevocable damage to your people, and potentially to the human race."

Willing myself, I changed back to my human form. The rags that had once been my clothes hung loosely from my muscular frame, scantily covering my now fully healed body.

"I cannot ask this of you brother," I said with a heavy sense of guilt as I approached Notak. I knew they would all be taking on a great risk.

"You have not asked anything of me, of us, sister. We have chosen this path on our own. We are all tired of living in fear of their return. It is already agreed, and the alliance sealed in blood," Notak said as he nodded to the group of unlikely fellows. I looked towards the group and noticed suddenly that all the palms of their hands, werewolf and vampire alike, were caked with dried blood and venom. They had already mostly healed though, even the werewolves.

It was then that I saw Aiden, standing with his hand extended to me. As I got closer I saw that it dripped with blood from a fresh cut in his palm. I took the knife he handed me and made a deep slice mark in the palm of my left hand. Our two hands joined together and the blood and venom mixed, sealing our proverbial bond to each other and the group. I grimaced a little as the venom stung, and Aiden did the same, upset that I was in pain.

"My people will forever be in your debt," I said, both to the Kathel coven and my own pack. It sounded strange how I had claimed the Kalapuya people as my own, but it felt right.

"There will be no debt owed. It is our duty as immortal creatures to protect the life that feeds us. We can only hope that, ultimately, this will bring about the end of the merciless reign of Josiah and the Xavier coven," Draigon said.

There was silence as we all accepted the gravity of the situation. And then the three werewolves parted and returned to the reservation for the first watch.

Aiden and I returned to the solitude of his chambers and I sat on the edge of his bed and pulled my knees into my chest. I looked down at my palm, and then his, to find with little surprise that they were both completely healed. My almost naked body shivered uncontrollably from both the nippy evening air and the somber circumstances that weighed so heavily on my mind. I felt utterly vulnerable and breakable.

Aiden grabbed a blanket and wrapped it around me to warm my physical body. Then he wrapped his arm around me to warm my troubled soul. He edged his nose closer and closer to my neck, smelling me in a sensual way. I closed my eyes slowly as his cool lips finally pressed against a vein in my neck like a kiss.

"Take it. It's yours," I quietly commanded him. I knew he was thirsty.

Gently, he sank his fangs into my neck, releasing my blood. I shut my eyes as I savored that long moment as he fed. I relished the erotic feelings his touch elicited.

"What do you desire more? My body? Or my blood?" I asked. I did not open my eyes as I awaited his answer. With forced restraint, he pulled himself away from my blood.

"I wish I could tell you that it is your body that I desire most," he said, while he gently brushed a strand of hair away from my face. "But in this existence, somewhere between the living and the dead, my thirst for blood is strongest," he said, with the sadness I had become accustomed to.

I let out a trembling breath, somewhat relieved to hear that he desired my body to some extent.

"It's a bit easier for me not to tear you part though when I have fresh blood in my system," he said, explaining his ability to tolerate the close proximity. He laid another kiss on my neck, just below the wound he had created which was already beginning to heal.

As I shut my eyes and savored his cool lips against my skin. I felt a little guilty for admitting to myself that I enjoyed when he drank my blood. Slowly, I pulled away from his touch, edging off the bed to stand inches away from him.

"I can give you both worlds," I said as I let the blanket fall to the floor, revealing my scantily clad body.

The moonlight glistened off of my bronze skin. The curves of my hips met the cascade of muscles in my abdomen, calling his attention. His eyes went to my breasts, golden brown and as smooth as rose petals. Then they rose a bit—up to my neckline—for several seconds. I knew he could see the blood coursing through my jugular veins through my thin skin.

I saw him swallow a forceful gulp. I quickly put my finger to his lips, shushing him. Erotically wrapping my arms around his neck, I straddled him.

Forcefully he grabbed my arms and broke my grip around his neck. I sat atop him, still straddling him with my strong legs. Slowly I cocked my head to one side as I challenged him. In one swift motion I tore what remained of my clothes off of my body.

His eyes meandered down the nakedness of my bronze skin, and for the first time I saw an almost completely human lust in his eyes.

I leaned in close to his lips and then stopped.

"Trust me," I whispered. I knew he could feel my breath against his skin as I spoke.

He sat there for a moment, contemplative.

"I don't want to hurt you," he said shaking his head in defiance. He stood up, dragging me with him and he tried to pry away from my hold.

I did not let go of the embrace.

I leaned my head back a bit, letting my eyes revel on the brawny muscle of his chest beneath his thin white t-shirt. Then I leaned in, pushing up on the tips of my toes to reach his lips.

"I love you, Aiden. I am yours, now and forever. In life, in death, and everything in between," I whispered. Gently, I placed a soft kiss on his hesitant lips.

Our eyes met again, and I could see the pleading in his two-toned eyes. But I did not relent. Gripping the back of his t-shirt, I tore it down the center of his back like a piece of paper, before stripping it off his perfect body.

I pulled his head to me, forcing my warm lips against his with a ravenous appetite that was not entirely my own. This time though, he submitted his delicious lips to mine. His left hand meandered to the small of my back with a gentleness that seemed meticulously practiced.

It was incredibly exciting—trusting my feeble, fragile little body to such a being.

I clawed at the zipper on his pants for a few moments, finally succeeding in getting it down. I burned for him in a way I never had before. It was sensual, predatory, erotic, and loving all at once.

In one motion he grabbed me below the knees and picked me up to a cradled position. He slowly turned and gently placed me on the bed. Our eyes never parted.

He laid me gently into the pillows as his lips began to slowly caress mine again. His hard, icy chest felt good against my burning breasts.

Our lips meshed together.

I savored every touch of his perfect fingers, every passionate kiss, every time his eyes met mine and burned a hole into my soul. They were eternal moments I would cherish forever, in life or death.

He kissed me down my neck, around my breast, down the center of my abdomen, to the funnel shape of my pelvis that called to him. My body trembled with anticipation.

He was so cautious at first, when we made love. Calculated and restrictive in a desperate attempt to control the beasts we both restrained within us, we tried to suffocate the deathly thirsts they contained.

Our bodies moved together as one, just as our lips had meshed moments before. We moved in sync, as if I could read his mind, and he mine.

As the physical intensity increased, I saw something different in his eyes. It was that familiar deathly look. I knew what he wanted. I could see it in his eyes.

I pulled his head forcefully to my neck, but he separated from me abruptly and threw me across the room. My body made a loud thud as it hit the wall.

"Enough! I want to drain you. Don't tempt me," he hissed at me.

The werewolf in me awakened then, and an anger entered my being. I clawed my neck with one quick sharp motion reopening the wound he had created just moments before, and I moved towards him quickly with a canine growl. I could feel the blood dripping down my neck and around my breasts. When I was a foot away from him, I stopped short.

"Give in to your temptation Aiden." With hybrid strength, I shoved him hard so that he fell back into the pillows. I straddled him again, letting the blood drip onto his lips. My eyes begged him to give in, my loins yearned for his presence again, and my blood boiled beneath my skin.

Endless seconds ticked by, interrupted only by the sound of dripping blood as it hit his face. I leaned my neck invitingly into his mouth, and finally I felt his fangs pierce gently into my soft skin, a cross between a kiss and a drink. It was slow and sensual.

He took me in every way possible, and my nails dug into his shoulders with the ecstasy of our physical merging, our spiritual connection, our bestial behavior. The venom that escaped his wounds burned under my skin, but I could barely feel it against the pleasure that so entirely enraptured me.

I began to feel lightheaded and faint from the loss of blood. I yanked away from him with the strength of three thousand horses, successfully breaking his grip from my neck. The blood gushed for a minute, and I licked my hand with my own saliva and placed it against the wound in my neck. Within seconds the bleeding had slowed, and in a few more, it had stopped and coagulated.

My body relaxed from the werewolf changes, the loss of blood helped to balance the human with the beast within me. I could feel that we were still joined, and now his eyes were refocused with a decidedly human intent and pleasure. Aiden turned me onto my back in one swift motion and a few moments later my nails ripped into his back for a different reason. I burned with a fire in my loins I could not comprehend. Aiden pushed up onto his arms, and I reveled at the site of my blood on his perfect fangs. His flawless face shown in the moonlight like some god frozen in time.

I wondered fleetingly then, how I got there. How I found a love so timeless with a being so perfect and timeless himself. I also thought how demented that thought might be.

My breath escaped me, my blood burned like lava, and then, simultaneously, we exploded in ecstasy. My screams could have been heard from a mile away.

The venom in his fluids burned like knives, but it lasted only seconds before the werewolf blood took control back.

We fell into each other and he pressed his cold chest into my breasts and ribcage to help control my wildly hot body temperature. My hand meandered to his shoulders and back where the deep gouges from my nails had previously been, but the marks were no longer there.

He had already healed.

Eventually he wrapped his naked body around mine, soothing the bruises that had risen on my back and hips from hitting the wall. And with our act of lust and love complete, I reveled in his embrace, feeling peace and contentment.

It was like nothing I had ever felt before.

I traced the moons on his fingernails in circles that had no beginning or end. I remember looking up at the full moon once more before passing into a deep sleep.

16   Blood Bath

"You two were busy last night." Enya said when she saw us enter the kitchen the next morning. I was bruised on the left side of my head and part of my shoulder where my body had hit the wall and bookshelf. The bite marks on my neck were still visible as well.

Draigon and Yuki froze in shock at the site of my disheveled body.

"I'm fine, I just need to hunt soon," I tried to reassure her.

Enya put her cup down, and leaned in closer to Aiden over the island in the middle of the kitchen.

"So it's possible?" Enya asked nodding suggestively towards me.

"Ma!" Aiden exclaimed in disbelief.

I heard Yuki let out a stifled, but amused laugh. Enya's inquisitive stare did not waver, and her demeanor demanded Aiden's response.

"Did I shag her?" he yelled in both embarrassment and shock. He looked from Enya, to Yuki, and then to Draigon, hoping that one of them would spare him from having to answer. The room was deathly silent.

"Yes! Alright? Happy?" he demanded.

"Impossible!" Draigon whispered without a movement.

"Apparently not," Yuki said with a wry smile she attempted to hide behind the cup she held in her hand. "Although I already figured as much with all the ruckus last night."

"Real funny, Yuki," Aiden mocked. "Shut up!" he demanded as he left the room and stormed out the front door.

I stood there for a minute, a little embarrassed and shocked.

"Um . . . I'm going to go," I said as I backed out of the kitchen slowly. "I should get to hunting . . . or something . . ." I trailed off trying to fill the uncomfortable silence that hung in the air as they all looked at me.

I found Aiden in the front yard leaning against a tree. Cautiously, I edged closer so that I could see his face. It was sad and haunted.

"I'm so sorry," he began. But I shushed him quickly by pressing a finger to his lips.

"I never imagined I'd be talking about sex with your family so soon—much less *ever*, for that matter," I said amused. "But they are right about one thing. Last night was impossible," I said.

Aiden looked at me inquisitively, trying to understand what I was saying.

"Impossibly, and utterly unbelievable," I whispered as I crept onto my tippy toes and planted a kiss on his cool lips.

"Now," I said, just as our lips parted. "I need to hunt. And then I think I'll have some learning to do," I said with a sly smile as I turned and bounded into the forest. A few seconds later, I had made a full change to my hybrid form and I hunted.

My life had changed from stagnant waters to a ripping waterfall. I barely recognized the life in which I resided. It was all very "impossible", just as Draigon had said. The more I thought about it, the more impossible and surreal it all seemed.

Vampire and Half Blood Werewolf—or whatever the hell I was. We had not only sworn our loyalty and lives to each other, but we had consecrated our love. And now in our beastly states, we simply existed together.

Internally, I laughed as I thought of how sick and twisted it all really was.

"Always be on your guard when in the presence of a vampire," Aiden said as he crouched low in preparation for attack. He lurched towards me with blazing speed, and I sidestepped barely in the nick of time, leaving an inch between myself and his stone-hard body.

We were in the great domed room where Aiden and I had shared our first dance. But this time, the dancing was imbued with a violent intent. The Kathel coven had united to prepare for the coming of Josiah and his followers. And this time, it was in my hybrid form that I pranced across the smooth floor.

"Use all your senses to anticipate where your attacker will come from," and then he lurched at me again. But this time I wasn't quite as fast, I felt his body hit me like a brick and I skidded across the floor almost twenty feet before flipping back onto all fours and instantly turning to face him again.

"Use your sense of smell to detect where they will be coming from," came Yuki's sweet voice from behind me. I should have smelled her there before I heard her voice, but I was having a hard time comprehending everything that was happening. As she finished the sentence, I felt the weight of her tiny body smashing into me from behind. I knew she was taunting me, just playing with me the way a cat would with a mouse.

They were so fast. I shook the frustration and dizziness away. I had to figure out how to fight them. I had to try harder.

From my right side I heard something, the flutter of wind. I picked up a scent. It was heavy and bold . . . Draigon.

In the blink of an eye my jaw opened, I turned to my right, and I gnashed my teeth at Draigon. He avoided me by a hair, changing directions in mid stride and jumping over me to avoid my sharp, half canine teeth.

"Good . . ." Draigon said in a hushed tone.

"You must completely attune with all your surroundings," I heard Enya say. But I wasn't sure where the voice came from, it seemed to echo and bounce from every direction, giving me no sense of its origin.

I closed my eyes and inhaled and exhaled deeply, all my nerves tingling in anticipation. I felt something, a tremor, almost undetectable. The hairs on my back stood up. She was above me and I didn't understand how I could know that with so much certainty, but I knew. One moment later I could almost taste her odor in the air above me.

I jumped to the side just as Enya careened down to the spot where I had been standing.

"Everything has a rhythm, a tone, a feel . . . learn the language of the earth and she will tell you the story. Let the spirits guide you," her angelic voice lilted as she touched her long, perfect fingers to the floor beneath her. The room was deathly still.

Suddenly, with a speed I never saw and could barely comprehend she had risen, turned, and snatched Aiden from mid-air, and then thrown him with a resounding thud to the ground. It was as if the ground had somehow told her that he was coming.

"Shite ma, not bad," Aiden said as he pulled himself off the floor with an amused laugh.

"I'll be needing a bit more practice, I think," she said.

"Impossible," I whispered in shock. I felt intimidated by their power, their finesse, and their speed. Lost within my thoughts of awe, I barely felt my body sliding across the floor. I didn't stop until I crashed into a wall. I jumped up to a full stand on my hind legs, and saw that it was Draigon that had taken me down.

"No matter what, NEVER let your guard down," Enya reminded me as she glided off behind her husband.

"And you had better start believing in the impossible," Draigon added with a knowing look in his eyes. I had turned their world upside down, and so had they done to mine. We both knew that our worlds united would entirely redefine the meaning of impossible.

"Sight, smell, hearing, touch, taste . . . your five human senses. They are heightened exponentially when you are in hybrid form. So use them. You must practice and learn what their full potential is," Aiden said as he stepped towards me in a non-aggressive stance.

I held my ground and kept my guard up, learning from my previous mistake.

"The only way you can defeat Josiah is if you embrace all that you are. Past, present, and future. In doing so, do not forget who you are," he said.

Cocking my head to one side for a moment, I contemplated his words and thought about what he meant by them.

"Anything and everything around you is a tool, a weapon, a friend, whatever you need it to be. Embrace all your abilities," Draigon elaborated.

There were a few moments of silence as they let the words sink in and then the bombardment of attacks came again. First Draigon, then Aiden, then Enya, and then Yuki. And then again, and again, and again. I did my best to utilize all my senses, but it was difficult to keep up with their combined speed and strength.

I felt like a child learning to walk. Up until today, I thought I knew what I was capable of. But now I felt naked and lost again, uncertain as to what I was.

The hits kept coming with relentless force. I felt my skin break or tear here and there under the bombardment. I heard my bones as they cracked under the force of the vampires' incredible strength. My grunts and moans were now audible in the air. And still I attempted to hit back, or at least misdirect them as they came at me. But it felt useless, and I felt badly beaten.

I collapsed to the ground in defeat.

"Enough!" Aiden commanded as he held up his closed fist to signal the coven to cease the attacks. Draigon and Enya left without a word.

"I hope you have a death wish," Yuki said smugly to Aiden. "Because if that's all she's got, it'll be our funeral." She gave me a deathly glare before she glided out of the room.

Aiden cocked his head to one side the way an owl or dog would as he inspected me. Our eyes met. We both knew that Yuki was right. But I also knew that both Aiden and I would die before allowing the covens to destroy our world.

I stood up and reverted back to my human form. The frustration in my face was undeniable. Aiden looked on, wordless, as the pieces of my broken body began to slowly mend themselves. It wouldn't be but a couple minutes before I would be completely healed.

In all the commotion, I hadn't realized how much destruction we had caused. There were several tiles on the floor that were dislodged or broken, music scores and other papers strewn everywhere, and the two walls where my body had hit it were shattered and crumbling. I looked down to where my feet had been planted, realizing that the moisture I stood in was a pool of my own blood.

I turned and slowly walked out into the forest, devastated. Even though I knew I possessed immense power inside of me, I felt helpless in harnessing it. And therefore, powerless as a defense to my people.

"Lakota!" Aiden called after me.

"Don't follow me. I must find the nature of the beast within me. I just need some time," I said with a voice that was not entirely my own. It was a powerful voice that held a strength that I heard but I did not feel I owned.

Aiden did not follow me.

In but a few moments, I had changed back to my hybrid self and I was running hard and fast.

At my little house on the reservation, Wakiza, Notak, and my warrior brothers were sitting in the front yard. There were slight looks of surprise, but I could tell that they were becoming accustomed to my new form. Within seconds, I had morphed back to my human form.

"Brothers, you must go to the Kathel coven and train with them. Father, Notak, you must gather the strongest of our human warriors and train with our werewolf brothers and vampire friends. This battle will not be easily won and we must prepare ourselves," I commanded. "The Kathel coven is waiting for you."

"Where are you going?" Notak demanded. I knew he could read the sadness in my eyes. I knew he could smell my fear and helplessness.

"I . . . must train. Alone," I said in barely a whisper.

There was silence in the air for a short moment as none of them dared to challenge me. I could not bear to see Notak's sad and worried eyes and I wished he could see how my heart bled for him.

"Go now!" I yelled as I quickly turned and morphed mid-air and bounded into the forest.

The sun and the moon came and went as I ran north until the blizzards of the Canadian wilderness nipped at my canine nose. I stopped in the midst of the snow-feathered trees and stood in still silence.

"Spirits of the earth and sky, ancestors of my brothers, my sisters," I screamed into the angry winds. "Mother, father," this time my words whispered as the pain of my parents' absence filled me.

"Help me . . ." I trailed off as I collapsed to my knees into the velvety soft snow. I shut my eyes against the emotional agony that seeped into my soul. I saw the faces of my mother and my father just like in my dream. I saw the black cloud that descended on them like a vapor. And then my memories ran with streams of blood as I watched them die in each other's arms. A rage I'd never admitted to myself boiled inside of me.

I screamed in rage as I threw my head back towards the sky.

Only the angry winds answered me and I bowed my head in turmoil. Against my closed eyelids, a cloud of blackness rose and thickened. Its dreary presence haunted me. But this time, I would not let fear take hold of me. I smiled as I invited the evil to show itself.

And then there he was, even though I had never once before remembered seeing his face.

Josiah.

He was tall and handsome, but his eyes were sinister and thirsty. There was something more too . . . .

I inhaled deeply as I let the nightmare envelope me. There was something in his eyes I hadn't expected to see . . . fear.

Suddenly, all the pieces fit. I accepted the reality of what the black cloud represented and a dread seventeen years in the making filled my gut. Josiah. He had killed my father for his uncommon werewolf strength, and my mother for their union together. He had to in order to release my anger, so that I might survive the change.

But I also saw the fear in Josiah's eyes, fear of what I might become. I now welcomed the fright I saw in his eyes. I relished it like a sweet apple fresh from the tree.

"You do have a weakness, my dear Josiah," I taunted aloud. "You fear those who are stronger than yourself. You fear being replaced."

I opened my eyes and rose with heavy conviction and purpose.

"You, Josiah, will fear me. You will witness the power and strength my mother and father gave me, and I will take my vengeance for the lives you took from my people. Your selfish desire for my blood, your greed for power will be your undoing. I will bring honor back to my people, and free them from the prison of fear you brought upon us," I spoke into the winds. "With your death, I will provoke Xavier himself. And I will destroy him and free us all from his reign on both our worlds."

I sprinted through the woods as fast as I could. Bounding and leaping from the sides of trees and boulders. I wove in and out of the dense forest with blinding speed.

I let my instincts take over. I let the beast within me emerge in all her glory. And in her strength, I found my own.

For days on end I trained. I learned to listen to the earth to hear every change in the wind, every leaf that moved, every branch that swayed.

I bled myself until I was almost too weak to move, and then I would push myself by training even harder. I made dozens upon dozens of arrows, spears, and knives with tips and blades to be dipped in werewolf blood. They were the weapons with which all my brothers were familiar and adept at handling. And they would assist striking down these undead monsters for good. So I fashioned harnesses and holsters from the skin of my meals with which to carry the arsenal I had developed.

My focus was undeterred, my mission held no room for error.

The moons came and went. My training and preparation was ceaseless. Enya was right—there was a rhythm. It was in everything around me, and it always had been. Everything began to make sense. All my senses were honed with an inhuman precision, and the young native girl I had always been merged with the beast within me. When I embraced all the parts of what I had become, an incredible peace came over me.

I could smell, see, hear, feel, and taste the world in an entirely different and incredibly powerful new way.

Inhaling deeply and gently touching the snowy earth beneath me with my fingers, I could now tell when a bird was about to leave its perch, or when an animal approached from miles away, or when the air changed.

I knew minutes before he came flying through the air towards me that Aiden had come. In a quick heartbeat, I snatched him from the air with my two very human hands, turned three hundred and sixty degrees and gently set him on the ground.

Aiden nodded his head in astonishment and shock.

"You've been busy, love," he said, bewilderment in his face as he looked upon my human form.

A sly smile crossed my face. My very, human face.

"The beast and the girl are one," I said with a satisfied demeanor. "I am no longer bound to the powers of one or the other. I am both united." I said, as I effortlessly morphed to my canine form and then back to human again.

We stood holding one another's gaze for several minutes before we became entangled in a mutual embrace. I closed my eyes against his cold chest, calmed by the strength I drew from him.

Slowly, I pulled away as a mist came over my eyes. It was a black vapor that seeped into my consciousness with a warning.

"Are you alright?" Aiden asked concerned at my sudden possession.

"They will be coming soon," I said as I strapped on my harness, which held my arrows and knives, swinging the bow over my shoulder.

"Help me with the rest," I told him. "We have work to do."

Aiden looked on with surprise and amusement, but he did as I commanded. I morphed effortlessly and bounded into the forest towards home. Aiden was by my side, easily paced with my speed.

Every muscle in my body was tensed and anxious. Every cell in my brain screamed caution into my ears. Every bone in my hybrid body quivered with anticipation of the inevitable.

When we returned to the familiarity of the Willamette, I morphed back to human form and stopped here and there to smell the air or to touch the forest floor. It felt as if the ground was shaking in fear. The unrest in the air disturbed me to the core.

"They are here," I said to Aiden who was a few steps behind me.

Our eyes met and without a word we acknowledged what had to be done. Aiden opened his mouth and an ear-shattering screech filled the air. It was as beastly as it was alien.

"The children and women have been taken to the Sanctuary. My family will be here soon," Aiden said, as he took my hands into his.

"Enya has seen it too. They are coming," I realized.

Aiden nodded affirmatively as he leaned into my lips and we shared in what might be our last kiss. A passionate, irrepressible kiss. Then he took my wrist to his lips and he drank. When he had finished, he whispered his love for me in his native tongue as he brushed a hair behind my ear.

"I love you, Aiden Kathel, in life and death," I said, as our eyes locked. "May the spirits be with us."

Aiden nodded his consent and without another word I bounded urgently towards the reservation to meet my brothers. My senses were honed acutely, my mind was prepared and alert.

"The coven will be here shortly," I said as I came skidding into the Communal area. About two dozen of our best warriors, my brother werewolves, and my father and brother stood around an open fire. I threw down the loaded satchels of weapons.

"What good are a bunch of primitive weapons going to do against the likes of them?" Notak asked in frustration.

I smiled as I met Notak's eyes. The hope and determination I felt spread to my brother.

"Werewolf blood is poisonous to vampires," I explained, without ever breaking our gaze. A silence hung in the air as the realization struck the warriors. "Get busy brothers."

"Do as she says, use your blood, coat the tips and blades," Notak commanded. Without another word, they did as they were told. And then they waited for my next command. The smell of fear in the air was undeniable. I could sense their anxiety and anticipation. But I could also see their determination and courage. There was an overwhelming sense of pride that moved through my soul.

"Brothers! Tonight we will take back our honor!" I yelled as I waved my bow high into the air. The cheers and war calls of my brothers filled the air. I lifted my head to the bright moon letting out a howl as I morphed to my hybrid form.

I circled around the blazing fire with a saunter that was no less than regal. The sound of drums began to fill the night sky and the warriors began the dance of war to summon the ancestors for strength.

Soon, Aiden and the coven had joined us. The war cries of my brothers met the howls of the pack. Enya and I both rose at the same time, and the drums, chanting, and dancing stopped abruptly as we did so. The air stood stagnant with the smell of death.

My human brothers fell back to a circle around the fire, and Aiden's coven and the werewolf pack stepped forward as the first defense. In my human form, I met Aiden's eyes one last time.

I didn't see them approach. They came on us like a swarm of angry bees. Draigon, Yuki, Aiden, Enya, and the three warrior werewolves collided with each of six undead bodies. The sounds of their alien screeches filled the air along with the wolf growls. In the midst of it all, there was a presence I could not ignore. A presence I had been awaiting for seventeen years.

He came from the mists of the forests like a demon on a black cloud. He was tall and handsome just as I had seen before. He glided towards me slowly, as if he were taunting me.

I should have been terrified, but his sinister eyes were just as I had seen before. And they held no secrets from me.

"So the daughter of the great werewolf martyr and the beautiful native survives," Josiah said.

I knew he was referring to my late parents.

"Half blood," he said with a snakelike hiss. He was within inches of my face now.

I did not move an inch and my eyes bore into his heartless soul. He took another moment to look around to see all the other vampires and werewolves engaged in fierce battle. And then he looked back to me with a burning fear in his eyes.

"You are beautiful like your mother," he said with a tsk. "So sad that you'll spend the rest of your days in a dungeon. With your blood, I will possess the most powerful bargaining chip in the history of vampires. Finally, I will become an Untouchable."

I closed my eyes and let the earth speak to me. Before he moved towards me, I could feel his intentions. I adeptly moved just enough to the side to avoid his sharp claws as they sliced through the air. And as I moved, my own protruded claws raked from his cheek clear across his chest.

He turned back to me in astonishment and horror. His wounds healed within seconds.

"I've been waiting for you Josiah," I taunted as I turned in the same moment to meet him. "I am all that you fear." A sly smile crossed my face.

"I fear no one," he said, his voice seething with disdain.

And then he unleashed his fury on me. I redirected his blows one by one, and lashed out at him when I could. He was very fast, and he was gaining on me. It was almost as if his rage fed his fury. But my practiced connection with the earth united with the beast within allowed me to read his frustrated attacks.

After several minutes of meaningless battle, he stopped and paced in front of me angrily.

"You are stronger than the last half blood," he commented, amused.

"You have no idea," I mocked him. Without breaking his gaze, I morphed to my hybrid form and howled the signal to unleash all the fury of my arsenal upon the invaders. And then I effortlessly morphed back to human.

"Kill them all!" he screamed in rage. A dozen of my Kalapuya brothers bombarded one vampire with the poisoned arsenal, then Aiden stepped in to deliver the final blow, tearing his heart out of his chest with a strength he had borrowed from my blood. The creature writhed in agony at the feet of Josiah.

Realizing quickly what Aiden had done, why he was so strong, Josiah's amused expression turned into a fury of rage. He came at me with renewed strength, again and again.

I fought as hard and as fast as I could. But the cries of my brothers falling around me distracted my focus. As I glanced over, I saw that the vampires wounded by my blood were feeding off my human brothers to heal faster. While those who were still strong were stripping the weapons away from my people faster than they could even comprehend.

I felt myself hurling through the air suddenly, and I realized that Josiah had hit me. With a loud crunch, my body hit a tree, and bark and branches broke away under the weight of my body. In a split second I had jumped up, thrust myself in a full sprint towards Josiah, and morphed into my hybrid form.

We exchanged blow after blow, neither one of us truly getting the better of the other. We danced our violent death steps for what felt like an eternity.

I could hear the painful yelps of my brother werewolves as they fell around me. I could smell the blood in the air from their wounds. At that moment, Josiah's sharp claws caught me in the abdomen. Wincing in pain, I tried to retaliate but Josiah had me in a bear-hug grip before I could even take a breath.

"Look at them, so fragile and weak," Josiah whispered into my ear with a hideous hiss.

I could smell the blood and death in the air before my eyes met the battlefield in front of me. So many bodies littered the ground, some wounded, some dying, and some dead. My heart sank like a boulder to the bottom of the ocean.

The coven and my werewolf brothers fought valiantly, but I could feel the hopelessness in the air. These vampires were centuries old and inhumanly strong from the hundreds of human lives they had consumed. Enya and Aiden had spent over two centuries attempting to find a way to end the Untouchables. If we couldn't even defeat vampires such as these, than what chance would anyone ever have against Xavier. Doubt began to enter my mind as I wondered if our death was imminent.

I caught the desperation in Notak's eyes. Wakiza was a fiery ball of revenge and justice, but I could sense that he saw his death nearing. Jesse let out an agonizing cry for help as one of the vampires pinned him down and prepared to decapitate him. His eyes met mine, full of desperation and pain.

With every ounce of strength I possessed I threw my head back into Josiah's, stunning him so I could break free. I bounded towards Jesse and smashed into the vampire atop him. With blinding speed I turned, grabbed two knives from my holsters, and sank them into his chest cavity. Aiden was beside me suddenly, as if I had summoned him. A split second later he snapped the vampires' neck and tore his head from his shoulders. The blood of his last feed spewed out and then his undead body collapsed to the ground.

As I looked back to Jesse to make sure he was alright, a dark figure descended on us. I could smell the blood before my mind could comprehend what had happened. As I exhaled in disbelief, my mind finally caught up with the horror of what had happened and I instantly regretted letting Jesse get involved in the fight.

Josiah stood there in front of me with Jesse held off the ground by no means of his own. Blood spilled from the young werewolf's back, and he slowly transformed back to his human self as Josiah yanked his claws from the boys back. Jesse collapsed to the ground with a lifeless thud.

17 LAST BREATH

"JESSE! NO!" I SCREAMED AS I MORPHED back to my human form and ran to his side. Josiah towered over me but did not strike me. I could sense that he was enjoying my agony.

"It's alright, Kota. Tell my mother that I love her. Tell her that father is alive," he gasped between bloody lungs. And then he went limp.

A cry of agony and loss escaped my trembling lips as Josiah began to laugh. I looked to find Aiden's saddened face, only to find him in the midst of a vicious battle with one of the vampires. Yuki and Enya were desperately trying to drive the vampires away from my human brothers. Our native lands had once again become a war zone.

"He was just a boy," I screamed at Josiah. "Damn you to hell." I stood and faced him head on again. My eyes burned with a hateful fire.

"You're humanity is your weakness," Josiah said with an amused smile as he towered over me.

He leaned in close to me and inhaled deeply. I could see the blood lust in his savage eyes.

"You know nothing of pain. But you will." He leaned in even closer to me but I did not step down. His scent was pungent and repulsive and I could feel the evil in his essence from a thousand unmentionable sins. "I will kill everyone you hold dear tonight. And you will watch as I destroy this place. I will break you, I will snuff out your humanity. I will suffocate all of your hope. I killed your father. I killed your mother." He hissed at me, just inches from my face now. "And now you will be mine," he whispered.

I lunged at him with claws protruded, but something hot and agonizing emanated from my midsection. Slowly I looked down.

Josiah's claws were inside my abdomen.

"Lakota!" I heard Aiden's desperate scream.

In one blindingly fast motion, Josiah thrust his other hand into my abdomen as well.

"Stop it! She's no use to you dead," came Aiden's pained voice. I looked over to find Aiden pinned against a tree. With a sickening feeling, I realized that the vampire who held him hostage wanted him to watch me.

"I should kill you. I want to kill you, just as your father killed my brother," Josiah hissed with a hatred that oozed from every word. "But you are the only living half blood, and your Aiden is right. You are useless to me dead. Of course, that does not mean I cannot make you suffer every day of your miserable life."

As he leaned into my neck to drink my blood, I deliberately grasped each one of his hands still thrust deep into my stomach.

"You will never have me," I said in a deep, unrecognizable voice. I closed my eyes and focused all the energy of my human and beastly existence on his hands. Slowly and painfully, I pulled them from my body with an impossible strength that rivaled his. Then I hit Josiah square in the chest with enough force to send him flying twenty feet into a tree behind him. His weight resounded against the trunk as it sent splinters everywhere from the impact.

He stood and watched as my wound began to heal. The look of disbelief was apparent in his hollow face.

In a tornado of strength I bounded towards the vampire that held my Aiden hostage. I leapt into the air and bit at him with my canine teeth but fell short by mere inches as I felt my body being pulled in the opposite direction. Josiah had caught my feet mid-air and sent my body flying. I crashed into the earth.

"They say a vampires' venom cuts like a knife for a werewolf. I wonder what it'll feel like for you," Josiah hissed. A fire burned on my neck.

I realized that Josiah was on top of me, and his fangs were sunk deep into my jugular vein. A split second later I was human again and an agonizing scream escaped my lips as his venom cut through my veins. It burned and coursed deeper and deeper into me with every heartbeat. It blazed like a hot knife. My screams grew louder and my breathing became labored as if my lungs had filled with the poisonous liquid.

My eyes went dark although they were still open. I could hear the unearthly screeches of a handful of vampires in battle again in the near distance. I turned my eyes to Aiden, blinking to clear the darkness. He had pushed the vampire holding him hostage back a bit, fighting with his augmented strength and desperately trying to break free. But I could sense that the strength of my blood running in his veins had begun to wane. He needed more.

My vision began to fade again and flashbacks of my life flew across my minds' eye. My mother, my father, Wakiza, Notak, and then Aiden.

Suddenly, I felt my body go completely limp and the sound of my screaming stopped. The agony however, never left.

A blackness came over me. A horrible weight that I could scarcely bear. It felt as if I was living in a nightmare I would never escape.

Against the blackness I saw the ghost of a face, a familiar face. The dark mist faded and the face became

very clear. It was my mother, and she was more beautiful than I ever could have imagined. The image played
like a movie against the darkness. I could hear her sweet
voice singing an old Kalapuya melody as she picked ber-
ries in the forest. I saw the terror in her face when something dark came over her.

"Be still, little one," I heard her say to me with desperation in her voice as she carried me into the cave. I
heard the pitter-patter of her feet. I heard her screams,
and then I saw the blood pouring from her neck.

I saw Wakiza then. He quickly whisked a half dozen
little children into the forest.

I saw three other vampires, one of them, Josiah. I
saw their teeth sinking into the bodies of my people. I
felt the terror of my people.

And like a dark savior from the depths of the forests,
I saw the metamorphosis of a magnificent, regal creature. It was my father, and he was the most beautiful
werewolf I had ever seen. He fought with strength and
a vengeance that made me proud. He struck them down,
one by one. Until only Josiah remained. I felt Josiah's
triumph as he tore at my father, I felt the warm blood
in his hands. I saw him fall with a thunderous roar to
the forest floor.

A bloody figure crawled to my father's side and my
mother looked up with pleading eyes. She begged Josiah
to spare him.

The vision almost ripped my heart from my chest.

The ground was no longer green with grass, it flowed with the blood of my fallen brothers and sisters, fathers and mothers, grandfathers and grandmothers. I could feel Josiah's self-satisfaction and it made me ill.

NO! The forest was a blur again as I heard the most torturous scream from my mother. But her desperate voice was dim now and it felt as if I was flying through the trees.

I could smell Wakiza's scent as if I was there, and Josiah peered through the brush at the old man and several women and young children. I recognized Notak's face in the little crowd of children. Just as Josiah was about to attack, my father appeared again as if out of nowhere. He ripped at Josiah, until I could feel the weakness that he once felt at my fathers' hand. But my fathers' wounds were too deep, and so I saw him fall.

I felt Josiah's weakened state, his desire to pursue the little ones. But his wounds prevented him for a few minutes and instead he sat to watch my father die. I saw my mother crawl to my fathers' side once again. I saw her lifeless body fall on top of his. I heard my mother's mouth utter one word before her last breath left her. I could feel Josiah's irritation that he had not caught it.

But I knew what she had said. I could see the way her lips formed the word, as if she were nursing the word in her death.

"Lakota . . ."

I watched as Josiah picked up the body of my mother and then he left the reservation.

There were flickers of light, of years gone past.

In a dark castle that sat on an island in some country far from here, I saw him lay my mother down into a coffin.

She was so still and yet so beautiful. I felt what Josiah felt for my mother. Both affection and pride.

I saw her agonizing change three days later, and I saw her rise from death in her coffin. Her face was still bronze, but the tone wasn't quite right. Her lips were blood red, and her brown eyes had a vivid rim of blue. She was beautiful, in an unearthly way. It was as if death itself had frozen her perfection as well as added its own compliments.

She was one of them. Eternally frozen in both her beauty and her death.

"You will be my eternal bride," I heard Josiah say softly.

I saw the sadness in her eyes, the pain of the lives she'd watched being taken, the child she left behind, the lover who sacrificed himself for her, and her own life now damned for eternity.

I saw the covens unite to sanctify their eternal unity. I saw her two-toned eyes filled with an indescribable sadness.

I watched her sit on a wooden bench by a great stained glass window, so still that she looked devoid of life.

"Cry for me, my beauty," I heard Josiah command of her.

Tears streamed down her face.

"You are my most treasured possession," Josiah said, as I watched his hand caress my mother's cheek.

I realized that it was odd that she could cry, that she held onto so much emotion as a vampire. Perhaps that was why Josiah loved her so much, she was the closest thing to human he would ever have.

I wondered if I would ever see my mother again as I felt Josiah drop my limp body to the forest floor, his act of cruelty complete. He had poisoned me with his venom, and if I survived, it would be days of intolerable pain until my werewolf blood would be able to destroy the venom. He wanted the memories of my past to haunt me. He wanted me to suffer.

"What have you done?" I heard Aiden scream.

"Don't worry Lakota, you will see your mother again very soon. And she will watch as I feed on you," he said, with a cruel laugh, taunting me.

The dark cloud that shrouded my eyes lifted suddenly. And I looked straight into his eyes. The intensity of my gaze must have surprised him, because he took a step back.

Something inside of my consciousness snapped like a tree in a lightning storm. A blood-curdling scream escaped from the depths of my lungs as the agony of a werewolf change combined with the torment of the venom.

For a few seconds I could see again with incredible clarity. I felt a fury that I had never felt before. The venom of the vampire merged with my hybrid blood. It was an unbearable sensation and it made me crazy with rage.

I lashed out my right hand. My claws dug deep into Josiah's ashen face, and I drove my other hand straight into his chest. It seemed effortless. It wasn't the strength of my human or my werewolf self, it was something much more. Much darker and more sinister. It was a power that was not my own.

"You shouldn't have done that. It was too much venom. I can feel it," I said. "You just killed the only living half blood," I told him. "I hope you don't have any friends or family, because Xavier will not be please."

My hand grabbed his black heart and I ripped it from his chest. He looked down in horror. The last thing I saw in his face was terror.

Then his eyes rolled to the top of his head and his body collapsed to the ground. As he fell, I realized that Aiden was standing a few feet back in utter shock, finally freed from his assailant with the help of Draigon and Enya. But it was too late for me and they looked on in astonishment.

A sigh of relief escaped my mouth as the world around me began to grow dim and I felt the agony of the venom beginning to overtake me. Aiden caught me as I collapsed to the ground.

I smiled as I inhaled his heavenly scent . . . honey and leather.

"Lakota, this isn't supposed to happen." I heard his desperate voice whisper. "Enya what's happening?"

"I don't know. Half bloods shouldn't die from our venom. Their blood is stronger."

"Aiden, it's ok. Is it over?" I struggled to ask.

Aiden nodded his confirmation.

In the near distance, I could hear the cries of my people. Mournful, painful cries . . . and they tormented my fading ability to hear. The smell of their spilled blood was still in the air, and my heart felt as if it had broken into a thousand pieces.

My vision blurred again, and the stars and moon above became but faint lights in the sky. I could feel my consciousness slipping away.

"In life and death . . ." I whispered weakly, "I love you."

"There is nothing we can do love. This is beyond our understanding," I heard Enya's motherly voice as a faint whisper.

Aiden did not respond. I felt a drop of something, something cold and wet on my forehead. A tear. I could feel Aiden rocking me back and forth in his arms as my heart began to slow . . . beat by beat.

More warm drops fell on my neck, my breasts, and one found its way to my mouth. It tasted bittersweet instead of salty. Almost like the venom.

I couldn't see anything, smell anything, or feel anything anymore. Even the sound of my own heart beating was absent.

The last thing I heard were the unearthly, agonizing screams of his honey and leather voice.

My eternal love. My Aiden.

And then there was darkness and my heart ceased to beat at all.

Acknowledgments

Thank you to my husband, my daughter, and my son for being so patient and understanding throughout the writing process. And to my mom and dad for nurturing my abilities and for providing me with the opportunities that helped me grow as a writer.

Thank you and hugs to Aspen Takahashi, my content editor, fellow supernatural genre fanatic, and best friend; for her invaluable insight, hard work, and constant support through all the years.

Many thanks to my editor, Deborah DeNicola, for helping to create Lakota's world in a way that would resonate with others while honoring my style of writing.

Thank you to Gary and Gwen Connolly, my gracious Irish friends and mentors for their invaluable contributions on Irish lifestyle, culture, and language.

A big thank you to my Production Manager Teddy Gyi, for his assistance and expertise in the film industry, marketing, and production. These were areas that I had originally dreaded, but Teddy helped make them simple and manageable.

Thank you to Darko Tomic, my illustration artist and cover designer, for his phenomenal talent and insight in creating artwork that truly captured everything I had dreamed of for the cover art.

A huge thank you to Oakridge, Oregon for the inspiration and for the wonderful people who make this little town so unforgettable.

Many thanks to the Willamette Forest Services; to Katie Isacksen, Public Affairs Specialist of the Middle Fork Ranger District, who provided much of the background research about Oakridge and the Forest Rangers; and to Tony Farque, Archeologist of the Sweet Home Ranger District, who was so gracious to share the history and lore behind the Kalapuya Native Americans.

And thank you to all my contributors and supporters, for their financial contributions and their moral support.

KAT SLOAN

is the author of The Lycanthropire Saga.
She is an accomplished writer, author, and
entrepreneur with a passion for all things
supernatural.

Her website is www.katsloan.com

Look for the next book in the series
COMING SOON!

THE LYCANTHROPIRE SAGA
FIRST BREED

www.ingramcontent.com/pod-product-compliance
Lightning Source LLC
Chambersburg PA
CBHW020917110726
47900CB00001B/189